The Author

ETHEL WILSON was born in Port Elizabeth, South Africa, in 1888. She was taken to England at the age of two after her mother died. Seven years later her father died, and in 1898 she came to Vancouver to live with her maternal grandmother. She received her teacher's certificate from the Vancouver Normal School in 1907 and taught in many local elementary schools until her marriage in 1921.

In the 1930s Wilson published a few short stories and began a series of family reminiscences which were later transformed into *The Innocent Traveller*. Her first published novel, *Hetty Dorval*, appeared in 1947, and her fiction career ended fourteen years later with the publication of her story collection, *Mrs. Golightly and Other Stories*. Through her compassionate and often ironic narration, Wilson explores in her fiction the moral lives of her characters.

For her contribution to Canadian literature, Wilson was awarded the Canada Council Medal in 1961 and the Lorne Pierce Medal of the Royal Society of Canada in 1964. Her husband died in 1966, and she spent her later years in seclusion and ill-health.

Ethel Wilson died in Vancouver in 1980.

THE NEW CANADIAN LIBRARY

General Editor: David Staines

ETHEL WILSON

Mrs. Golightly and Other Stories

With an Afterword by David Stouck

M&S

Canadian Cataloguing in Publication Data

Wilson, Ethel, 1888-1980
Mrs. Golightly and other stories

(New Canadian library)
Includes bibliographical references.
ISBN 0-7710-8956-2

I. Title.   II. Series.

PS8545.I62M7 1990   C813'.54   C90-093953-2
PR9199.3.W5M7 1990

Printed and bound in Canada

Published by arrangement with Macmillan of Canada

McClelland & Stewart Inc.
The Canadian Publishers
481 University Avenue
Toronto, Ontario
M5G 2E9

Contents

ONE

Mrs. Golightly and the First Convention

M RS. GOLIGHTLY was a shy woman. She lived in Vancouver. Her husband, Tommy Golightly, was not shy. He was personable and easy to like. He was a consulting engineer who was consulted a great deal by engineering firms, construction firms, logging firms in particular, any firm that seemed to have problems connected with traction. When he was not being consulted he played golf, tennis, or bridge according to whether the season was spring, summer, autumn or winter. Any time that was left over he spent with his wife and three small children of whom he was very fond. When he was with them, it seemed that that was what he liked best. He was a very extroverted sort of man, easy and likeable, and his little wife was so shy that it just was not fair.

At the period of which I write, Conventions had not begun to take their now-accepted place in life on the North American continent. I am speaking of Conventions with a capital C. Conventions with a small c have, of course, always been with us, but not as conspicuously now as formerly. In those days, when a man said rather importantly I am going to a Convention, someone was quite liable to ask What is a Convention? Everyone seemed to think that they must be quite a good thing, which of course they are. We now take them for granted.

Now Mr. Golightly was admirably adapted to going to Conventions. His memory for names and faces was good;

he liked people, both in crowds and separately; he collected acquaintances who rapidly became friends. Everyone liked him.

One day he came home and said to his wife, "How would you like a trip to California?"

Mrs. Golightly gave a little gasp. Her face lighted up and she said, "Oh Tom . . . !"

"There's a Western and Middle Western Convention meeting at Del Monte the first week of March, and you and I are going down," said Mr. Golightly.

Mrs. Golightly's face clouded and she said in quite a different tone and with great alarm, "Oh Tom . . . !"

"Well, what?" said her husband.

Mrs. Golightly began the sort of hesitation that so easily overcame her. "Well, Tom," she said, "I'd have to get a hat, and I suppose a suit and a dinner dress, and Emmeline isn't very good to leave with the children and you know I'm no good with crowds and people, I never know what to say, and – "

"Well, *get* a new hat," said her husband, "get one of those hats I see women wearing with long quills on. And *get* a new dress. Get *twenty* new dresses. And Emmeline's fine with the children and what you need's a change, and I'm the only one in my profession invited from British Columbia. You get a hat with the longest feather in town and a nice dinner dress!" Mr. Golightly looked fondly at his wife and saw with new eyes that she appeared anxious and not quite as pretty as she sometimes was. He kissed her and she promised that she would get the new hat, but he did not know how terrified she was of the Convention and all the crowds of people, and that she suffered at the very thought of going. She could get along all right at home, but small talk with strangers – oh, poor Mrs. Golightly. These things certainly are not fair. However, she got the dress, and a new hat with the longest quill in town. She spent a long time at the hairdresser's; and how pretty she looked and how disturbed she felt! "I'll break the quill every time I get into the car, Tom," she said.

"Non-*sense*," said her husband, and they set off in the car for California.

Mrs. Golightly travelled in an old knitted suit and a felt hat pulled down on her head in observance of a theory which she had inherited from her mother that you must never wear good clothes when travelling. The night before arriving at Del Monte a car passing them at high speed side-swiped them ever so little, but the small damage and fuss that resulted from that delayed them a good deal. The result was that they got late to bed that night, slept little, rose early, and had to do three hundred miles before lunch. Mrs. Golightly began to feel very tired in spite of some mounting excitement, but this did not make her forget to ask her husband to stop at the outskirts of Del Monte so that she could take her new hat out of the bag and put it on. Mr. Golightly was delighted with the way his wife was joining in the spirit of the thing. "Good girl," he said, which pleased her, and neither of them noticed that nothing looked right about Mrs. Golightly except her hat, and even smart hats, worn under those circumstances, look wrong.

How impressive it was to Mrs. Golightly, supported by her hat, to approach the portals of the fashionable Del Monte Hotel. Large cars reclined in rows, some sparkling, some dimmed by a film of dust, all of them costly. Radiant men and women, expensively dressed (the inheritors of the earth, evidently), strolled about without a care in the world, or basked on the patio, scrutinizing new arrivals with experienced eyes. Mrs. Golightly had already felt something formidably buoyant in the air of California, accustomed as she was to the mild, soft and (to tell the truth) sometimes deliciously drowsy air of the British Columbia coast. The air she breathed in California somehow alarmed her. Creatures customarily breathing this air must, she thought, by nature, be buoyant, self-confident – all the things that Mrs. Golightly was not. Flowers bloomed, trees threw their shade, birds cleft the air, blue shone the sky, and Mrs. Golightly, dazzled, knocked her hat crooked as she got out of the car, and she caught the long quill on the door. She felt it snick. Oh, she thought, my darling quill!

No sooner had they alighted from their car, which was seized on all sides by hotel minions of great competence, than her husband was surrounded by prosperous men who said, "Well Tom! And how's the boy! Say Tom this is great!" And Tom turned from side to side greeting, expansive, the most popular man in view. Mrs. Golightly had no idea that Tom had so many business friends that loved him dearly. And then with one accord these prosperous men turned their kindly attention to Mrs. Golightly. It overwhelmed her but it really warmed her heart to feel that they were all so pleased that she had come, and that she had come so far, and although she felt shy, travel-worn and tired, she tried to do her best and her face shone sweetly with a desire to please.

"Now," said the biggest of the men, "the boys are waiting for you, Tom. Up in one three three. Yes in one three three. And Mrs. Golightly I want you to meet Mrs. Allyman of the Ladies' Committee. Mrs. Allyman meet Mrs. Tom Golightly from British Columbia. Will you just register her please, we've planned a good time for the ladies, Tom . . . we'll take good care of Tom, Mrs. Golightly." And Mr. Golightly said, "But my wife . . . " and then a lot of people streamed in, and Tom and the other men said, "Well, well, *well*, so here's Ed! Say, Ed . . . " and the words streamed past Mrs. Golightly and Tom was lost to her view.

A lump that felt large came in her throat because she was so shy, and Tom was not to be seen, but Mrs. Allyman was very kind and propelled her over to a group of ladies and said, "Oh this is the lady from British Columbia, the name is Golightly isn't it? Mrs. Golightly I want you to meet Mrs. Finkel and Mrs. Connelly and Mrs. Magnus and – pardon me I didn't catch the name – Mrs. Sloper from Colorado. Oh there's the President's wife Mrs. Bagg. Well Mrs. Bagg did you locate Mr. Bagg after all, no doubt he's in one three three. Mrs. Golightly I'd like to have you meet Mrs. Bagg and Mrs. Simmons, Mrs. Bagg, Mrs. Finkel, Mrs. Bagg, and Mrs. Sloper, Mrs. Bagg. Mrs. Golightly is all the way from British Columbia, I think that's where you come from, Mrs. Golightly?" Mrs. Allyman, speaking continually, seemed to say all this in one breath. By the time that Mrs. Golightly's vision had cleared (although she felt rather dizzy), she saw that all these ladies were chic, and that they wore hats with very long quills, longer even than hers, which made her feel much more secure. However, her exhilaration was passing; she realized that she was quite tired, and she said, smiling sweetly, "I *think* I'd better find my room." The hubbub in the hotel rotunda increased and increased.

When she reached her room she found that Tom had sent the bags up, and she thought she would unpack, and lie down for a bit to get rested, and then go down and have a quiet lunch. Perhaps she would see Tom somewhere. But first she went over to the window and looked out upon the incredible radiance of blue and green and gold, and the shine of the ethereal air. She looked at the great oak trees and the graceful mimosa trees and she thought, After I've tidied up and had some lunch I'll just go and sit under one of those beautiful mimosa trees and drink in this . . . this largesse of air and scent and beauty. Mrs. Golightly had never seen anything like it. The bright air dazzled her, and made her sad and gay. Just then the telephone rang. A man's strong and purposeful voice said, "Pardon me, but may I speak to Tom?"

"Oh I'm sorry," said Mrs. Golightly, "Tom's not here."

"Can you tell me where I can get him?" asked the voice very urgently.

"I'm so sorry . . . ," faltered Mrs. Golightly.

"Sorry to troub . . . " said the voice and the telephone clicked off.

There. The Convention had invaded the bedroom, the azure sky, and the drifting grace of the mimosa tree outside the bedroom window.

"I think," said Mrs. Golightly to herself, "if I had a bath it would freshen me, I'm beginning to have a headache." She went into the bathroom and gazed with pleasure on its paleness and coolness and shiningness, on the lavish array of towels, and an uneven picture entered and left her mind of the bathroom at home, full, it seemed to her, of the essentials for cleaning and dosing a father and mother and three small children, non-stop. The peace! The peace of it! She lay in the hot water regarding idly and alternately the soap which floated agreeably upon the water, and the window through which she saw blue sky of an astonishing azure.

The telephone rang. She dripped to the telephone. "Is that Mrs. Goodman?" purred a voice.

"No no, not Mrs. Goodman," said Mrs. Golightly, wrapped in a towel.

"I'm *so* sorry," purred the voice.

Mrs. Golightly got thankfully into the bath and turned on some more hot water.

The telephone rang.

She scrambled out, "Hello, hello?"

"There's a wire at the desk for Mr. Golightly," said a voice, "shall we send it up?"

"Oh dear, oh dear," said Mrs. Golightly, wrapped in a towel, "well . . . not yet . . . not for half an hour."

"Okay," said the voice.

She got back into the bath. She closed her eyes in disturbed and recovered bliss.

The telephone rang.

"Hello, hello," said Mrs. Golightly plaintively, wrapped in a very damp towel.

"Is that Mrs. Golightly?" said a kind voice.

"Yes, oh yes," agreed Mrs. Golightly.

"Well, this is Mrs. Porter speaking and we'd be pleased if you'd join Mrs. Bagg and Mrs. Wilkins and me in the Tap Room and meet some of the ladies and have a little drink before lunch."

"Oh thank you, thank you, that will be just lovely, I'd

love to," said Mrs. Golightly. Away went the sky, away went the birds, away went the bath, and away went the mimosa tree.

"Well, that will be lovely," said Mrs. Porter, "in about half an hour?"

"Oh thank you, thank you, that will be lovely . . . !" said Mrs. Golightly, repeating herself considerably.

She put on her new gray flannel suit which was only slightly rumpled, and straightened the tip of her quill as best she could. She patted her rather aching forehead with cold water and felt somewhat refreshed. She paid particular and delicate attention to her face, and left her room looking and feeling quite pretty but agitated.

When she got down to the Tap Room everyone was having Old-Fashioneds and a little woman in gray came up and said, "Pardon me but are you Mrs. Golightly from British Columbia? Mrs. Golightly, I'd like to have you meet Mrs. Bagg (our President's wife) and Mrs. Gillingham from St. Louis, Mrs. Wilkins from Pasadena; Mrs. Golightly, Mrs. Finkel and – pardon me? – Mrs. Connelly and Mrs. Allyman of Los Angeles."

Mrs. Golightly felt confused, but she smiled at each lady in turn, saying "How do you do," but neglected to remember or repeat their names because she was so inexperienced. She slipped into a chair and a waiter brought her an Old-Fashioned. She then looked round and tried hard to memorize the ladies nearly all of whom had stylish hats with tall quills on. Mrs. Bagg very smart. Mrs. Wilkins with pince-nez. Little Mrs. Porter in gray. Mrs. Simmons, Mrs. Connelly and Mrs. Finkel in short fur capes. Mrs. Finkel was lovely, of a gorgeous pale beauty. Mrs. Golightly sipped her Old-Fashioned and tried to feel very gay indeed. She and Mrs. Connelly who came from Chicago found that each had three small children, and before they had finished talking a waiter brought another Old-Fashioned. Then Mrs. Connelly had to speak to a lady on her other side, and Mrs. Golightly turned to the lady on her left. This lady was not talking to anyone but was quietly sipping her Old-Fashioned. By this time Mrs. Golightly was feeling unusually bold and responsible, and quite like a woman of the world. She thought to herself, Come now, everyone is being so lovely and trying to make everyone feel at home, and I must try too.

So she said to the strange lady, "I don't think we met, did we? My name is Mrs. Golightly and I come from British Columbia." And the lady said, "I'm pleased to meet you. I'm Mrs. Gampish and I come from Toledo, Ohio." And Mrs. Golightly said, "Oh isn't this a beautiful hotel and wouldn't you like to see the gardens?" and then somehow everyone was moving.

When Mrs. Golightly got up she felt as free as air, but as if she was stepping a little high. When they reached the luncheon table there must have been about a hundred ladies and of course everyone was talking. Mrs. Golightly was seated between two perfectly charming people, Mrs. Carillo from Little Rock, Arkansas, and Mrs. Clark from Phoenix, Arizona. They both said what a cute English accent she had and she had to tell them because she was so truthful that she had never been in England. It was a little hard to talk as there was an orchestra and Mrs. Golightly and Mrs. Carillo and Mrs. Clark were seated just below the saxophones. Mrs. Golightly couldn't quite make out whether she had no headache at all, or the worst headache of her life. This is lovely, she thought as she smiled back at her shouting companions, but how nice it would be to go upstairs and lie down. Just for half an hour after lunch, before I go and sit under the mimosa tree.

But when the luncheon was over, Mrs. Wilkins clapped her hands and said, "Now Ladies, cars are waiting at the door and we'll assemble in the lobby for the drive." And Mrs. Golightly said, "Oh hadn't I better run upstairs and see whether my husband ... " But Mrs. Wilkins said again, "Now Ladies!" So they all gathered in the lobby, and for one moment, one moment, Mrs. Golightly was still.

Oh, she thought, I feel awful, and I am so sleepy, and I

feel a little queer. But she soon started smiling again, and they all got into motor cars.

She got into a nice car with some other ladies whom she did not know. They all had tall quills on their hats which made it awkward. Mrs. Golightly was the smallest and sat in the middle. She turned from side to side with great politeness. Flick, flick went the quills, smiting against each other. Well, we'd better introduce ourselves, she thought. But the lady on her right had already explained that she was Mrs. Johnson from Seattle, so she turned to her left and said to the other stranger, "Do tell me your name? I'm Mrs. Golightly and I come from British Columbia."

The other lady said a little stiffly, "Well, I'm Mrs. Gampish and I come from Toledo, Ohio," and Mrs. Golightly felt awful and said, "Oh Mrs. Gampish, how stupid of me, we met in the Tap Room, of course! So *many* people!" "Oh, it's quite all right," said Mrs. Gampish rather coldly. But she and Mrs. Johnson soon found that their husbands both had gastric ulcers and so they had a very very interesting conversation. Mrs. Golightly did not join in because she had nothing to offer in the way of an ulcer, as she and Tom and the children never seemed to be ill and the ladies did not appear to need sympathy. She dodged this way and that behind Mrs. Gampish and Mrs. Johnson, interfering with their quills, and peering at gleaming Spanish villas enfolded in green, blazing masses of flowers, a crash and white spume of breakers, a twisted Monterey pine – they all rushed dazzling past the car windows – villas, pines, ocean and all. If I were courageous or even tactful, thought Mrs. Golightly, I could ask to sit beside the window where I want to be, and these ladies could talk in comfort (the talk had moved from ulcers to their sons' fraternities), which is what they wish, but she knew that she was not skilful in such matters, and it would not do. Oh, she yearned, if I could ever be a woman of the world and achieve these simple matters!

Then all the cars stopped at a place called Point Lobos, and everybody got out.

Mrs. Golightly sped swiftly alone toward the cliffs. She stood on a high rock overlooking the vast ocean, and the wind roared and whistled about her. She took off her hat as the whistling, beating broken quill seemed to impede her. She looked down and could hardly believe the beauty that lay below her. Green ocean crashed and broke in towering spray on splintered rocky islets, on the cliffs where she stood, and into swirling, sucking, rock-bound bays and caves. In the translucent green waves played joyous bands of seals, so joyous that they filled her with rapture. Bellowing seals clambered upon the rocks, but the din of wind and ocean drowned their bellowing. The entrancement of sea and sky and wind and the strong playing bodies of the seals so transported Mrs. Golightly that she forgot to think, Oh I must tell the children, and how Tom would love this! She was one with the rapture of that beautiful unexpected moment. She felt someone beside her and turned. There was Mrs. Carillo with a shining face. They shouted at each other, laughing with joy, but could not hear each other, and stood arm in arm braced against the wind, looking down at the playing bands of seals.

As the party assembled again, Mrs. Golightly stepped aside and waited for Mrs. Gampish and Mrs. Johnson to get in first. Then she got in, and sat down beside the window. Conversation about Point Lobos and the seals became general, and Mrs. Johnson who was in the middle found herself turning from side to side, bending and catching her quill. They then became quiet, and the drive home was peaceful. I shall never forget, thought Mrs. Golightly, as the landscape and seascape flashed past her rather tired eyes, the glory of Point Lobos, and the strong bodies of the seals playing in the translucent water. Whatever happens to me on earth, I shall never never forget it.

When she arrived at the hotel she discovered that she was nearly dead with excitement and noise and fatigue and when Tom came in she said, because she was so simple and ignorant, "Oh darling, can we have dinner somewhere quietly tonight, I must tell you about all those seals." Tom looked shocked, and said, "Seals? But darling, aren't you having a good time? I was just talking to Mr. Bagg and he tells me that you made a great hit with his wife. This is a Convention, you know," he said reprovingly, "and you can't do *that* kind of thing! Seals indeed! Where's your programme? Yes, Ladies' Dinner in the Jacobean Room, and I'll be at the Men's." And Mrs. Golightly said, "Oh, Tom . . . Yes, of course, I know, how stupid of me . . . I'm having the *loveliest* time, Tom, and we had the *loveliest* drive, and now I'm really going to have a proper bath and a rest before I dress." And Tom said, "*Fine!* But can I have the bathroom first because . . . " and then the telephone rang and Tom said, "Yes? Yes, Al, what's that? In the Tap Room? In fifteen minutes? Make it twenty, Al, I want to have a bath and change. Okay, Al . . . That was Al, dear. I'll have to hurry but you have a good rest." And then the telephone rang and it was Mrs. Wilkins and she said, "Oh Mrs. Golightly, will you join Mrs. Porter and me and some of the ladies in my room one seven five for cocktails at six o'clock? I do hope it won't rush you. One seven five. Oh that will be lovely." "Oh, yes, that will be lovely," said Mrs. Golightly. She put her hands to her face and then she took out her blue dinner dress and began pressing it, and away went the bath and away went the rest and away went the mimosa tree. Tom came out of the bathroom and said, "Whyever aren't you lying down? That's the trouble with you, you never will rest! Well, so long darling, have a good time." He went, and she finished pressing her dress and put it on.

The next time Mrs. Golightly saw Tom was downstairs in the hotel lobby as she waited with some of the other ladies to go into the ladies' dinner. Tom was in the middle of a group of men who walked down the centre of the lobby. They walked almost rolling with grandeur or something down the lobby, owning it, sufficient unto themselves, laughing together at their own private jokes and unaware of anyone else. But Mr. Golightly's eyes fell on his wife. He saw how pretty she looked and was delighted with her. He checked the flow of men down the lobby and stepped forward and said, "Terry, I want you to meet Mr. Flanagan; Bill, this is my wife." A lively and powerful small man seized Mrs. Golightly's hand and held it and looked admiringly at her and said, "Well, Mrs. Golightly, I certainly am pleased to meet you. I've just got Tom here to promise that you and he will come and stay with Mrs. Flanagan and me this fall when the shooting's good up at our little place in Oregon – now, no argument, it's all settled, you're coming!" What a genial host! It would be a pleasure to stay with Mr. Flanagan.

Tom beamed in a pleased way, and Mrs. Golightly's face sparkled with pleasure. "Oh Mr. Flanagan," she said, "how kind! Tom and I will just *love* to come." (Never a word or thought about What shall we do with the children – just "We'd love to come.") "So *that's* settled," said Mr. Flanagan breezily, and the flow of men down the hotel lobby was resumed.

At dinner Mrs. Golightly sat beside a nice woman from San Francisco called Mrs. de Kay who had once lived in Toronto so of course they had a lot in common. Before dinner everyone had had one or two Old-Fashioneds, and as the mists cleared a bit, Mrs. Golightly had recognized Mrs. Bagg, Mrs. Connelly, dear Mrs. Carillo, and beautiful Mrs. Finkel. How lovely was Mrs. Finkel, sitting in blonde serenity amidst the hubbub, in silence looking around her with happy gentle gaze. You could never forget Mrs. Finkel. Her face, her person, her repose, her shadowed eyes invited scrutiny. You gazed with admiration and sweetly she accepted your admiration. While all around her were vivacious, Mrs. Finkel sat still. But now Mrs. Finkel and Mrs. Carillo were far down the table and Mrs. Golightly conversed with Mrs. de Kay as one woman of the world to another. How well I'm coming along! she thought, and felt puffed up.

During the sweet course she became hot with shame! She had not spoken a word to the lady on her left who wore a red velvet dress. She turned in a gushing way and said to the lady in the red dress who, she realized, was not speaking to anyone at the moment, "Isn't this a delightful dinner! We haven't had a chance of a word with each other, have we, and I don't believe we've met, but I'm Mrs. Golightly from British Columbia."

The lady in the red cut-velvet dress turned towards Mrs. Golightly and said clearly, "I am Mrs. Gampish, and I come from Toledo, Ohio." Their eyes met.

Mrs. Golightly remained silent. Blushes flamed over her. She thought, This is, no doubt, some dreadful dream from which I shall soon awake. And still the chatter and clatter and music went on. Mrs. Golightly could not think of anything to say. Mrs. Gampish continued to eat her dessert. Mrs. Golightly attempted to smile in a society way, but it was no good, and she couldn't say a thing.

After dinner there was bridge and what do you suppose? Mrs. Golightly was set to play with Mrs. Magnus and Mrs. Finkel and Mrs. Gampish. Trembling a little, she stood up.

"I think I will go to bed," she said. She could not bear to think of Mrs. Gampish being compelled to play bridge with her.

"No, *I* shall go to bed," said Mrs. Gampish.

"No, do let me go to bed," cried Mrs. Golightly, "I simply insist on going to bed."

"And *I* insist on going to bed too," said Mrs. Gampish firmly. "In any case I have a headache." Mrs. Magnus and Mrs. Finkel looked on in amazement.

"No no, I shall go to bed," said Mrs. Golightly in distress.

"No, *I* shall go to bed," said Mrs. Gampish. It was very absurd.

Mrs. Bagg hurried up. "Everything all set here?" she said in a hostess voice.

Mrs. Gampish and Mrs. Golightly said, speaking together, "I am going to bed."

"Oh, don't both go to bed," pleaded Mrs. Bagg,

unaware of any special feeling. "If one of you must go to bed, do please one of you stay, and I will make the fourth."

Mrs. Golightly considered and acted quickly. "If Mrs. Gampish *really* wants to go to bed," she said, timidly but with effect, "I will stay . . . a slight headache . . . " she said bravely, fluttering her fingers and batting her eyelashes which were rather long.

Mrs. Gampish did not argue any more. She said good night to the ladies, and left.

"Oh do excuse me a minute," said Mrs. Golightly, flickering her eyelashes, and she caught Mrs. Gampish at the elevator. Mrs. Gampish looked at her with distaste.

"I want to tell you, Mrs. Gampish," said Mrs. Golightly with true humility, and speaking very low, "that I have never been to a Convention before, and I want to confess to you my stupidity. I am not really rude, only stupid and so shy although I have three children that I am truly in a whirl. Will you be able ever to forgive me? . . . It would be very kind of you if you feel that you could. Oh, please do try."

There was a silence between them as the elevators came and went. Then Mrs. Gampish gave a wan smile.

"You are too earnest, my child," she said. ("Oh how good you are," breathed Mrs. Golightly.) "I wouldn't myself know one person in this whole Convention – except Mrs. Finkel and no one could forget her," continued Mrs. Gampish, "and I never knew you each time you told me who you were *until* you told me, so you needn't have worried. If you want to know why I'm going to bed, it's because I don't like bridge and anyway, I *do* have a headache."

"Oh I'm so glad you *really* have a headache, no I mean I'm so sorry, and I think you're perfectly sweet, Mrs. Gampish, and if ever you come to Canada . . . " and she saw the faintly amused smile of Mrs. Gampish going up in the elevator. "Well I never," she said, but she felt happier.

She turned, and there was Tom hurrying past. "Oh Tom," she called. He stopped.

"Having a good time darling?" he said in a hurry. "D'you want to come to the meeting at Salt Lake City next year? " and he smiled at her encouragingly.

"Oh Tom," she said, "I'd adore it!" (What a changed life. Del Monte, Mr. Flanagan's shooting lodge, Salt Lake City, all in a minute, you might say.)

"Well, well!" said Tom in surprise and vanished.

On the way to her bedroom that night Mrs. Golightly met Mr. Flanagan walking very slowly down the hall.

"How do you do, Mr. Flanagan!" said Mrs. Golightly gaily. She felt that he was already her host at his shooting lodge.

Mr. Flanagan stopped and looked at her seriously as from a great distance. It was obvious that he did not know her. "How do you do," he said very carefully and with a glazed expression. "Did we meet or did we meet? In any case, how do you do." And he continued walking with the utmost care down the corridor.

"Oh . . . ," said Mrs. Golightly, her eyes wide open . . . "oh . . . " It was probable that Mr. Flanagan invited every-one to the shooting lodge. The shooting lodge began to vanish like smoke.

When she entered the bedroom she saw that in her hurry before dinner she had not put her hat away. The quill was twice bent, and it dangled. She took scissors and cut it short. There, she thought, caressing and smoothing the feather, it looks all right, doesn't it? She had felt for a moment very low, disintegrated, but now as she sat on the bed in her blue dinner dress she thought, Mr. Flanagan isn't a bit afraid to be him and Mrs. Gampish isn't a bit afraid to be her and now I'm not a bit afraid to be me . . . at least, not much. As she looked down, smoothing her little short feather, a dreamy smile came on her face. Seals swam through the green waters of her mind, Mrs. Finkel passed and repassed in careless loveliness. Mrs. Gampish said austerely, "Too earnest, my child, too earnest." The ghost of the mimosa tree drifted, drifted. Salt Lake City, she thought fondly . . . and then . . . where? . . . anticipation . . . a delicious fear . . . an unfamiliar pleasure.

Mrs. Golightly was moving out of the class for beginners. She is much more skilful now (how agile and confiding are her eyelashes!) and when her husband says, "There's going to be a Convention in Mexico City" (or Chilliwack or Trois Rivières), she says with delight, "Oh *Tom* . . . !"

TWO

Haply the soul of my grandmother

CLOWN: What is the opinion of Pythagoras concerning wild
   fowl?
MALVOLIO: That the soul of our grandam might haply inhabit
   a bird.

TWELFTH NIGHT, Act IV, Scene ii.

"IT IS AIRLESS," said Mrs. Forrester.
"Yes there is no air," said the woman half beside her
half in front of her. The mouth of the tomb was no longer
visible behind them, but there was light. They stepped
carefully downwards. Mrs. Forrester looked behind her at
her husband. She was inexcusably nervous and wanted a
look or a gleam of reassurance from his face. But he did
not appear to see her. He scrutinized the yellow walls
which looked as if they were compounded of sandstone
and clay. Marcus seemed to be looking for something, but
there was nothing on the yellowish walls not even the
marks of pick and shovel.

Mrs. Forrester had to watch her steps on the stairs of
smoothed and worn pounded sandstone or clay, so she
turned again, looking downwards. It did not matter
whether she held her head up or down, there was no air.
She breathed, of course, but what she breathed was not air
but some kind of ancient vacuum. She supposed that this

absence of air must affect the noses and mouths and lungs of Marcus and of the woman from Cincinnati and the guide and the soldier and that she need not consider herself to be special. So, although she suffered from the airlessness and a kind of blind something, very old, dead, she knew that she must not give way to her impulse to complain again, saying, "I can't breathe! There is no air!" and certainly she must not turn and stumble up the steps into the blazing heat as she wished to do; neither must she faint. She had never experienced panic before, but she recognized all this for near panic. She stiffened, controlled herself (she thought), then relaxed, breathed the vacuum as naturally as possible, and continued her way down into the earth from small light to light. They reached the first chamber which was partly boarded up. Looking through the chinks of the planking they seemed to see a long and deep depression which because of its shape indicated that, once, a body had lain there, probably in a vast and ornate coffin constructed so as to magnify the size and great importance of its occupant. The empty depression spoke of a removal of some long object which, Mrs. Forrester knew, had lain there for thousands of years, hidden, sealed, alone, yet existing, in spite of the fact that generations of living men, know-alls, philosophers, scientists, slaves, ordinary people, kings, knew nothing about it. And then it had been suspected, and then discovered, and then taken away somewhere, and now there was only the depression which they saw. All that was mortal of a man or woman who had been all-powerful had lain there, accompanied by treasure hidden and sealed away by a generation from other generations (men do not trust their successors, and rightly), till only this great baked dried yellowish aridity of hills and valleys remained, which was called the Valley of the Kings. And somewhere in the valley were dead kings.

Peering between the boards and moving this way and that so as to obtain a better view, they saw that a frieze of figures ran round the walls above the level of the depression. The figures were all in profile, and although they were only two-dimensional, they had a look of intention and vigour which gave them life and great dignity. There was no corpulence; all were slim, wide of shoulder, narrow of hip. Mostly, Mrs. Forrester thought, they walked very erect. They did not seem to stand, or, if they stood, they stood as if springing already into motion. She thought, peering, that they seemed to walk, all in profile and procession, towards some seated Being, it might be a man, or it might be sexless, or it might be a cat, or even a large bird, no doubt an ibis. The moving figures proceeded either with hieratic gesture or bearing objects. The colours, in which an ochreous sepia predominated, were faintly clear. The airlessness of the chamber nearly overwhelmed her again and she put out her hand to touch her husband's arm. There was not much to see, was there? between these planks, so they proceeded on downwards. The guide, who was unintelligible, went first. The soldier followed them.

If ever I get out of this, thought Mrs. Forrester. The airlessness was only part of an ancientness, a strong persistence of the past into the now and beyond the now which terrified her. It was not the death of the place that so invaded her, although there was death; it was the long persistent life in which her bones and flesh and all the complex joys of her life and her machine-woven clothes and her lipstick that was so important to her were less than the bright armour of a beetle on which she could put her foot. Since all three of the visitors were silent in the tomb, it was impossible to know what the others felt. And anyway, one could not explain; and why explain (all this talk about "feelings"!).

The farther down the steps they went the more the air seemed to expire, until at the foot of the steps it really died. Here was the great chamber of the great king, and a sarcophagus had been left there, instructively, perhaps, so that the public, who came either for pleasure or instruction, should be able to see the sort of sight which the almost intoxicated excavators had seen as they removed the earth and allowed in the desecrating air – or what passed for air.

Since Mrs. Forrester was now occupied in avoiding falling down and thereby creating a small scene beside the sarcophagus which would annoy her and her husband very much indeed and would not help the lady from Cincinnati who had grown pale, none of the guide's talk was heard and no image of the sarcophagus or of the friezes or of the tomb itself remained in her mind. It was as a saved soul that she was aware of the general turning up towards the stairs, up towards the light, and she was not ashamed, now, to lay her hand upon her husband's arm, really for support, in going up the stairs.

They emerged into the sunlight which blinded them and the heat that beat up at them and bore down on them, and all but the two Egyptians fumbled for their dark glasses. The soldier rejoined his comrade at the mouth of the tomb, and the guide seemed to vanish round some cliff or crag. The two soldiers were unsoldierly in appearance although no doubt they would enjoy fighting anyone if it was necessary.

Marcus and Mrs. Forrester and the lady from Cincinnati whose name was Sampson or Samson looked around for a bit of shade. The lion-coloured crags on their left did of course cast a shade, but it was the kind of shade which did not seem to be of much use to them, for they would have to climb onto farther low crags to avail themselves of the shade, and the sun was so cruel in the Valley of the Kings that no European or North American could make shift to move one step unless it was necessary.

"Where's that guide?" said Marcus irritably, of no one, because no one knew. The guide had gone, probably to wave on the motor car which should have been waiting to pick them up. Mrs. Forrester could picture him walking, running, gesticulating, garments flowing, making all kinds of gratuitous movements in the heat. We're differently made, she thought, it's all those centuries.

"I think," said Mrs. Sampson timidly, "that this s-scems to be the best p-place."

"Yes," said Mrs. Forrester who was feeling better though still too hot and starved for air, "that's the best place. There's enough shade there for us all," and they moved to sit down on some yellow rocks which were too hot for comfort. Nobody talked of the tomb which was far below the ground on their right.

Mrs. Forrester spoke to her husband who did not answer. He looked morose. His dark brows were concentrated in a frown and it was obvious that he did not want to talk to her or to anybody else. Oh dear, she thought. It's the tomb – he's never like that unless it's really something. They sat in silence, waiting for whatever should turn up. The two soldiers smoked at some distance.

This is very uncomfortable, this heat, thought Mrs. Forrester, and the tomb has affected us unpleasantly. She reflected on Lord Carnarvon who had sought with diligence, worked ardently, superintended excavation, urged on discovery, was bitten by an insect – or so they said – and had died. She thought of a co-worker of his who lay ill with some fever in the small clay-built house past which they had driven that morning. Why do they do those things, these men? Why do they do it? They do it because they have to; they come here to be uncomfortable and unlucky and for the greatest fulfilment of their lives; just as men climb mountains; just as Arctic and Antarctic explorers go to the polar regions to be uncomfortable and unlucky and for the greatest fulfilment of their lives. They have to. The thought of the Arctic gave her a pleasant feeling and she determined to lift the pressure that seemed to have settled on all three of them which was partly tomb, no doubt, but chiefly the airlessness to which their lungs were not accustomed, and, of course, this heat.

She said with a sort of imbecile cheerfulness, "How about an ice-cream cone?"

Mrs. Sampson looked up at her with a pale smile and Marcus did not answer. No, she was not funny, and she subsided. Out of the rocks flew two great burnished-winged insects and attacked them like bombers. All three ducked and threw up their arms to protect their faces.

"Oh ... " and "oh ... " cried the women and forgot about the heat while the two vicious bright-winged insects charged them, one here, one there, with a clattering hiss. Mrs. Forrester did not know whether one of the insects had hit and bitten Marcus or Mrs. Sampson. She had driven them away, she thought, and as she looked around and her companions looked up and around, she saw that the insects, which had swiftly retired, now dived down upon them again.

The car came round a corner and stopped beside them. There was only the driver. The guide had departed and would no doubt greet them at the hotel with accusations and expostulations. They climbed into the car, the two women at the back and Marcus – still morose – in front with the driver. The car started. The visit to the tomb had not been a success, but at all events the two insects did not accompany them any farther.

They jolted along very fast in the dust which covered them and left a rolling column behind. At intervals the driver honked the horn because he liked doing it. In the empty desert he honked for pleasure. They had not yet reached the trail in the wide sown green belt that bordered the Nile.

The driver gave a last honk and drew up. As the dust settled, they saw, on their right, set back in the dead hills, a row of arches, not a colonnade but a row of similar arches separated laterally a little from each other and leading, evidently, into the hills. They must be tombs, or caves. These arches were black against the dusty yellow of the rock. Mrs. Forrester was forced to admit to herself that the row of arches into the hills was beautiful. There seemed to be about twenty or thirty arches, she estimated when she thought about it later.

There they sat.

"Well, what are we waiting for?" Marcus asked the driver.

The driver became voluble and then he turned to the women behind, as Marcus, who was impatient to get on, did not seem to co-operate.

"I think he has to w-wait a few minutes for someone who m-may be there. He has to pick someone up unless they've already gone," said Mrs. Sampson. "He has to w-wait."

The driver then signified that if they wished they could go up to the tombs within the arches. Without consultation together they all immediately said no. They sat back and waited. Can Marcus be ill? Mrs. Forrester wondered. He is too quiet.

Someone stood at the side of the car, at Mrs. Forrester's elbow. This was an aged bearded man clothed in a long ragged garment and a head-furnishing which was neither skull cap nor tarboosh. His face was mendicant but not crafty. He was too remote in being, Mrs. Forrester thought, but he was too close in space.

"Lady," he said, "I show you something" ("Go away," said Mrs. Forrester), and he produced a small object from the folds of his garment. He held it up, between finger and thumb, about a foot from Mrs. Forrester's face.

The object on which the two women looked was a small human hand, cut off below the wrist. The little hand was wrapped in grave-clothes, and the small fingers emerged from the wrapping, neat, gray, precise. The fingers were close together, with what appeared to be nails or the places for nails upon them. A tatter of grave-clothes curled and fluttered down from the chopped-off wrist.

"Nice hand. Buy a little hand, lady. Very good very old very cheap. Nice mummy hand."

"Oh g-go away!" cried Mrs. Sampson, and both women averted their faces because they did not like looking at the small mummy's hand.

The aged man gave up, and moving on with the persistence of the East he held the little hand in front of Marcus.

"Buy a mummy hand, gentleman sir. Very old very nice very cheap, sir. Buy a little hand."

Marcus did not even look at him.

"NIMSHI," he roared. Marcus had been in Egypt in the last war.

He roared so loud that the mendicant started back. He rearranged his features into an expression of terror. He shambled clumsily away with a gait which was neither running nor walking, but both. Before him he held in the air the neat little hand, the little raped hand, with the tatter of grave-clothes fluttering behind it. The driver, for whom the incident held no interest, honked his horn, threw his hands about to indicate that he would wait no longer, and then drove on.

When they had taken their places in the boat with large sails which carried them across the Nile to the Luxor side, Mrs. Forrester, completely aware of her husband's malaise but asking no questions, saw that this river and these banks and these tombs and temples and these strange agile people to whom she was alien and who were alien to her had not – at four o'clock in the afternoon – the charm that had surprised her in the lily green and pearly cool scene at six o'clock that morning. The sun was high and hot, the men were noisy, the Nile was just water, and she wished to get Marcus back to the hotel.

When they reached the hotel Marcus took off his outer clothes and lay on the bed.

"What is it, Marc?"

"Got a headache."

It was plain to see, now, that he was ill. Mrs. Forrester rang for cold bottled water for Marcus to drink and for ice for compresses. She rummaged in her toilet case and found that she had put in a thermometer as a sort of charm against disease. That was in Vancouver, and how brash, kind, happy, and desirable Vancouver seemed now. Marcus had a temperature of 104°.

There were windows on each side wall of the room. They were well screened and no flies could, one thought, get in; so, by having the windows open, the ghost of the breeze that blew off the Nile River entered and passed out of the room but did not touch Marcus. There was, however, one fly in the room, nearly as dangerous as a snake. Mrs. Forrester took the elegant little ivory-handled fly switch that she had used in Cairo and, sitting beside her husband, flicked gently when the fly buzzed near him.

"Don't."

"All right, dear," she said with the maddening indulgence of the well to the sick. She went downstairs.

"Is that compartment still available on the Cairo train tonight?" she asked.

"*Si*, madame."

"We will take it. My husband is not well."

"Not well! That is unfortunate, madame," said the official at the desk languidly. "I will arrange at once."

It was clear that the management did not sympathize with illness and would prefer to get rid of sick travellers immediately.

Mrs. Forrester went upstairs and changed the compress. She then went and sat by the window overlooking the Nile. She reflected again that this country, where insects carried curses in their wings, made her uneasy. It was too old and strange. She had said as much to Marcus who felt nothing of the kind. He liked the country. But then, she thought, I am far too susceptible to the power of Place, and Marcus is more sensible; these things do not affect him in this way, and, anyway, he knows Egypt. However high the trees and mountains of her native British Columbia, they were native to her. However wide the prairies, she was part of them. However fey the moors of Devon, however ancient Glastonbury or London, they were part of her. Greece was young and she was at home there. The Parthenon in ruins of glory was fresh and fair. And Socrates, drinking the hemlock among his friends as the evening sun smote Hymettus . . . was that last week . . . was he indeed dead? But now . . . let us go away from here.

Below the window, between a low wall and the river,

knots of men stood, chattering loudly – Egyptians, Arabs, Abyssinians, and an old man with two donkeys. The air was full of shouting. They never ceased. They shouted, they laughed, they slapped their thighs, they quarrelled. No one could sleep. The sickest man could not sleep in that bright hot loud afternoon. This was their pleasure, cheaper than eating, drinking, or lust. But she could do nothing. The uproar went on. She changed the compress, bending over her husband's dark face and closed eyes and withdrawn look.

It's odd (and she returned to the thought of this country which in spite of its brightness and darkness and vigour was fearful to her), that I am Canadian and am fair, and have my roots in that part of England which was ravaged and settled by blond Norsemen; and Marcus is Canadian and is dark, and before generations of being Canadian he was Irish, and before generations of being Irish – did the dark Phoenicians come? – and he finds no strangeness here and I do.

In the late evening Marcus walked weakly onto the Cairo train. The compartment was close, small, and grimy. The compressed heat of the evening was intense. They breathed dust. Mrs. Forrester gently helped her husband on to the berth. He looked round.

"I can't sleep down here!" he said. "You mustn't go up above in all this heat!" But he could do no other.

"I shan't go up," she said consolingly. "See!" and she took bedclothes from the upper berth and laid them on the floor beside his berth. "I shall be cooler down here." There she lay all night long, breathing a little stale air and grit which entered by a small grid at the bottom of the door. "Oh . . . you sleeping on the floor . . . !" groaned Marcus.

And outside in the dark, she thought, as the train moved north, is that same country that in the early dawning looks so lovely. In the faint pearl of morning, peasants issue from huts far apart. The family – the father, the ox, the brother, the sons, the children, the women in trailing black, the dog, the asses – file to their work between the lines of pale green crops. There again is something hieratic, ageless, in their movements as they file singly one behind the other between the green crops, as the figures on the frieze had filed, one behind the other. Here and there in the morning stand the white ibis, sacred, unmolested, among the delicate green. How beguiling was the unawareness, and the innocency. Then, in that morning hour, and only then, had she felt no fear of Egypt. This scene was universal and unutterably lovely. She . . .

"A LITTLE HAND," said her husband loudly in the dark, and spoke strange words, and then was silent.

Yes, buy a little hand, sir, nice, cheap, very old. Buy a little hand. Whose hand?

When morning came Marcus woke and looked down in surprise.

"Whatever are you doing down there?" he asked in his ordinary voice.

"It was cooler," said his wife. "Did you sleep well?" and she scrambled up.

"Me? Sleep? Oh yes, I think I slept. But there was something . . . a hand . . . I seemed to dream about a hand . . . What hand? . . . Oh yes, that hand . . . I don't quite remember . . . in the tomb . . . you didn't seem to notice the lack of air in that tomb, did you . . . I felt something brushing us in there . . . brushing us all day . . . That was a heck of a day . . . Where's my tie?"

He stood up weakly. Without speaking, Mrs. Forrester handed her husband his tie.

Marcus, whose was that little hand, she thought and would think . . . whose was it? . . . Did it ever know you . . . did you ever know that hand? . . . Whose hand was it, Marcus? . . . oh let us go away from here!

THREE

On Nimpish Lake

S ANDHILL CRANES fly high over Nimpish Lake. Geese fly high too. They fly south from the vast north-lands beyond the Arctic watershed. They fly strongly, with outstretched necks. Their heads are thrust forward. Their voices are raised in harsh and musical clamour. Why do they cry, cry, cry, as they fly. Is it jubilation or argument or part of the business of flying. Who knows how much they see of the forests of British Columbia as they fly south. How much do they see of the mountains and valleys in their spearhead flight, and how much do they see of human habitation. Their old leader seeks a lake that he knows, or a chain of lakes, where they will camp for the night. They will circle down when the wise old leader sees his lake. They will circle down talking their vehement goose talk. There they will rest where they are safe in protected places, or where they are remote from men. Perhaps they will stay for a few days. Some of these strong geese are tired. The wise old leader knows.

Nimpish Lake is far to find. You drive inland for a day, and then next morning you leave the rugged highway and drive on a narrow winding road through the sage brush along waggon tracks, over the cattle ranges, up into the hills through the forest of crowded little pines. The forest seems quiet. You think there is little life in these high woods, for you see and hear no birds there. But perhaps you hear a chipmunk scolding or you see a squirrel carrying great whiskers of grass dried by the summer. He is making his winter home. He needs plenty of grass, because in these parts winter is long and severe for little hibernating creatures. When you reach the cabin beside Nimpish Lake you will see the gray whiskey-jacks who love the neighbourhood of man – what cheeky birds they are and how endearing – and magpies sometimes, and the pretty kingfisher, the osprey and the eagle. The rapacious hawk keeps to the open country. Before you see the lake through the trees you will hear the loons laughing and crying on the water. The loon is the true owner of the lake, and the loon's melodious unhappy cry is the true voice of these regions.

The lame man and his little brother rowed away from the cabin on Nimpish Lake. They rowed across the lake to a sunken log that they knew, where there was a pool and sometimes there were good fish. "Look," cried the little boy, pointing, "geese!" His brother stopped rowing. They both looked upwards. "Cranes," said the big brother. "Geese," said the little boy, "no, it's cranes!" The high silvery trumpeting of the sandhill cranes came clearly and magically to them. The fluid arrow of birds passed swiftly over the tranquil lake, over the hills to the south, and vanished from sight. The sound of the silvery trumpeting became only the memory of a sound in the still air. It is always like this on Nimpish Lake in late September. Nimpish Lake, five thousand feet up in the hills, the geese and cranes flying south, the aspens turning to honey gold after the first frost, and all the creatures getting ready for winter.

The lake with a wooded shore-line of thirty miles provides many a little bay for fishing and for protection from the sudden lake storms, but only a few for landing. Towards one of these bays with its narrow strip of silt and shingle the two brothers rowed when lunch time seemed to come. On the mild and deceptive mirror of the lake's expanse there was only one other boat. This boat also approached the narrow beach, but uncertainly.

The little boy rowed. The lame man, seated in the stern, cast and silently cast. He selected a dimple on the sweet surface of Nimpish Lake and there he dropped his fly. The occupant of the other boat behaved in a more lively and less expert fashion. He cast with abandon. He lashed his line into strange and unproductive curves. He caught himself. He detached himself. He seized the oars and rowed splashingly. His boat was the centre of commotion upon the waters. The Kamloops trout drew off from his vicinity and eyed each other in their disagreeable way. They stared, flickered, and darted away. They flickered up staring. Staring they flickered away.

"Gosh, look at that man," said the little boy. "Gosh Hughie just look at him. Look at that Mr. Leander."

"You look at your own rowing," said the big brother. "Hey, you're putting us into the reeds, keep out, keep out. *Now* look where you are! Never mind about Mr. Leander. *That's* better." The little boy struggled and righted the boat again. He still looked with bright eyes at Mr. Leander. Mr. Leander had come all the way from Salt Lake City to catch a fish, and the little boy was sure he never would. And so it was.

But now the morning fishing was over, and the brothers reached the little bay. When Mr. Leander arrived it was clear to the recumbent sandwich eaters that he had not enjoyed himself. The big brother was sympathetic. He gave friendly words and then abruptly fell asleep on the piney shingle. He could do that. The little brother could not do that, and besides he was awake to every emanation from the shining lake and sky and to the handsome Mr. Leander lolling beside him. Mr. Leander had lighted a large cigar. How urban, how elegant Mr. Leander looked as he lounged on the shingle smoking his large cigar. Somehow, just by sitting there in his good clothes and smoking his cigar Mr. Leander transformed the primitive and charming shores of the remote lake into a deserted club. He talked in a slow pleasing growl. He smoked, and occasionally he also spat, simply for pleasure, without any explanation. From where he sat his expectorations fell neatly into the limpid lake. The little boy watched and appreciated.

"My," said Mr. Leander softly, "isn't this lake a picture? I certainly love this lake." Spit, right into the clear water that lapped deliciously the little beach. "I'm just crazy about this lake. I'm just crazy about Nature anyway. I thought I'd like to stay here a week but I think I'd get kinder restless." Spit. "How old are you?"

"Going on eleven," said the little boy.

"He your brother?" inquired Mr. Leander.

"Yes sir, half brother," said the little boy.

"Quite a bit older'n you," said Mr. Leander.

"Twenny years older," said the little boy.

"Well, he's a very, very lovely man," growled Mr. Leander gently. "He's as common as an old shoe and a very, very lovely man," and he spat. The little boy said nothing. Hughie, a very lovely man. Hughie, as common as an old shoe. He felt hurt. Hughie, as common as an old shoe. No, Mr. Leander didn't mean that kind of common. He meant comfortable and nice to have.

The lame man woke up and felt at once the warm bliss of the day. Mr. Leander got up unwillingly. He had to try again. They pushed away in the two boats. The brothers rowed slowly along the tulé reeds that lined the shore. The little boy had the fishing-rod.

"Gosh Hughie," said the little boy, "you should have seen him spit. He just did *this* . . . " and the little boy spat. Again. Again. He began to admire Mr. Leander.

"Here *look* out, *look* out," said the big brother suddenly aware of him, "you stop that! You row now, and I'll fish as far as the beaver house."

The handsome Mr. Leander stopped rowing. He leaned forward looking at the bottom of the boat. He was thinking. An osprey circled overhead. Sometimes the big brother made a cast. Sometimes he played a fish. Vigour had gone out of the day. Sky and silent lake breathed a charm. The dreaming little boy rowed slowly. The osprey circled above. Not far from the boat floated a loon and her two big babies. Out of the silence the loon uttered her startled and melancholy laughing cry. Her laugh clattered over the lake and was thrown back by the shores. The vacuous but musical cry of the loon spoke to all the creatures on the lake. All the creatures listened. The laugh ceased abruptly and the two big babies swam closer to their mother. Then the loons dived. One. Two. Three. The sky and the lake blazed with the outrageous colours of the setting sun. The little boy rowed very slowly. The trout, beautiful and exasperating, began to jump and jump from the shining surface of the lake. They jumped all around the exasperated Mr. Leander. They jumped near the idling brothers. Splash here. Splash there. Little fountains of water arose far and near in the placid lake, and there came the delayed "plop" of the jumping fish. The osprey dropped from high and hit the water in an explosion of flying spray. The osprey shook itself like a dog, and flew up carrying in its talons a silver fish. It was getting cold, so the big brother took over the oars from the little boy and rowed through the coloured water out into the lake towards home.

Overhead came the sound of high music. They looked up. High in the flaming sky drove a spearhead of great birds flying south. The clamour came nearer. The little boy's brown face turned to the sky. "Oh Hughie, it's geese isn't it?" he said.

"Yes. Geese. Just look at them," said the lame man, gazing upwards. He gazed until the clamorous flying shaft had passed like a filament from sight and sound. He felt a queer exaltation, a sudden flash that was deepest envy of the wild geese, strongly flying and crying together on their known way, a most secret pain.

FOUR

From Flores

U P AT FLORES Island, Captain Findlay Crabbe readied his fishboat the *Effie Cee* for the journey home and set out in good spirits while the weather was fair. But even by the time he saw the red shirt flapping like mad from the rocky point just north of the Indian's place the wind had freshened. Nevertheless Fin Crabbe told the big man at the wheel to turn into shore because there must be some trouble there and that Indian family was pretty isolated. As the man at the wheel turned the nose of the boat towards the shore, the skipper listened to the radio. The weather report was good, and so he went out on the small deck well satisfied and stood there with his hands on his hips, looking at the shore where the red flag was.

The third man on the fishboat was just a young fellow. Up at Flores Island he had come down to the float with his gear all stowed in a duffel bag and asked the skipper to take him down to Port Alberni. He was an anxious kid, tall, dark, and thin-faced. He said he'd pay money for the ride and he spoke of bad news which with a young man sounds like parents or a girl and with an older young man sounds like a wife or children or a girl. Fin Crabbe said shortly that the boy could come, although the little *Effie Cee* was not geared for passengers. He didn't need to pay.

Captain Crabbe was small. He had come as an undersized boy to the west coast of Vancouver Island and there he had stayed. He had been fairish and was now bald. His eyes were sad like a little bloodhound's eyes and pink under, but he was not sad. He was a contented man and rejoiced always to be joined again with his wife and his gangling son and daughter. Mrs. Crabbe's name was Effie but she was called Mrs. Crabbe or Mom and her name had come to be used only for the *Effie Cee* which was by this time more Effie than Mrs. Crabbe was. "I'm taking home an Indian basket for Mrs. Crabbe," the skipper might say. "Mrs. Crabbe sure is an authority on Indian baskets." Fin Crabbe was his name up and down the coast but at home he was the Captain or Pop, and so Mrs. Crabbe would say, "The Captain plans to be home for Christmas. The Captain's a great family man. I said to him 'Pop, if you're not home for Christmas, I'll . . . !' " Thus they daily elevated each other in esteem and loved each other with simple mutual gratification. In bed no names were needed by Mrs. Crabbe and the Captain. (When they shall be dead, as they will be, what will avail this happy self-satisfaction. But now they are not dead, and the Captain's wife as often before awaits the Captain who is on his way down the coast from Flores Island, coming home for Christmas.)

Fin Crabbe had planned for some time to reach Port Alberni early in Christmas week and that suited Ed, the big crewman, too. Ed was not a family man although he had a wife somewhere; but what strong upspringing black curly hair he had and what black gambling eyes. He was powerful, not to be governed, and a heller when he drank. He was quick to laugh, quick to hit out, quick to take a girl, quick to leave her, a difficult wilful volatile enjoying man of poor judgment, but he got along all right with little Fin Crabbe. He did not want to spend Christmas in Flores Island when there was so much doing in Alberni and Port Alberni.

Captain Crabbe's family lived in Alberni proper which to the dweller in a city seems like a fairly raw small town at the end of a long arm through the forest to nowhere, and to the dweller up the coast or in the Queen Charlottes seems like a small city with every comfort, every luxury, motor cars speeding in and out by the long road that leads through the forest to the fine Island Highway, lighted streets, plumbing, beer parlours, a hospital, churches, schools, lumber mills, wharves. It lives for and on trees and salt water. Behind it is a huge hinterland of giant forests. Before it lies the long tortuous salt-water arm of the open sea.

Captain Crabbe, as the bow of the *Effie Cee* turned towards the pine-clad but desolate and rocky shore, cutting across the tricky undulations of the ocean, again gave his habitual look at the sky, north and west. The sky was overclouded but so it usually is in these parts at this time of year. Since these rocky shores are not protected as are the rocky shores of the British Columbia mainland by the long stretches of sweet liveable gulf islands and by the high barrier of mountainous Vancouver Island itself, the west coast of the island lies naked to the Pacific Ocean which rolls in all the way from Asia and breaks upon the reefs and rocks and hard sands, and the continuous brewing of weather up in an air cauldron in the north seethes and spills over and rushes out of the Gulf of Alaska, often moderating before it reaches lower latitudes; but sometimes it roars down and attacks like all hell. The fishboat and tugboat men know this weather well and govern themselves accordingly. Next morning perhaps the ocean smiles like a dissolute angel. The fishboat and tugboat men know that, too, and are not deceived. So that although Fin Crabbe knew all this as well as he knew his own thumb, he did not hesitate to turn the *Effie Cee* towards the shore when he saw the red shirt flapping at the end of the rock point but he had no intention of stopping there nor of spending any time at all unless his judgment warranted it, for on this trip his mind was closely set to home.

The turning aside of the fishboat in her journey irked the young passenger very much. Since the weather report on the radio was fairly good and anyway he was used to poor weather, he felt no concern about that. But here was delay and how much of it. He did not know how often he had read the letter which he again took out of his pocket, not looking at big Ed nor at little Captain Crabbe but frowning at the letter and at some memory. He was possessed entirely, usurped, by impatience for contact, by letter, by wire or – best of all – by speech and sight and touch with the writer of this letter. Now that he had started on the journey towards her, now that he had started, now that he was on his way, his confusion seemed to clear. He read again in the letter: "Dear Jason I am very unhappy I dont know I should tell you Ive thought and thought before I wrote you and then what kind of a letter because I could say awful things and say you must come to Vancouver right away and marry me or believe me I could just cry and cry or I could write and say plain to you O Jason do I beseech you think if we couldnt get married right away. I could say I love you and I do."

The young man folded the letter again. He looked with distaste at the red flag that signified an Indian's trouble and his own delay and his mind ran backwards again. The letter had found him at last and only two days ago. He had left the camp and had crossed to Flores and there an old man with a beard had told him that Fin Crabbe was all set to go to Alberni the next morning, and he had enquired for Captain Crabbe. As he had walked up and down the float pushing time forward, sometimes a violence of joy rose in him and surprised him. This was succeeded by a real fear that something would happen to prevent the fishboat from leaving, would prevent them reaching Alberni very soon, while all the time Josie did not even know whether he had received the letter. Many feelings were induced in him by what Josie had written, and now he thought ceaselessly about her to whom, only three days before, he had barely given a thought. He unfolded the letter again.

"I gess I dont know too much about love like in the

pictures but I do love you Jason and I wouldnt ever ever be a person who would throw this up at you. I dont sleep very good and some nights I threton to myself to kill myself and tho I am awful scared of that maybe that would be better and easiest for us all and next night I say no. Lots of girls go through with this but what do they do with the Baby and no real home for it and then I am bafled again and the time going."

Jason, looking out to the ocean but not seeing it, was aware of a different Josie. If a person had told me, he thought, that I'd want to get married and that I'd be crazy for this baby I'd say they were crazy, I'd say they were nuts, and impatience against delay surged over him again. The boat neared the mouth of the bay.

"One thing I do know I couldnt go back to the prairies with the Baby," (no, that's right, you couldn't go back) "so where would the Baby and me go. Mother would let me feel it every day even if she didnt mean to tho she would take us but Father no never. Then I think its the best thing for the Baby I should drown myself its quite easy in Vancouver its not like the prairies I do mean that."

The skipper was talking back and forth to the crewman at the wheel and the *Effie Cee* slowed down. There were beams of sunshine that came and went.

"I cant believe its me and I do pitty any poor girl but not begging you Jason because you must decide for yourself. Some people would pay no attention to this letter but I kind of feel youre not like some people but O please Jason get me a word soon and then I can know what. Josie."

From the pages arose the helpless and lonely anguish of little Josie and this anguish entered and consumed him too and it was all part of one storm of anxiety and anger that she was alone and she so quiet, and not her fault (he said), and impatience rose within him to reach a place where he could say to her Don't you worry kid, I'm coming! He thought with surprise Maybe I'm a real bad guy and I never knew it, maybe we're all bad and we don't know it. He read once more: "I am bafled again and the time is going . . . I do love you Jason." He put his head in his hands with dumb anger that she should be driven to this, but as soon as he reached a telephone in Alberni everything would be all right. As he suddenly looked up he thought he would go mad at this turning off course for any sick guy, or any kid who'd been crazy enough to break an arm. In his frustration and impatience there was an infusion of being a hero and rushing to save someone. Some hero, he said very sourly to himself, some hero.

The *Effie Cee* slowed to a stop and a black volley of cormorants, disturbed, flew away in a dark line. There was an Indian and an Indian woman and a little boy in a rowboat almost alongside the fishboat. The little boy was half lying down in an uncomfortable way and two rough sticks were tied to his leg. Three smaller children stood solemnly on the rocky shore looking at the two boats. Then they turned to play in a clumsy ceremonial fashion among the barnacled rocks. They did not laugh as they played.

Jason put the letter in his pocket and stood up. The rowboat jiggled on the water and Captain Crabbe was bending down and talking to the Indian. He listened and talked and explained. The Indian's voice was slow and muffled, but not much talk was needed. Anyone could see. "Okay," said the skipper and then he straightened himself and turned to look at Ed and Jason as much as to say . . . and Jason said, "Better I got into the rowboat and helped him lift the kid up," and the skipper said "Okay."

All this time the woman did not say anything. She kept her hands wrapped in her stuff dress and looked away or at the child. Jason slipped over the side and the rowboat at once became overcrowded which made it difficult for him and the Indian to lift the child up carefully without hurting him and without separating the boats. The Indian child made no sound and no expression appeared on his face so no one knew how much pain he suffered or whether he suffered at all. His eyes were brown and without meaning like the dusky opaque eyes of a fawn. The Indian spoke to his wife and she reached out her hands and held on to the fishboat so that the two craft would not be parted. Jason and the father succeeded in slipping their arms – "This way," said Jason, "see? do it this way" – under the child and raised him gradually up to where Ed and the skipper were kneeling. Everyone leaned too much to one side of the rowboat and Jason tried to steady it so that they would not fall with the child into the sea. All this time the woman had not spoken but had accepted whatever other people did as if she had no rights in the matter. When the child was safely on board, Jason sprang onto the deck and at once, at once, the *Effie Cee* turned and tore away with a white bone of spume in her mouth and a white wake of foam behind, leaving the Indians in the rowboat and the children on the shore looking after her.

"Best lay him on the floor, he'd maybe roll off of the bunk," said Fin Crabbe when they had lifted the child inside. "Mustn't let you get cold, Sonny," he said, and took down a coat that swung from a hook. The child regarded him in silence and with fear in his heart. One two another white man taking him to some place he did not know.

"Make supper Ed, and I'll take the wheel," said the skipper. The boat went faster ahead, rising and plunging as there was now a small sea running.

What'd I better do, thought Fin Crabbe and did not consult the crewman who hadn't much judgment. There were good reasons for going on through and trying to make Alberni late in the night or in early morning. That would surprise Mrs. Crabbe and she would be pleased, and the young fella seemed desperate to get to Alberni on account of this bad news; but here was this boy he'd taken aboard and the sooner they got him into hospital the better. I think it's his hip (he thought), I could turn back to Tofino but it'd be dark then and would he be any better off landing him in the dark and likely no doctor. Anyway I can make Ucluelet easy and spend the night. I don't like to take no chances but all in all I think we'll go on. And they went on.

Evening came and black night. It was winter cold outside and Jason crowded into the wheelhouse and looked out at the dark. The coming of night brought him nearer the telephone, so near he could all but touch it, but he could not touch it.

The *Effie Cee* could not make much speed now and ploughed slowly for hours never ending, it seemed to Jason, through water that had become stormy and in the dark she followed a sideways course so that she could cut a little across the waves that were now high and deep. Ed had the wheel and Captain Crabbe stood beside him. The storm increased. The boat's nose plunged into the waves and rose with the waves and the water streamed over. There was a wallowing, a sideways wallowing. The little fishboat became a world of noise and motion, a plunging, a rising, a plunging again. Jason wedged the child against the base of the bunk. The child cried out, and vomited with seasickness and fear. "Now now," said Jason, patting him. "Try the radio again," said Captain Crabbe.

Jason fiddled with the radio. "Can't seem to get anything," he said.

"Let me," said the skipper.

"Bust," he said.

But now the storm rapidly accelerated and the waves, innocent and savage as tigers, leaped at the *Effie Cee* and the oncoming rollers struck broadside and continuously. The little boy made sounds like an animal and Jason, in whom for the first time fear of what might come had struck down all elation and expectation, took the child's hand and held it. The little plunging boat was now the whole world and fate to Jason and to Fin Crabbe and to the Indian boy but not to Ed who had no fear. Perhaps because he had no love he had no fear. Standing over the wheel and peering into the dark, he seemed like a great black bull and it was to Jason as though he filled the cabin.

Ed turned the boat's nose towards shore to get away from the broadside of the waves. Fin Crabbe shouted at him to be heard above the storm. The boat had been shipping water and Jason, crouching beside the shaking child in a wash of water, heard the words "Ucluelet" and "lighthouse" and "rocks" but Ed would not listen. The skipper went on shouting at him and then he seized the wheel. He pushed the big man with all his strength, turning the wheel to starboard. Jason and the Indian child saw the big man and the little man fighting in the small space, in the din of the ocean, the howl of the wind, for possession of the wheel. As quick as a cat Ed drew off and hit the older man a great blow. Fin Crabbe crumpled and fell. He lay in the wash of the water at Ed's feet and Ed had his way, so the fishboat drove inshore, hurled by the waves onto the reefs, or onto the hard sand, or onto the place that Ed knew that he knew, whichever the dark should disclose, but not to the open sea. Captain Crabbe tried to raise himself and Jason crawled over towards him.

The skipper could not stand in the pitching boat. He looked up at Ed who was his executioner, the avenger of all that he had ever done, driving on against death for sure.

The thought of the abandonment of Josie (for now a belief was formed terribly in him that she was to be abandoned) pierced Jason through and through and then in the immediate danger the thought of Josie was no longer real but fled away on the wind and water, and there was nothing but fear. Without knowing what he did, he seized and held the child. Never could a man feel greater despair than Jason in the walnut shell of a reeling boat soon to be cracked between land and water. Ed, bent over the wheel, knowing everything, knowing just where they were, but not knowing, looked only forward into the blackness and drove on. The sea poured into the boat and at the same minute the lights went out and they were no longer together. Then the *Effie Cee* rose on a great wave, was

hurled upwards and downwards, struck the barnacled
reef, and split, and the following seas washed over.

A few days later the newspapers stated that in the recent
storm on the west coast of Vancouver Island the fishboat
Effie Cee was missing with two men aboard. These men
were Findlay Crabbe aged fifty-six and Edward Morgan
aged thirty-five, both of Alberni. Planes were continuing
the search.

A day or two afterwards the newspapers stated that it
was thought that there might have been a third man
aboard the *Effie Cee*. He was identified as Jason Black
aged twenty-two, employed as a logger up the coast near
Flores Island.

On the second morning after the wreck of the *Effie Cee*
the skies were a cold blue and the ocean lay sparkling and
lazy beneath the sun. Up the Alberni Canal the sea and air
were chilly and brilliant but still. Mrs. Crabbe spent the
day waiting on the wharf in the cold sunshine. She stood
or walked or sat, accompanied by two friends or by the
gangling son and daughter, and next day it was the same,
and the next. People said to her, "But he didn't set a day?
When did he *say* he'd be back?"

"He never said what day," she said. "The Captain
couldn't ever say what day. He just said the beginning of
the week, maybe Monday was what he said." She said "he
said, he said, he said" because it seemed to establish him
as living. People had to stop asking because they could not
bear to speak to Mrs. Crabbe standing and waiting on the
busy wharf, paying the exorbitant price of love. They
wished she would not wait there because it made them
uncomfortable and unhappy to see her.

Because Josie did not read the papers, she did not know
that Jason was dead. Days had passed and continued to
pass. Distraught, alone, deprived of hope and faith (two
sovereign remedies) and without the consolation of love,
she took secretly and with terror what she deemed to be
the appropriate path.

The Indian, who had fully trusted the man who took his

son away, heard nothing more. He waited until steady fine weather came and then took his family in his small boat to Tofino. From there he made his way to Alberni. Here he walked slowly up and down the docks and at last asked someone where the hospital was; but at the hospital no one seemed to know anything about his only son.

FIVE

God help the young fishman

THE OLD FISHMAN stepped out for a bit of lunch. The elderly lady said to the young fishman, "I'd like a nice bit of cod."

The young fishman went to the window, took up a fillet of cod and balanced it tentatively on waxed paper on his hand. "How's this?" he said.

"I don't like it filleted. I like it in the piece."

"Then how's this. A nice small fish. Tail end. A matter of two pound or maybe a pound and three quarters."

Another customer came in, and stood waiting.

"Did you say a pound and *three* quarters?"

"I'll weigh it . . . there it is . . . all but two pounds."

"I'd like it with the skin off, and I'd like you to fillet it."

The young man looked at the latter half of the fish and said, "Well lady, that's filleted fish I showed you first in the window. You said you'd rather have the piece . . . "

Another customer came in.

"What I mean is, it's not so tasty when the fillet runs *that* way. Anyone'll tell you it's not so tasty."

"It's off of the same fish, lady."

"Well, it's not so tasty."

"Did you say you wanted it skinned?"

"Skinned? No, I don't want it skinned."

"You *do* know, lady" (knife hung in air), "it'll cost you more filleting this piece?"

"How much more?"

"Okay okay I'll fillet it . . . seventy-nine cents. Is there anything else?"

"No, nothing else."

Another customer came in.

"Oh just a minute just a minute," said the elderly lady, "have you got a crab?"

"Say lady . . . I . . . there's a customer here . . . "

"All right then. You attend to that other party and I'll . . . "

The customer said, "I'd like a nice piece of salmon in the piece for boiling. Centre cut, about two and a half pounds, well not less than two and a half pounds and certainly not more than three . . . haven't you any white salmon, we like it much better than the red. . . . "

"No lady, only the red."

"Haven't you any of the pink?"

"No lady, only the red."

"I don't know whether I can wait," said the elderly lady, "but I *would* like to have a crab . . . "

"Let me see that middle piece," said the customer. "Oh . . . that's near the head end. That wouldn't do. My husband . . . Well, *that* piece. All right. Not more than three pounds."

"How's this?" asked the young fishman, laying his knife along the silver skin.

"I can't see. You're standing in the way."

"Did you say it was okay?"

"No. I say you're standing in the *way*. I can't see."

"Oh . . . well, *now* can you see?"

Another customer came in.

"Yes, now I can see. Oh that's not enough . . . just a leetle . . . no, that's too much. Oh I forgot to ask you how much is it?"

"Eighty-five."

"Well, move the knife a bit to the right then . . . there . . . that should do."

The fishman cut the fine thick silver red-fleshed fish. He weighed it. "Three and a quarter."

"Three and a *quarter*! I said not more than three! Couldn't you cut a steak off? Yes, just about . . . "

"Okay . . . that will be two fifty-five."

"Oh stop stop, I *am* sorry to ask you to undo it but couldn't you slip in a bit of that nice parsley for sauce . . . thank you *so* much. *Good-bye* . . . oh I forgot . . . *do* excuse me" (smiling winningly at the next customer), "my cousin asked me to get her two salmon steaks one for tonight and one for tomorrow night but I think she must have made a mistake. Better give me one salmon steak and one large fillet of sole. Or two small . . . oh, here she comes! She'd better choose! Hello Lucile how are you. There's some nice sole. And before you wrap that up again, just a teeny bit of shrimp meat, enough for sandwiches . . . no, that's too much. Oh thank you! Forty-five cents? Good-bye."

"Two salmon steaks or let me see," murmured the cousin.

"How much did you say the crabs were?" asked the elderly lady.

"Forty cents and fifty cents."

"They used to be twenty-five cents."

"They're forty cents and fifty cents."

"Which are the forty cent ones?"

Another customer came in.

"That's forty cents."

"And is the other one fifty cents?"

"Yes mam."

"It doesn't look any bigger to me."

"Well it's bigger all right."

"It looks the same to me."

"Well it's bigger all right. Which one would you like, lady?"

"I'd like to feel the claws. I always like to feel the claws. No, turn it over."

"Say lady. . . . "

"I'll take the forty cent one but I don't feel satisfied."

The fishman wrapped up the crab and said nothing but "Forty cents."

"Do *you* think, I mean as a fish person do *you* think it *really* makes a difference if there's an R in the month," asked the next customer. "Oysters I mean."

"We wouldn't keep them lady if they wasn't fresh."

"But what is your *own* opinion?"

The young fishman looked sideways and said nothing.

"Well then, I'll take a pint . . . I suppose you couldn't give me three quarters of a pint?"

"Pints and half pints is the way they come."

"Oh I do think it was nicer when they used to come in bulk!" The fishman did not express an opinion.

"Seventy-five cents," he said and looked about him at the customers. "Next?" he said.

"Two herrings," said a bad-tempered looking woman with a dark moustache.

"Did you say two herrings?" said the young fishman with light in his eyes.

"You heard me," snapped the customer.

What a lovely lady, thought the young fishman, what a lovely lady. He looked tenderly, earnestly at the bad-tempered-looking woman in whom all the sins of woman were forgiven on account of two herrings.

Still the young man gazed. Something was held suspended. The fish shop seemed to dream.

What's wrong with him, the bad-tempered-woman thought uneasily. God, what's he looking at; and instinctively she covered her moustache with her hand.

The young fishman gave her the small parcel and unwillingly withdrew his eyes from her. "Next," he said, and resumed.

Another customer came in.

Sometime he will take the fish knife to the whole lot of them.

SIX

We have to sit opposite

E VEN IN the confusion of entering the carriage at Salzburg, Mrs. Montrose and her cousin Mrs. Forrester noticed the man with the blue tooth. He occupied a corner beside the window. His wife sat next to him. Next to her sat their daughter of perhaps seventeen. People poured into the train. A look passed between Mrs. Montrose and Mrs. Forrester. The look said, "These people seem to have filled up the carriage pretty well, but we'd better take these seats while we can as the train is so full. At least we can have seats together." The porter, in his porter's tyrannical way, piled their suitcases onto the empty rack above the heads of the man with the blue tooth, and his wife, and his daughter, and departed. The opposite rack was full of baskets, bags and miscellaneous parcels. The train started. Here they were. Mrs. Montrose and Mrs. Forrester smiled at each other as they settled down below the rack which was filled with miscellaneous articles. Clinging vines that they were, they felt adventurous and successful. They had travelled alone from Vienna to Salzburg, leaving in Vienna their doctor husbands to continue attending the clinics of Dr. Bauer and Dr. Hirsch. And now, after a week in Salzburg, they were happily on their way to rejoin their husbands, who had flown to Munich.

Both Mrs. Montrose and Mrs. Forrester were tall, slight and fair. They were dressed with dark elegance. They knew that their small hats were smart, suitable and becoming, and they rejoiced in the simplicity and distinction of their new costumes. The selection of these and other costumes, and of these and other hats in Vienna had, they regretted, taken from the study of art, music and history a great deal of valuable time. Mrs. Montrose and Mrs. Forrester were sincerely fond of art, music and history and longed almost passionately to spend their days in the Albertina Gallery and the Kunsthistorische Museum. But the modest shops and shop windows of the craftsmen of Vienna had rather diverted the two young women from the study of art and history, and it was easy to lay the blame for this on the museums and art galleries which, in truth, closed their doors at very odd times. After each day's enchanting pursuits and disappointments, Mrs. Montrose and Mrs. Forrester hastened in a fatigued state to the café where they had arranged to meet their husbands who by this time had finished their daily sessions with Dr. Bauer and Dr. Hirsch.

This was perhaps the best part of the day, to sit together happily in the sunshine, toying with the good Viennese coffee or a glass of wine, gazing and being gazed upon, and giving up their senses to the music that flowed under the chestnut trees. (Ah Vienna, they thought, Vienna, Vienna.)

No, perhaps the evenings had been the best time when after their frugal pension dinner they hastened out to hear opera or symphony or wild atavistic gypsy music. All was past now. They had been very happy. They were fortunate. Were they too fortunate?

Mrs. Montrose and Mrs. Forrester were in benevolent good spirits as they looked round the railway carriage and prepared to take their seats and settle down for the journey to Munich to meet their husbands. In their window corner, opposite the man with the blue tooth, was a large hamper. "*Do* you mind?" asked Mrs. Montrose, smiling sweetly at the man, his wife, and his daughter. She prepared to lift the hamper on which the charming view from the carriage window was of course wasted, intending to move it along the seat, and take its place. The man, his wife, and his daughter had never taken their eyes off Mrs. Montrose and Mrs. Forrester since they had entered the carriage.

"*If* you please," said the man loudly and slowly in German English, "*if* you please, that place belongs to my wife or to my daughter. For the moment they sit beside me, but I keep that place for my wife or my daughter. That seat is therefore reserved. It is our seat. You may of course use the two remaining seats."

"I'm sorry," said Mrs. Montrose, feeling snubbed, and she and Mrs. Forrester sat down side by side on the two remaining seats opposite the German family. Beside them the hamper looked out of the window at the charming view. Their gaiety and self-esteem evaporated. The train rocked along.

The three continued to stare at the two young women. Suddenly the mother leaned toward her daughter. She put up her hand to her mouth and whispered behind her hand, her eyes remaining fixed on Mrs. Montrose. The daughter nodded. She also stared at Mrs. Montrose. Mrs. Montrose flushed. The mother sat upright again, still looking at Mrs. Montrose, who felt very uncomfortable, and very much annoyed at blushing.

The man ceased staring at the two young women. He looked up at the rack above him, which contained their suitcases.

"Those are your suitcases," he asked, or rather announced.

"Yes," said Mrs. Montrose and Mrs. Forrester without smiles.

"They are large," said the man in a didactic manner, "they are too large. They are too large to be put on racks. A little motion, a very little motion, and they might fall. If they fall they will injure myself, my wife, or my daughter. It is better," he continued instructively, "that if they fall, they should fall upon your heads, not upon our heads.

That is logical. They are not my suitcases. They are your
suitcases. You admit it. Please to move your suitcases to
the opposite rack, where, if they fall, they will fall upon
your own heads." And he continued to sit there motionless. So did his wife. So did his daughter.

Mrs. Montrose and Mrs. Forrester looked at the suitcases in dismay. "Oh," said Mrs. Forrester, "they are so
heavy to move. If you feel like that, please won't you sit
on this side of the carriage, and we will move across,
under our own suitcases, though I can assure you they will
not fall. Or perhaps you would help us?"

"We prefer this side of the carriage," said the man with
the blue tooth. "We have sat here because we prefer this
side of the carriage. It is logical that you should move your
suitcases. It is not logical that my wife, my daughter and I
should give up our seats in this carriage, or remove your
suitcases."

Mrs. Montrose and Mrs. Forrester looked at each other
with rage in their hearts. All their self-satisfaction was
gone. They got up and tugged as the train rocked along.
They leaned resentfully across the erectly sitting man, and
his wife and his daughter. They experienced with exasper-
ation the realization that they had better make the best of
it. The train, they knew, was crowded. They had to remain
in this carriage with this disagreeable family. With much
pulling and straining they hauled down the heavy suitcases. Violently they removed the parcels of the German
family and lifted their own suitcases onto the rack above
their heads, disposing them clumsily on the rack. Panting
a little (they disliked panting), they settled down again side
by side with high colour and loosened wisps of hair. They
controlled their features so as to appear serene and unaware of the existence of anyone else in the railway carriage, but their hearts were full of black hate.

The family exchanged whispered remarks, and then
resumed their scrutiny of the two young women, whose
elegance had by this time a sort of tipsy quality. The girl
leaned toward her mother. She whispered behind her

hand to her mother, who nodded. Both of them stared at Mrs. Forrester. Then they laughed.

"Heavens!" thought the affronted Mrs. Forrester, "this is outrageous! Why can't Alice and I whisper behind our hands to each other about these people and make them feel simply awful! But they wouldn't feel awful. Well, we can't, just because we've been properly brought up, and it would be too childish. And perhaps they don't even know they're rude. They're just being natural." She breathed hard in frustration, and composed herself again.

Suddenly the man with the blue tooth spoke. "Are you English?" he said loudly.

"Yes – well – no," said Mrs. Forrester.

"No – well – yes," said Mrs. Montrose, simultaneously.

A derisive look came over the man's face. "You must know what you are," he said, "either you are English or you are not English. Are you, or are you not?"

"No," said Mrs. Montrose and Mrs. Forrester, speaking primly. Their chins were high, their eyes flashed, and they were ready for discreet battle.

"Then are you Americans?" said the man in the same bullying manner.

"No," said Mrs. Montrose and Mrs. Forrester.

"You can't deceive *me*, you know," said the man with the blue tooth, "I know well the English language. You *say* you are not English. You *say* you are not American. What, then, may I ask, are you? You must be something."

"We are Canadians," said Mrs. Forrester, furious at this catechism.

"*Canadians*," said the man.

"Yes, Canadians," said Mrs. Montrose.

"This," murmured Mrs. Forrester to Mrs. Montrose, "is more than I can bear!"

"What did you say?" said the man, leaning forward quickly, his hands on his knees.

"I spoke to my friend," said Mrs. Forrester coldly, "I spoke about my bear."

"Yes," said Mrs. Montrose, "she spoke about her bear."

"Your bear? Have you a bear? But you cannot have a bear!" said the man with some surprise.

"In Canada I have a bear. I have two bears," said Mrs. Forrester conceitedly.

"That is true," said Mrs. Montrose nodding, "she has two bears. I myself have five bears. My father has seven bears. That is nothing. It is the custom."

"What do you do with your bears?" asked the man.

"We eat them," said Mrs. Forrester.

"Yes," said Mrs. Montrose, "we eat them. It is the custom."

The man turned and spoke briefly to his wife and daughter, whose eyes opened wider than ever.

Mrs. Montrose and Mrs. Forrester felt pleased. This was better.

The man with the blue tooth became really interested. "Are you married?" he asked Mrs. Forrester.

"Yes," she replied. (We'll see what he'll say next, then we'll see what we can do.)

"And you?" he enquired of Mrs. Montrose. Mrs. Montrose seemed uncertain. "Well, yes, in a way, I suppose," she said.

The man with the blue tooth scrutinized Mrs. Montrose for a moment. "*Then*," he said, as though he had at last found her out, "if you are married, where is your husband?"

Mrs. Montrose took out her pocket handkerchief. She buried her face in her hands, covering her eyes with her handkerchief. She shook. Evidently she sobbed.

"Now you see what you've done!" said Mrs. Forrester. "You shouldn't ask questions like that. Just look at what you've done."

The three gazed fascinated on Mrs. Montrose. "Is he dead or what is he?" asked the man of Mrs. Forrester, making the words almost quietly with his mouth.

"Sh ! !" said Mrs. Forrester very loudly indeed. The three jumped a little. So did Mrs. Montrose.

There was silence while Mrs. Montrose wiped her eyes.

She looked over the heads opposite. The wife leaned toward her husband and addressed him timidly behind her hand. He nodded, and spoke to Mrs. Forrester.

"Well," he said, "at least you admit that *you* have a husband. If you have a husband then, where is he?"

"Oh, I don't know," said Mrs. Forrester lightly.

"No, she doesn't know," said Mrs. Montrose.

The three on the opposite seat went into a conference. Mrs. Montrose and Mrs. Forrester did not dare to look at each other. They were enjoying themselves. Their self-esteem had returned. They had impressed. Unfavourably, it is true. But still they had impressed.

The man with the blue tooth pulled himself together. He reasserted himself. Across his waistcoat hung a watch chain. He took his watch out of his pocket and looked at the time. Then to the surprise of Mrs. Montrose and Mrs. Forrester he took another watch out of the pocket at the other end of the chain. "You see," he said proudly, "I have two watches."

Mrs. Montrose and Mrs. Forrester were surprised, but they had themselves well in hand.

Mrs. Montrose looked at the watches disparagingly. "My husband has six watches," she said.

"Yes, that is true," nodded Mrs. Forrester, "her husband *has* got six watches, but my husband, like you, unfortunately has only two watches."

The man put his watches back. Decidedly the battle was going in favour of the two young women. How horrid of us, he was so pleased with his watches, thought Mrs. Montrose. Isn't it true that horridness just breeds horridness. We're getting horrider every minute. She regarded the man, his wife and his daughter with distaste but with pity.

"You *say*," said the man, who always spoke as though their statements were open to doubt, which of course they were, "that you come from Canada. Do you come from Winnipeg? I know about Winnipeg."

"No," said Mrs. Montrose, and she spoke this time

quite truthfully, "I come from Vancouver." Mrs. Forrester remained silent.

"And you, where do you come from?" persisted the man in a hectoring tone, addressing Mrs. Forrester. Mrs. Forrester remained silent, she had almost decided to answer no more questions.

"Oh, do not tell, please do not tell," begged Mrs. Montrose in an anguished way.

"No," said Mrs. Forrester importantly, "I shall not tell. Rest assured. I shall not tell."

"Why will she not tell?" demanded the man. He was tortured by curiosity. So was his wife. So was his daughter.

"Sh ! !" said Mrs. Montrose very loudly.

The man seemed ill at ease. By this time nothing existed in the world for him, or for his wife, or for his daughter but these two Canadian women who ate bears.

"How is it," asked the man, "that you no longer buy my trousers?"

"I beg your pardon?" faltered Mrs. Montrose. For a moment she lost ground.

"I said," replied the man, "why is it that you no longer buy my trousers?"

The ladies did not answer. They could not think of a good answer to that one.

"I," said the man, "am a manufacturer of trousers. I make the most beautiful trousers in Germany. Indeed in the world." (You do not so, thought Mrs. Forrester, picturing her husband's good London legs.) "For three years I receive orders from Winnipeg for my trousers. And now, since two years, yes, since 1929, I receive no more orders for my trousers. Why is that?" he asked, like a belligerent.

"Shall we tell him?" asked Mrs. Forrester, looking at Mrs. Montrose. Neither of them knew why he had received no more orders for his trousers, but they did not wish to say so. "Shall we tell him?" asked Mrs. Forrester.

"You tell him," said Mrs. Montrose.

"No, *you* tell him," said Mrs. Forrester.

"I do not like to tell him," said Mrs. Montrose, "I'd rather you told him."

The man with the blue tooth looked from one to the other.

"Very well. I shall tell him," said Mrs. Forrester. "The fact is," she said, looking downward, "that in Canada men no longer wear trousers."

"What are you saying? That is not true, never can that be true!" said the man in some confusion.

"Yes," said Mrs. Montrose, corroborating sombrely. "Yes, indeed it is true. When they go abroad they wear trousers, but in Canada, no. It is a new custom."

"It is the climate," said Mrs. Forrester.

"Yes, that is the reason, it is the climate," agreed Mrs. Montrose.

"But in Canada," argued the man with the blue tooth, "your climate is cold. Everyone knows your climate is cold."

"In the Arctic regions, yes, it is really intensely cold, we all find it so. But not in Winnipeg. Winnipeg is very salubrious." (That's a good one, thought Mrs. Montrose.)

The man turned and spoke rapidly to his wife. She also turned, and looked askance at her daughter. The expressions of the man, his wife, and his daughter were a blend of pleasure and shock. The two liars were delighted.

At last the man could not help asking, "But they *must* wear something! It is not logical."

"Oh, it's logical, all right!" said Mrs. Forrester.

"But what *do* they wear?" persisted the man.

"I never looked to see," said Mrs. Montrose. "*I* did, I looked," said Mrs. Forrester.

"Well?" asked the man.

"Oh, they just wear kilts," said Mrs. Forrester.

"Kilts? What are kilts? I do not know kilts," said the man.

"I would rather not tell you," said Mrs. Forrester primly.

"Oh," said the man.

Mrs. Montrose took out her vanity case, and inspected herself, powder puff in hand.

"I do not allow my wife and daughter to paint their faces so," said the man with the blue tooth.

"No?" said Mrs. Montrose.

"It is not good that women should paint their faces so. Good women do not do that. It is a pity."

(Oh, Alice, thought Mrs. Forrester in a fury, he shall not dare!) "It is a pity," she hissed, "that in your country there are no good dentists!"

"Be careful, be careful," whispered Mrs. Montrose.

"What do you mean?" demanded the man with the blue tooth.

(She will go too far, I know she will, thought Mrs. Montrose, alarmed, putting out her hand.)

"In our country," said the rash Mrs. Forrester, "anyone needing attention is taken straight to the State Dentist by the Police. This is done for aesthetic reasons. It is logical."

"I am going to sleep," said Mrs. Montrose very loudly, and she shut her eyes tight.

"So am I," said Mrs. Forrester, in a great hurry, and she shut her eyes too. This had been hard work but good fun for Mrs. Montrose and Mrs. Forrester. They felt, though, that they had gone a little bit too far. It might be as well if they slept, or pretended to sleep, until they reached Munich. They felt that outside their closed eyes was something frightening. The voice of the man with the blue tooth was saying, "I wish to tell you, I wish to tell you . . . " but Mrs. Montrose was in a deep sleep, and so was Mrs. Forrester. They sat with their eyes tightly closed, beside the hamper which still occupied the seat with the view by the darkening window. Mrs. Montrose had the inside corner, and so by reason of nestling down in the corner, and by reason of having an even and sensible temperament, she really and truly fell asleep at last.

Not so Mrs. Forrester. Her eyes were tightly closed, but her mind was greatly disturbed. Why had they permitted themselves to be baited? She pondered on the collective mentality that occupied the seat near to them (knees almost touching), and its results which now filled the atmosphere of the carriage so unpleasantly. She had met this mentality before, but had not been closely confined with it, as now. What of a world in which this mentality might ever become dominant? Then one would be confined with it without appeal or relief. The thought was shocking. She felt unreasonably agitated. She felt rather a fool, too, with her eyes shut tightly. But, if she opened them, she would have to look somewhere, presumably at the family, so it seemed safer to keep them closed. The train sped on. After what seemed to her a very long time, she peeped. The wife and daughter were busy. The husband sat back, hands on knees, chin raised, expectant, eyes closed. His wife respectfully undid his tie, his collar, and his top shirt button. By this time the daughter had opened the hamper, and had taken from it a bottle and a clean napkin. These she handed to her mother. The wife moistened the napkin from the bottle and proceeded to wash her husband, his face, his ears, round the back of his neck, and inside his shirt collar, with great care. "Like a cat," thought Mrs. Forrester, who had forgotten to shut her eyes.

The man with the blue tooth lowered his raised chin and caught her. "You see," he said loudly, "you see, wives should look properly after their husbands, instead of travelling alone and . . . " But Mrs. Forrester was fast asleep again. The whole absurd encounter had begun to hold an element of terror. They had been tempted into folly. She knew – as she screwed up her closed eyes – that they were implicated in fear and folly.

The two young women took care to sleep until the train reached Munich. Then they both woke up.

Many people slept until they reached Munich. Then they all began to wake up.

SEVEN

The Birds

H AVING WRITTEN down that dreadful day, I will not spend much time on subsequent emotions. I spoke last night of pride. Let me recommend it. When circumstances reduce us to being alone and unhappy, pride is a good companion. Pride does not sound a very religious quality and it is not. Religion is a great help as long as one does not turn into a spaniel. That, of course, is not really religion, becoming too submissive. You have heard of "a pride of lions", "a pace of asses", an "exaltation of larks"? I have read of "a submission of spaniels", and I think, to a point only, that is good. Pride is cold comfort but good, too. I could submit, but I could not show submission. When I went to see Cora the following day, I took my pride with me. I had not dared to set it down, night nor day. I had to see Cora as naturally as possible and I thought, Once this interview is over successfully, things will be easier. That is the way people talk but that is not the way things are. Things work in a sort of inverse fashion; that is to say, if your interview with Cora is successful you are still as unhappy as ever; but if your interview is a flop, then you are worse off than ever – if that is possible.

During these extra bad days I took particular care of my appearance and tried to seem nonchalant, which is rather a contradiction in terms. I ambled into Cora's study where she was doing her bills and signing her cheques. Oh hello, she said, and finished addressing an envelope.

She looked up pleasantly. How's the aunt? she said.

Well, said the aunt, how's the nephew?

He's well. He's adorable.

It was five months since the little twin had faded and faded and faded and died. Cora had recovered her elegant delicate appearance of health. The infinite pathos of the fading and death of the little baby, and her cruel loss, had reduced her pitifully; but now all the current of life and love had begun to swell again, and the whole current flowed and encompassed the baby John with his little body so like the other little body. I do think that Johnny saved her.

He's out, she said, Bessy has him out but they'll soon be back. Sit down and we'll have some tea. What have you been doing?

I was very nervous and had to keep myself from fidgeting or from walking up and down.

We didn't go up Jervis Inlet, I said, after all.

Jervis Inlet? Were you going? Was it nice? said Cora vaguely, looking down the driveway.

I told you, I said, we didn't go.

Cora's eyes strayed back to me. We? she asked.

Oh Cora, I said (and I was on edge), you knew the Doucettes were coming!

Oh yes of course, the Doucettes! she murmured, drawing her thoughts from the driveway to the incomparably insignificant Doucettes.

Yvette . . . she's married? asked Cora.

Cora, I said, I've come to tell you that . . . that . . . (How does one tell a final thing? With what colour or tone does one shade it, adorn it, present it?) I have decided not to be married.

Then Cora's full attention was on me. Her eyes went a lighter blue and she stared.

You don't mean what you're saying!

Yes. I do.

But what . . . what – and her eyes swept my hands – you've kept that ring!

Platonic, my dear, not romantic. We didn't quarrel.

Darling! Cora seldom said darling, but she was deeply moved. She leaned towards me and looked over into my face and said, But you love him! You must be so unhappy! What has happened? Tell me! Tell me! What did he do?

Remember that I was suffering and fighting to protect myself; and remember that there were two things that I could do. I could hold on to my pride and not reveal myself; or I could yield to my desire to lean upon my sister's shoulder and accept her love, and weep and weep, and always regret it. But I rejected this invitation to weep although it came from Cora's heart, and it would be – in time – resented that I had rejected the invitation, the proffered love, the desire to know. I held fast.

Cora dear, I said, it's not as bad as you think. Accept it and don't ask me . . .

I could act no longer. What, I said, is that mark on the window pane? Cora turned to look.

The Peakes' house faced west and south and there were great sheets of glass of the kind called view windows. You looked through the windows – hardly observing them, they were so clear – on to a lawn and clumps of maples and dogwoods. Between the trees a path sloped down toward the beach and over all the sun shone. The trees were full of birds. Little birds cast themselves into the air as if they were wild with joy. Earlier in the year this garden was full of birdsong.

That? said Cora and she came to the window and traced the mark with her finger nail. It was a bird, see! she said, the beak, and here was a wing. There's another. I think, yes, here, see! the beak and both wings. And I saw the partial and ghostly outline of a bird.

They dash at the window, Cora said, and we often find them fallen. The gardener finds them outside beside the windows.

Stunned? I said.

Oh, worse. Their mouths are split and sometimes their bodies are broken.

Horrible, horrible. Do they live? I said.

For a while, poor things, and she turned to me again, because she had to know.

I looked out of the window at the living birds who were tossing themselves in the air and flying from tree to tree, and a moment of revelation came to me and I was a bird and the birds were I. The birds flew and flew with speed and attack in the clear air, and in the clear window was reflected to them the familiar sky and the flowers and the trees, and so each day some little bird flew into this familiar reflection and dashed itself against the real glass and fell, with its mouth split and its bones broken by the passion of its flight. Here was the dim mark of its death. And yesterday I had bashed my head against the reality that was waiting for me, invisible, and had nearly broken my neck. The thought of the merry birds and the birds in the years to be, falling outside the window, sickened me. A bird is so free.

I must go, I said, I promised to meet Miriam but I had to come and tell you.

Cora took me by the wrists. She was hurt by this . . . this exclusion.

You *must* stay, she said. You *must* stay. Have dinner here, stay the night, anything. I can't bear you to go off and me knowing nothing!

Cora, I said, Cora, don't ask me. I can't stay. And I went.

How un-loving and un-trusting Cora must have thought me, because she did not know, I think, that I had to protect myself. It is no wonder that she felt repulsed, and became, as before, so unaware, and thus I came to live again in the annex of my sister's mind.

I joined Miriam who was waiting near the Library, and the love that flowed from her needed not a word nor a sound nor a touch. I thought, Some day I can tell Miriam about those birds, but not today.

EIGHT

A drink with Adolphus

I

"WELL I CAN'T do both," said Anne Gormley. "If I go with you I can't go to the Moxons' " ("What you mean is you can't go with that Thibeaudeau boy to the Moxons'," said her mother) "and if I don't go with you I *can* go with Tibby and I like going to the Moxons' and it *is* a party and it'll go on and on the way I like it. I'm sorry of course," said the beautiful girl shaking back her hair, "that you'll have to take a taxi but I do hate that kind of party that goes home at seven, sheer waste, and you know that's when you'll want to come home because you're scared of being late for dinner – you darling darling," she said, almost surrounding her mother with sudden cajoling love, "we like different parties. Okay by you?"

"I suppose so but this isn't a party. It's just us." And, as so often, she stopped herself saying out loud to her youngest child, "I'd like you to have been brought up in my generation, my young lass, just for about two years."

"I'll order your taxi for you."

"Not yet," said Mrs. Gormley who was lame and had to do her hair and make the best of herself and go downstairs rather slowly.

"Oh why do you go!" said Anne, her affection smiting her a little. "You don't *haf*to!"

"Yes," said her mother at the mirror, "that's three Saturdays now. I do have to. It's just us. To see the view.

The house is old but he's mad about the view on Capitol hill. That's why Adolphus bought it. I can't *not* go and your father'll be delighted not to have to."

Before walking downstairs, crabwise, Mrs. Gormley looked in on her husband but there was nothing to see except a great lump in the bed. "I'm going to have a drink with old Adolphus. Goodbye Hamish," she said, but only a muffled sound came from the bed. In the hall she met Ah Sing the cook.

"I takem hot lum Mister Doctor," said Ah Sing. "I fixem he cold"

"Yes do, Ah Sing," said Mrs. Gormley in the rather effusive way that she had the habit of employing to the Chinese cook whom she and the children had loved, feared, and placated for twenty years.

The taxi, proceeding eastwards, sped through mean streets and then began to climb. Mrs. Gormley looked towards the north at the salt waters of the inlet, gently snoring against the foot of the hill. The thought of going all this way to have a drink with Adolphus bored her and the fact of paying for a taxi both ways bored her still more; but she would enjoy the view. Adolphus was not a friend by selection, rather by happening. He was the kind of person that she had known, fortuitously, for so many years that he was designated "friend". They had lived near each other in childhood and Dolly had played with her big brothers and had survived to be called Adolphus. That was all. Therefore Mrs. Gormley was bored in anticipation and it was expecting too much of Hamish who had not been brought up with Dolly Bond to want to spend one of his precious Saturday afternoons admiring Dolly's new house. Now that the years spun faster and faster, Saturdays came hurtling towards Mrs. Gormley like apples thrown. She was still a fool for optimism and thought each week (after all these years with the children), But next Saturday Hamish and I will really "do" something, even if it's only staying at home. But come Saturday, and Hamish would say "I may be late home from the hospital and then I have some calls to make." He would arrive home late for dinner (he – the only one permitted by Ah Sing) and Saturday spun past them again without even being seen.

"Please stop," said Mrs. Gormley to the taxi-man, "and I'll have ten cents' worth of view."

The view was certainly superb and worth more than ten cents. She looked down the slope at the configuration of the inlet and on the wooded shores which now were broken by dwellings, by sawmills, by small wharves, by squatters' house-boats that were not supposed to be there, by many little tugs and fishboats moored and moving with vees of water in their wakes. But her eyes left the shores and looked down across the inlet, shimmering like silk with crawling waves where the tidal currents through the Second Narrows disturbed the waters. She looked farther on to where the dark park lay, dark green and black with pines and cedars against the bright skies of coming evening, at the ocean and islands beyond (so high she was above the scene), and across at the great escarpment of mountains still white with winter's snow. In ten cents' worth of time, she thought – and she was very happy islanded, lost, alone in this sight – there's nearly all the glory of the world and no despair, and then she told the taxi-man to drive on.

Adolphus Bond's new house was nice and rather shabby but, Mrs. Gormley told herself, it was a credit to Adolphus and it had something that these flat caricatures of houses hadn't got, although their insides were charming. The taxi arrived, and she was greeted by Adolphus and other sounds.

"It's so good of you to come," said Adolphus kindly as he helped her out of the car.

"So sorry about Hamish," said Mrs. Gormley at the same moment, stepping down not gracefully but with care.

"Too bad you had to get a taxi, someone would have fetched you," said Adolphus, kindest of men.

"You see it came on so suddenly," said Mrs. Gormley simultaneously. "One moment no cold, the next moment the worst cold you ever saw in your life but as usual he refuses inhalations. Ah Sing is giving him a hot rum and lemon and butter and honey, good enough to make anyone have a cold on purpose," but Adolphus did not hear. Neither of them listened to the other.

"This is the cupboard," he said. "Let me."

"I see you have a party," said Mrs. Gormley, "I thought it was just us. If I'd known I'd have worn a smarter dress. In honour of the new house. Who have you?"

"Oh, some people," said Adolphus vaguely. "So I see," she said for how could it be otherwise; but Adolphus was steering her towards wide and wide-open doors and then across a room towards a fine long and deep window which intimated a sloping lawn, a fir tree perhaps, and some lovely scene beyond. "This is the library," he said although nothing corroborated the statement.

Sounds of voices came from all around. Guests had scattered, and some had gone out of the french windows on to the lawn, adding to and subtracting from the view. Mrs. Gormley felt herself seized round the waist from behind. Two hands clasped themselves in front of her and a man's voice said (breath fanning the back of her neck), "At last, little one, at last! At last I have you!"

"Well really! How unfamiliar!" said Mrs. Gormley, wishing she were still slender, "this is very pleasant but who do you suppose it is? Is there some mistake?"

"Pay no attention. He's been to a wedding," murmured Adolphus rather crossly in her ear. Mrs. Gormley stood still and tried to avoid falling over backwards upon the person to whose body she was firmly clamped in an unusual manner.

"Perhaps if you'd tell me . . . " she began, unable to do anything about it.

"This is the view, you see," said Adolphus frowning at the view.

"Yes but . . . " said Mrs. Gormley perceiving that she

was now unclasped. A tall slight fair man in a gray suit stood in front of her.

"Jonathan Pascoe . . . " remarked Adolphus, . . . "you see how the garden slopes away, affording . . . "

"How do you do Mr. Pascoe . . . Yes I do see, Dolly, and what trees!"

"At last we have met!" said the man in the gray suit, indicating something somewhere with his long hands and smiling gently.

"But I have never seen you before!" said Mrs. Gormley.

"Neither have I," said the wedding guest and was no longer there. Adolphus explained the view.

"It is beautiful, beautiful, but I should like to sit down somewhere," said Mrs. Gormley and Adolphus led her back into the centre of the room and to a large high chair from which she could see out of the window. A black poodle dog, walking on his hind legs, pushed past them, strode down the library, out of the french windows, and disappeared.

"What a peculiar thing for a dog to do! I didn't know you had a dog, or whose dog is it?" she asked.

"What dog," said Adolphus, "this is Mr. Leaper."

"How do you do," said Mrs. Gormley and was surprised when Mr. Leaper said he was well. He's very literal, she thought. She sat down upon the high comfortable chair and looked around her. The wedding guest was not among the vivacious strangers in the room which though solid enough had a dream-like irrelevance. The large black rims of Mr. Leaper's glasses intimidated her.

"I have just been in Spain and my wife has been in Portugal," he said.

"Have you a dog?" asked Mrs. Gormley and Mr. Leaper said, "We used to have a monkey but it stole and we became involved in legal difficulties." Someone put a glass in her hand. Adolphus was fulfilling his duties elsewhere.

A young man who had the appearance of a hired waiter stood in front of her. On the tray were familiar-looking pieces of coloured food that she had seen somewhere before and some small spheres unfamiliar in appearance but, it seemed, edible.

"What are these do you suppose?" asked Mrs. Gormley tentatively. The young man became suffused by a dark spreading blush.

"I think," he said, speaking very low, "I heard some person call them hot ovaries."

"Did you really say hot ovaries?" said Mrs. Gormley very much interested and looking at him affectionately because he was so young, so awkward, blushing there. "Uh-huh," said the young waiter who was some mother's son.

"I wouldn't if I were you," said Mr. Leaper as if to a child. "When we were in Spain . . . "

"Parmee parmee," said a maid with a tray, pushing between them.

"What does she mean – 'parmee'?" asked Mr. Leaper.

"I think she means 'pardon me'," said Mrs. Gormley. "You were saying when you were in Spain?"

"We had too many eggs."

"I thought so too," she said, "but" (warmly) "there are compensations – what about the El Grecos?"

"We never had any of those," said Mr. Leaper gloomily. "Of that I am sure, as I noted down our meals very carefully in my diary."

"In your diary?" enquired Mrs. Gormley. "What else do you write in your diary?"

"I write my personal reflections and impressions," said Mr. Leaper looking very queer.

"Do you mean after a party like this? How alarming."

Mr. Leaper looked at her intently through his black-rimmed glasses and Mrs. Gormley felt uneasy. From the next room came shrieks of laughter.

"Parmee parmee," said the maid, pushing back again. There was Adolphus, looking engagingly kind. He brought up a nut-brown girl, a sad man, and a young friend of

Mrs. Gormley's with a dark beard. Beards are usually dark, she thought, why. They do not even know they have legs, these people, she thought with a pang, smiling at them. They do not know how pleasant it is at a party to move, move on, move on, negotiate yourself elsewhere, get away from Mr. Leaper who does not like eggs in Spain and will write about us in his diary, give him a chance poor thing. "I am going to show them the house," said Adolphus.

"Oh, do!" said Mrs. Gormley in her gushing way, and Adolphus, the nut-brown girl, the sad young man, and the young man with the beard went to look at the house. Mrs. Gormley and Mr. Leaper began to talk in earnest about Spain and the prices there. God, thought Mrs. Gormley, what would I give to have Hamish's cold, " . . . but cheaper still in Portugal!" she said, smiling, mustering pleasure and charm if any.

Evening had really fallen now. People had drifted away, to look at the house, to fill their glasses again in the dining-room, and wasn't the drawing-room full of music or something? The maid stood at the library door and threw a quick glance into the nearly empty room. Then she turned away. Mrs. Gormley, talking to Mr. Leaper, looked beyond him through the long windows unobscured now by people, on to the garden which was only faintly green in the twilight. A pale moon hung high, and upon the inlet the moonlight fell, and fell upon the garden, casting still faint shadows from a great cedar tree. The garden and the moonlight and the cedar shadows were made to walk in, but Mrs. Gormley, continuing to sit, continued also to fabricate things like "the Savoy . . . Dorchester . . . a quite humble little place on Ebury Street . . . Claridge's" (how snob can we get, talking like this, impressing each other but probably not. I sound as if Hamish and I stayed in these places, and she mimicked herself "a quite humble little place"). In the garden something moved. It could not be a large moth, but like a large moth the wedding guest danced all alone under the moon. His gray flannel arms rose and fell again. Perhaps he was flying. He advanced, flapping his arms in the haunted mystical evening, he retreated, stepping high and slowly below the cedar tree. How beautiful he was and he must have been happy. Mrs. Gormley longed to be out there dancing with the free slowly dancing wedding guest. She longed it until (sitting there smiling, with immobile hips and legs) she nearly burst, but she did not say to Mr. Leaper, "Look, there is Jonathan Pascoe whoever he is dancing in the scented moonlight like a large gray flannel moth." She could not share the wedding guest (whom she loved to see dancing under the moon) with Mr. Leaper. As she turned to agree that one could not do better than a good small hotel she saw that the young man with a beard had come to sit as if exhausted in a large chair opposite.

"Where's Anne, I suppose she wouldn't come. Your dog bit me," he said morosely.

"It's not my dog whose dog is it?" said Mrs. Gormley, "you know I haven't got a dog, Ozzie!"

"I think the government will be out in six weeks," he said, "and serve them right."

"Oh why do you think that? Whatever makes you think that?" she asked eagerly but he looked suspicious and did not answer.

"Let me fill your glass," said Mr. Leaper and did not return. Mrs. Gormley and the young man with a beard sat at peace and looked for some time at the very good carpet. She raised her head and saw that Jonathan Pascoe was leaning against the doorway.

"Little one," he said, "you are so beautiful, may I kiss you?"

"Yes, please do," said Mrs. Gormley laughing, "I need a kiss badly. I think it would do me good. How did the moonlight feel? And then will you get me a taxi. I want to go home."

II

Upon his return home from Mr. Bond's party, Mr. Leaper did not write in his diary as usual. He was agitated. Perhaps some part of his thin protective covering had been abrased, split, broken. However, a few nights later, he wrote:

"As you know, I make it a rule to write up my diary just before retiring at night. Mabel knows this and respects my privacy for a time which varies from a few minutes (I make registers of the seasons, bursting of buds, etc.) to quite a protracted period, even an hour. She then knocks and says in that clear voice of hers Beddy-byes and I bring my writing to a conclusion, that is, I stop writing. I hesitate to commit to paper the effect of that word Beddy-byes (which I even find it difficult to write) upon me. There may have been a time when it did not cause me to wince, but I do not remember. I cannot bring myself to tell Mabel (for whom I have such a regard) to say something else, nor can I be unmoved by it. I have no doubt that in the larger things of life Religion is a great comfort, but I do not think that Religion provides an answer in a relatively small matter like this. However.

Some years ago Mabel gave me a nicely bound book with the specially embossed words *Diary – S.B. Leaper* upon the cover. Although I appreciated the gift, it has not been useful, as I find a pad of typing paper easier on the whole. The book had a feeling of permanence which did not put me at my ease, and I found that I could not cross out what I had written without a sensation of waste.

Last night I was in a disturbed frame of mind owing to an unpleasant experience on the previous evening and I did not write my diary. However, tonight I have adjusted my feelings somewhat and will record the evening party which Mabel and I attended, given by my friend Mr. Adolphus Bond, one of the kindest of men. When I say "my friend", perhaps I overstep and should rather say acquaintance. A cousin of mine married a cousin of his who has since passed away.

Mr. Bond lives in a charming house complete with garden. He is a bachelor of many interests and has a wide and scattered social and business acquaintance and so Mabel and I did not see many familiar faces. In fact none. Mr. Bond, a genial host, introduced me to a young man with a dark beard whose name seemed to be Ozzie who was talking to a handsome lively girl. I did not hear Ozzie's other name but I thought I heard Mr. Bond say before he left us that he was a nephew of the Leader of the House. I was going to say by way of joke What House? because I had noticed in the telephone book that very day the House of Liqueurs, the House of Charm, the House of Drapes and the House of Sport but decided not to. Although I make it a rule never to bring up the subjects of politics and religion in strange company, it seemed safe to refer to my satisfaction at the recent elections, with a passing reference to the young man's uncle Mr. Robertshaw. The young man Ozzie became almost violent and referred to his uncle's party as a lot of bloody fools. I was silent, but the girl was amused and laughed heartily. It seems that Ozzie is an artist which one might have suspected from his beard, but as Mabel says, that is no proof.

There was a slight lull in the conversation and turning to the window I remarked on the lengthening of the days. I said that I made the practice of recording the position of the sun in my diary. The young man Ozzie said, very rudely I thought, "Your *what*? Do you mean you write a diary?"

I said, "Certainly I write a diary," whereupon he said, "If I can believe that I can believe anything." Silence fell and then the girl said, "Ozzie you great oaf some day somebody's going to hit you. You'd better apologize," and Ozzie said to me, "I beg your pardon. I had no business to say that but I never met anyone who wrote a diary before."

I received his apology as best I could and as I heard Mabel's clear voice ringing out from the neighbouring room I thought I would join her. I smiled and withdrew but I must confess that I was shaken as I had always regarded the writing of a diary as a natural affair and apparently there are some people who find it strange. The uncomfortable feeling of not resembling other people persisted with me and that is one reason why I did not feel in the mood for writing yesterday.

Before I reached the door I was stopped by my host who had on his arm an elderly woman who appeared to be lame, by the name I think of Gormley or Gormer. He introduced us and found her a chair and we were left together. Thinking the matter over later, I came to the conclusion that Mr. Bond, unintentionally no doubt, had left me – as Mabel sometimes says – holding the bag, for owing to Mrs. Gormley's lameness a certain sense of "noblesse oblige" made me spend most of the rest of the time at the party conversing with her. I did not find her an interesting woman and Mabel remarked afterwards that I seemed embittered at the close of the evening.

In an endeavour to avoid inflammable subjects I told this Mrs. Gormley that we had recently been in Spain. That conversational opening usually promotes lively response. People either wish to go to Spain or they have been in Spain, and a certain enthusiasm follows. Mrs. Gormley's only response was to make some enquiry about a dog. I saw at once that she must be a very unintelligent woman. I mentioned the monkey Chiko which we had some years ago but did not go further as Chiko led us into very unfortunate legal proceedings. I well remember that we had to give Chiko to the Monkey House in Stanley Park. Mabel and I have often remarked that when we went to visit Chiko there, it was impossible to distinguish him from the other monkeys. They all seemed to have the same anxious expression and a similarity of feature. I did not tell Mrs. Gormer anything further.

An embarrassing moment occurred at once. Owing to

the strike among waiters, all available experienced waiters are employed in the various hotels and restaurants and very few can be found for private parties. This accounts, I think, for the young hobbledehoy who served us at Mr. Adolphus Bond's party. When this Mrs. Gormer asked him (very rudely, I thought) what certain of the hors d'oeuvres contained, he said he did not know but thought they were hot ovaries. Mrs. Gormer seemed very much amused at this, but that shows the kind of woman she is.

We then had a long conversation on foreign travel. I said that in Spain we had too many eggs and she said Yes, but what about the el grecos. I had to admit that we did not have any. We then spoke about hotel accommodation. While I was telling her my impressions of the hotels in London she looked past me and at the windows behind my head, looking into the garden. I would, at any other time, have thought she was in a trance, but she responded with moderate intelligence to my remarks. I think it must be a bad habit of hers and I must say it is very disagreeable.

We were just discussing the Royal York Hotel in Toronto when the young man Ozzie entered the room. He flung himself down in a large chair opposite us and appeared quite exhausted. He too said something about a dog. I did not stay to enquire but gladly made this an opportunity to leave on the pretext of bringing Mrs. Gormer another drink. When I arrived at the bar which had been set up in the dining-room I saw Mabel leaning against the bar surrounded by other people, and talking very loudly. I was instantly alarmed, remembering that occasion in Winnipeg. She saw me and shouted "Hi!" (a greeting I particularly dislike) and went on laughing and talking. I did not join them but filled Mrs. Gormer's glass and my own. I drank my own and then decided to have a re-fill. I then carried Mrs. Gormer's glass and my own back to the library. I stopped at the door because it was partially blocked by a tall thin man in a gray suit who spoke the following words to someone in the room: "Little one, little one, you are so beautiful, may I kiss you?"

I looked under the extended arm of the man in gray, taking care not to spill the drinks, in order to see whom he might be addressing, but only Mrs. Gormer looking different and the man called Ozzie were in the room. The remark of the man in the gray suit then seemed unintelligible as Mrs. Gormer is far from beautiful but he may not have been quite sober.

What was my surprise to hear this Mrs. Gormer thereupon urge the man in gray to kiss her which he did with, I must say, considerable respect, but without passion which was understandable. She made the plea that she needed a kiss. I found the whole episode quite incomprehensible. I decided to drink Mrs. Gormer's whiskey as well as my own – did not re-enter the room but returned to the bar.

On the way home I have never known Mabel so outrageous except on that occasion in Winnipeg. She called me a sourpuss and used other terms which I shall never be able to forget. I went so far as to say that a little attention always goes to her head which seemed to annoy her excessively. She was driving the car and I must confess that some very strange thoughts came into my mind. You can imagine that on our arrival at home I was in no condition to write my diary. I sometimes think that whereas some people are born to joy, I was born to sorrow.

This morning I purchased a small safe and brought it home. I told Mabel that I had been asked to keep some of the Firm's papers in a safe in our house. I shall also keep my diary there which permits me the freedom of expression that I sometimes require but which in daily life I seem unable to enjoy. A man must have a friend even if it is only himself.

Before I stop, I will mention an item in the paper that has touched and moved me very much tonight. A man in Illinois or is it Iowa is undergoing trial for the murder of his wife. The thing that impressed me was that he and his wife had seemed to live a devoted and harmonious life together.

"I must have another party," said Adolphus, busy with his lists.

NINE

I just love dogs

WELL, SAID my friend from Vancouver, one Saturday I had lunch at the Club, you know, the Ladies'
Club. I was leaving, and had just turned the corner of
Dunsmuir Street, going down to Granville Street (that's
our principal business street), and there, right out on the
sidewalk beside the bank building, on the corner of Granville and Dunsmuir, but up a bit, lay the body of an
enormous yellow-haired collie, apparently very old, and it
was all stiff-looking. A beautiful dead dog.

There was no one near but an old lady with a string bag
and little parcels, and she was poking the dog with her
walking-stick, and saying, Poor dog, poor dog, what a
shame to leave it here. And I felt just the same, and I said,
Oh, dear, the poor dog, what can we do? And she said, I
don't know, dearie, but someone ought to get the Society
for the Prevention of Cruelty to Animals. Oh, yes, I said,
someone ought to telephone Inspector Snape at once. (I
wanted her to know that I knew about the S.P.C.A. too,
and who was the head of it, and everything.) The old lady
said quite simply, Inspector Snape is dead, he has been
dead for over six months. I felt rather taken aback,
because I'd been so pleased about knowing about Inspector Snape, but I said, Oh, well, it's no good telephoning
Inspector Snape. All this time the old lady kept on poking
the dog in different parts, but he never stirred. We felt just
terrible, he was such a lovely dog.

Then the old lady said, Inspector Perkins, he's the new man. And I said, Oh, yes, someone ought to telephone Inspector Perkins then, and the old lady said, Well, dearie, I'd go and telephone Inspector Perkins in a minute, only my husband is sick in bed, has been for three days. He gets these attacks, so I don't think I'd better telephone Inspector Perkins. Couldn't you do that, dearie? I was just trying to work that out in my head when a lady came up in a purple velvet hat. Oh, she said, look at the poor dog! Isn't that dreadful, and such a lovely dog too. My, she said. I just love dogs. I'm crazy about dogs. I like dogs a whole lot better than I like people. The old lady with the string bag and I said, yes, indeed, we did too, and I think we all felt a bit better after that. But, there lay the dog, all stiff.

This is terrible, said the lady in the purple hat, this beautiful dog lying here dead, and nobody doing one thing. And she looked round at me and at the old lady with the string bag, who kept on prodding the dog's ear with her walking-stick. I don't know why she kept on doing that.

So I said, yes, indeed, it was terrible, and someone ought to telephone the S.P.C.A. So the lady in the purple hat looked very stern and very practical and said yes, that someone ought to telephone Inspector Snape at once. So the old lady and I said, both speaking together, But Inspector Snape is dead, he has been dead for over six months. The lady in the purple hat seemed a little taken aback by this. But, we said, there is Inspector Perkins, and she said, Oh, well then, we must telephone Inspector Perkins at once.

Well, dearie, said the old lady, who was still prodding the body of the dog, and he certainly was a lovely dog, I'd go, only I don't feel that I can. I'd go in a minute, she said, only my husband is sick in bed. He has been for three days, and I think if you and this young lady (she meant me) went, it would be nice.

Just then some young men came up, and they said, Gosh, look at the dead dog, but they didn't seem to mean to do anything about it. They just stood and looked at the body of the dog. That seemed to make the lady in the purple hat very very angry, and she said, well, anyway I am going to telephone Inspector Perkins, and I said, I will go too. Let us go together, I said, let us go across to the Supreme Drug Store and telephone Inspector Perkins on the pay phone. And the old lady said, yes, do, dearie, and I will stay here with the dog.

So the lady in the purple hat and I went across the road to the Supreme Drug Store, and left the old lady and the young men standing beside the dog. The old lady was still poking it here and there with her stick, and she seemed by this time to be sort of owning the dog, and in a way, I suppose, it was her dog, as she'd found it first. And the crowd was growing round the dog, and people were saying, oh, what a pity, what a beautiful dog, why doesn't someone do something.

But the lady in the purple hat and I felt, I think, that we were the kind of people who really do things, though I'm sure I wouldn't have known what to do if it hadn't been for her. Well, we hurried across the street to the Supreme Drug Store, and all the way she kept saying how fond she was of dogs, and I said I was, too. And she said she loved her dog far better than she loved most human beings. In fact, she loved her dog far, far better than she loved her older brother, and I tried to think of something equally strong to say, only we haven't got a dog, and by the time we reached the pay phone in the Supreme Drug Store, you'd think we both hated the whole human race, and thought dogs should be in parliament.

I am shy anyway about speaking to strangers, very shy, even on the telephone, so I said, please do let me give you this nickel, and then you can speak to Inspector Snape – no – Perkins. And she said, oh no, I wouldn't think of it, and I said, no really, you must. So by the time we had talked about the nickel quite a bit, she put my nickel in the pay phone, and got Inspector Perkins's office. He wasn't at his office, this being Saturday. So I found another nickel, and she got his house, and he was away for the week-end, and so was Mrs. Perkins, the maid said.

She was very very angry at this. I felt quite angry too, and the lady in the purple hat said it was an outrage, and what was to prevent a valuable dog from dying on a Saturday afternoon, and there was the head of the S.P.C.A. away for the week-end. So I said it was an outrage too, and whatever should we do?

So she said, I'm going straight up Granville Street, two blocks, till I come to the traffic policeman, and I'm going to bring him right down here, whether he wants to or not, and see that something is done about this, and right away too. She was very very angry. Yes do, I said, because I knew I would never sound angry enough to make any traffic policeman leave his place, I should just make it sound silly, so I said, yes, do, and I will go back to the dog.

By this time the lady in the purple hat and I were feeling very important only she was feeling more important than I was, because I can never manage to feel as important as other people, although I do try, and she set off, her eyes flashing, and round the corner and up Granville Street, which was very very crowded, and I went back across to the dog.

When I arrived back at the dog a large crowd had gathered, and the old lady with the string bag was giving a kind of lecture to all the people, and poking with her stick, and when she saw me coming, she pointed at me with her stick, and all the people turned and looked at me, and I still tried to feel important. But when all the people looked at me, I stopped feeling important at once and blushed and explained about the lady in the purple hat going for the policeman, and all the people said, oh, what a good thing, and what a valuable dog, and wasn't it too bad!

Just at that moment I heard the queerest whistle, you know, the kind of whistle that families have, and boys, like a signal it was. Well, it was a special kind of whistle, like that, and done twice. We all turned and looked, and there, driving up Dunsmuir Street from Granville Street was a large car, driven by a young man, and the back door was open. The young man drove slower and slower, as he reached the crowd, and at the same moment as the young man whistled the second time, the dog sprang to its feet and wagged its tail – my, he had a marvellous tail – and shot through the crowd and into the car. And the boy slammed the door and drove quickly away. The car had an Oklahoma licence. Everyone was too astonished to speak. It was the queerest feeling. A minute ago there had been the dog dead, as you might say, and us all bound together, feeling very important, and very sorry about the dog, and the next minute there was the dog alive and gone, and us all feeling pretty silly.

Well, I hadn't time but to think how funny it all was, and I turned to speak to the old lady with the string bag. But she was away up Dunsmuir Street, walking very fast with her stick. And all the crowd just wasn't there, and where the dog had been was nothing, and there was just me. And I looked quickly towards Granville Street to see if the lady with the purple hat was coming, very angry, with the policeman, and no doubt the policeman very angry too, and I couldn't see her in the crowds of people walking up and down Granville Street. So I went very quickly to where my car was parked and drove home.

And when I told my husband that evening, all he said was for me to cultivate that dog's disposition. He said that dog had fine qualities. But I didn't get over feeling silly for days, and I was so mad at myself that I hadn't even gone into a store and watched for the lady in the purple hat and the policeman exploding at each other down Granville Street to where there was no dog.

TEN

The corner of X and Y streets

W E OFTEN had our dinner at Kettner's in Soho. Naturally there were plenty of continental or Oriental restaurants in Soho, but there was something over and around and beneath good food and pleasant wine at the unspectacular Kettner's so we went there for choice without quite knowing why.

It must have been in 1947, because that was the first year that I had been in London following the bombing. In a weak-kneed way I had been afraid to see bombed England and especially bombed London. My husband had been there during the war but I had had only my desperate imaginings. One night we came out of Kettner's after dinner and stood for a few minutes at the entrance. The sky was blue-black over London with many stars. We looked to left and right, very comfortable, very easy, ready for anything. X Street stopped a little distance to our right and in the not-much-lighted night we saw at the end of the street the façade of a bombed and gutted church. Very theatrical it looked against the blue-black and the stars, as though the characters would soon come out and sing, or do their murder. The doorman said something to us that struck me as poetic and unlike a doorman. But what are doormen like? What is anybody like? One never knows, and I have never been able to remember what the doorman said; only that it was truly poetic. We walked along the pavement – which was narrow – to the bombed

church, and increasingly the feeling of the night and the
past and the theatre of the gutted church combined. No
doubt in the daylight the church would be mere stone and
dingy at that, inhabited by cats.

We turned back and when we arrived again at Kettner's,
on the corner of X and Y streets we really did hear music.
Some subdued light came from Kettner's windows but
there was not much illumination outside. Light from a
high lamp fell on the figure of a man standing in the street
at the far left-hand corner of the intersection. He was tall
and large and dressed in a way that gave him a clean but
gypsy appearance. Because he kept his head raised, looking up at the lamp or at least toward the sky which was
very dark around the light of the lamp, the light fell full
on his face and showed it as pale, large, intelligent, with
pale gold straight hair that straggled across the large brow.
If he had any expression in his face one would say he
looked sad, or quenched, and detached from that street
corner and from people. He played an accordion and
played it very well and, all the time he played, his large
pale face was tilted up toward the dark sky as if he did not
care for us or our sixpences. He did not court us for
sixpences. He looks, I thought, like a young Oscar Wilde,
after all the disillusion. Where does he live. I thought,
what does he do, and why does he have to play the accordion in Soho with a tin for coins hanging from his shoulder? The tin seemed an affectation of something foreign to
him. I said to W., "He looks like a young Oscar Wilde,
doesn't he?" but W. was intent on the player.

By this time other people had gathered, and stopped,
and stood like shadows on the two other street corners
facing the large but not fat pale man playing the accordion. There were shadows where we stood too, but
because our eyes had become accustomed we saw in front
of us a tall and graceful girl with long hair waving to her
shoulders. She stood leaning on a taller young man beside
her and suddenly she began to sing. She simply "lifted her
voice" and sang. She sang with the accordion player who

did not even look at her but all the standing shadows turned to look. Her voice was full of music and she sang with beautiful deliberation. She sang song after song and then, suddenly, she stopped. The accordion player paid no attention and went on playing. A taxi driver with a small dark face, wearing a white cotton coat and a peaked cap, stood beside us, leaning on his taxi.

"That ain't music, miss," said the taxi driver as one who really knows. "Come on now, miss, you can't call *Song of Love* music, now can you. Opra now, that's music, but not *Song of Love*. That's common, *Song of Love* is."

As if the girl knew that someone stood behind her she turned and said to me, "Don't you think *Song of Love* is music?" and I said, "When you sing it, it is," and so it was. There was that kind of freedom between people standing there.

The girl did not sing any more, so. W. and I went across the street to the accordion player and dropped a shilling into his tin. He did not seem to observe us and did not thank us, but continued his lost gaze of extreme disillusion upward as he played. From the shadows at the opposite corner stepped a small strange man in black. He stood for a moment looking about him as it were grotesque and lost. All the shadows watched. Then he began to dance. He danced slowly like a marionette, as if invisible strings from the high dark pulled and dropped his legs, his hands, his elbows, ordering his movements. He wheeled and danced and all the while as the light fell on him too, we saw his eyes as in caverns, raking the standing shadows for something he wanted that must have been sympathy or at least understanding. He was not drunk.

Then he spoke at intervals.

"I'm a seaman, I am," he said to us all as he danced his wheeling balancing dance. "I'm a seaman, I am . . . I bin in strange ports wot you'll never see . . . I bin in big ships," and his eyes travelled over the shadows. "You'll never see things like wot I seen in them places . . . I bin in ships in them foreign ports . . . I seen terrible things . . .

I'm a seaman, I am," and all the while he danced slowly, turning this way and that, balancing and wheeling.

We were very much surprised by this stranger, and his dances. Everything – light, shadows, time, distance seemed to focus on him. There was silence somewhere, and we turned to look at the accordion player who seemed to have stopped playing, but he was not there. We turned to look at the dancer, but he had gone. The girl and her boy were not there. The shadows were no longer shadows but people walking up and down X and Y streets. Had these things happened? Yes, and they had left no trace as dreams leave no trace. Something had snapped and ended and now everything was ordinary and we all became strangers again, walking up and down Soho. W. and I went pub-crawling after that until we finished up at the Café Royal where there were plenty of ghosts if one could see them.

This year I heard that Oscar Wilde used to frequent Kettner's. I do not understand these things but for ten minutes there had been something simple and complicated and timeless on the corner of X and Y streets.

ELEVEN

"To keep the memory of so worthy a friend"

O NE OF THE advantages of being lame is that one can sit and think without the shame of being lazy and with no apology to anyone. And so I often think and think about the two actors Henry Condell and John Heminge, and I can never get to the end of the wonder of what they did and what they do in the world today, even though not even their dust remains – unless it was wiped off a London window sill this morning. Scholars know about them, of course, even amateur scholars like myself; but one is inclined to take them for granted, like the unicorn, and that is not fair to such great and humble men.

The last time but one that my husband and I were in London, we said, "We will not go home without finding the place where Condell and Heminge were buried." But London began to exercise her manifold arts, and we went home without trying to find the church of St. Mary the Virgin Aldermanbury.

Next time we arrived from Portugal on a Tuesday night in May, and on Wednesday morning we hailed a taxi, looked at the taxi driver, said "St. Mary the Virgin Aldermanbury," and experienced at once a feeling of disquiet.

The mind of the London taxi driver is a wonderful organism. His taxi is an extension of himself. He needs only a word to start him off, taxi and all, by devious routes to any place, however obscure, in the London area. Twice only I have found him not knowing: once when I wanted to go to Great Turnstile (there is, of course, no turnstile; Great Turnstile has other fame), and now when we wanted to go to St. Mary the Virgin Aldermanbury, and the expression of not knowing came on the taxi driver's face. "Down in the City, beyond the bombed part behind St. Paul's," we said, and he nodded.

Down in the City he stopped. "Well, 'ere we are," he said pleasantly, and indicated the little church of St. Mary Aldermary. We did not blame him although this was not what we wanted. St. Mary Aldermary would not do, but we got out. I leaned against St. Mary Aldermary, which Stow said, " . . . is elder than any church of St. Marie in the Citie," and my husband went up a side street. I saw him in conversation with a policeman and a taxi driver. Another policeman joined me, a very nice man, but he did not know where St. Mary the Virgin Aldermanbury might be. He wanted to know if I would mind telling him why we wanted to go there, and also where I came from. As I could not begin telling him about the burial place of Condell and Heminge and what they had done and why they were important to me, I continued to lean against St. Mary Aldermary and said that I came from British Columbia, which interested him very much. When we were well into the climate of British Columbia my husband arrived in another taxi and I had to leave the policeman.

The new taxi driver was young and keen and anxious to find this place that he did not know. We drove up Love Lane and past Little Love Lane and past the Roman Wall and past the empty air of St. Alphege, and Cripplegate, with all the bombed area on one side, and gutted walls, and now large blocks of buildings arising (incongruous) on the other side, and found ourselves in Little Love Lane again and then went down Love Lane once more. After doing this kind of thing for some time we saw a dark wall of survival and on it the words carved in stone, grimily decipherable, St. Mary the Virgin Aldermanbury. I experienced that spring at the heart which is so rare. There was no entrance available on that side, so we rounded the corner and stopped at a small garden that was enclosed – except for the paved entrance – by a railing, and we had found what we came to seek.

All that can be seen of St. Mary the Virgin Aldermanbury is gutted walls, and windows that have a fey look, as though invisible glass segments remain. This must be because of the illogical effects of blast or because spiders have spun their webs; but it is probably mainly blast, not spiders. The small church is from the fifteenth century, but Sir Christopher Wren rebuilt it in the seventeenth.

Across the rough road a large new building rises, an uninvited handsome stranger in uniform. Behind lies bombed area, like craters of the moon. You enter the small neat garden on which the gutted church wall abuts. The path is of ancient paving stones. Two green trees survive and flourish, giving a prettiness and humanity to the bombed scene. On the left, beside a wall, is a long jumbled pile of stone. Will it ever be used? The ancient stones were part of the destroyed church. There are some benches in the small, unlikely garden, and naturally one sits (no one else is there) and becomes lost in speculation and in admiration and in gratitude.

For this was the place where the two men worshipped and were buried, where their wives were buried and their children were baptized and married and buried – the two authentic friends who, after the death of their fellow actor William Shakespeare, collected his works, and so those works remain to us. That is what John Heminge and Henry Condell did for Shakespeare and for themselves and for posterity, and then – a few years later – they died, and were buried here in St. Mary the Virgin Aldermanbury, the church of their parish, and their life here was over; and now we are here, and soon we shall be gone, and others will listen to Shakespeare and read him, and will owe these men a great and unpayable debt.

Here are the first names on the list of twenty-six actors of Richard Burbage's company of players which Condell and Heminge have placed at the beginning of the First Folio. The introduction and the plays themselves display the irrelevance of spelling that later assumed, and now assumes, a static importance.

Thus they list:

THE NAMES OF THE PRINCIPALL ACTORS
IN ALL THESE PLAYES

William Shakespeare
Richard Burbadge
John Hemmings . . .
Henry Condell . . .

Condell is eighth on the list.

Then come the plays, arranged according to the considered decision of Heminge and Condell as Comedies, Histories, Tragedies, instead of chronologically, to the manifold pleasant despairs of literary scholars and historians.

One does not need to be a scholar, or not a scholar, to sit on a bench in this small garden and feel the immediacy of Henry Condell and John Heminge of this parish. Three hundred years go by very easily. In spite of footnotes, quartos, contexts, interpretations, inconsistencies, arguments, and psychology (a new invention, Sirs), scholars are human and would not be impervious to this place.

Sitting there, I needed to know what these two men of Burbage's company of players looked like, and what their daily and nightly friend and fellow actor Shakespeare looked like. (I remembered that Burbage, Heminge, and Condell were the three actor friends who were mentioned in friendship in Shakespeare's will.) I needed to know what clothes they wore, and when they spoke would I understand them plainly? They worked with him, and acted with him, sat and ate with him, and drank with him. They played in his plays, and after his death they sat down and with infinite labour they with their intimate knowledge compiled the First Folio of his plays.

Sitting there in the small neat garden of St. Mary the

Virgin Aldermanbury where these two men feel near at hand, one does not embark on argument. The men, the plays, are there, so clear; but for a moment one marvels that men and women of these distant days take trouble to ignore the fact of the two men (fellow actors with Shakespeare) who collected the plays. These two men lived here, and died, and were buried here; the people of these distant latter days take great trouble to think up theories based on fancy or irresponsible choice; they choose to attribute the plays to anyone except "our so worthy Friend and Fellow, Shakespeare"; they turn away from those two solid men, Condell and Heminge of this parish, as if they have never heard their names – and perhaps they have not–and pursue their fantasy.

Now let us read the words on a small plaque near the ground, and also the words graven on the sides of a pedestal in the centre of the garden. (Garden? It is an innocent plot of green, hardly a garden.) Upon the pedestal is a bust of Shakespeare. It is not authentic. It rather resembles the bust in Westminster Abbey, which is not authentic either, or the Chandos portrait. As the Christ of Renaissance and pre-Renaissance art became a visual Christ for generations of people, so this is the visual and symbolic Shakespeare; no assertions are made, and no harm is done.

Here, then, are the words we read on the ground plaque:

ST. MARY THE VIRGIN ALDERMANBURY

NOTICE

This pleasant garden full of memories of Shakespeare, and his friends, Heminge and Condell, wardens of this church, is open to all who need rest and quiet. Gratitude is due to American friends who helped to restore the garden to its present condition, and co-operation in keeping it fresh and tidy will be much appreciated.

Here follow some of the words graven on the sides of the pedestal:

JOHN HEMINGE

lived in this Parish upwards of forty-two years and in which he was married. He had fourteen children thirteen of whom were baptized, four buried and one married here.

He was buried here October 12, 1630. His wife was also buried here.

HENRY CONDELL

lived in this Parish upwards of thirty years. He had nine children eight of whom were baptized here and six buried. He was buried here December 29, 1627. His wife was also buried here.

The date of the First Folio being 1623, Heminge and Condell did not long survive the completion of their work. The second side of the pedestal bears these words:

The fame of Shakespeare rests on his incomparable Dramas. There is no evidence that he ever intended to publish them and his premature death in 1616 made this the interest of no one else. Heminge and Condell had been co-partners with him in the Globe Theatre Southwark and from the accumulated Plays there of thirty-five years with Great Labour selected them. No men then living were so competent having acted with him in them for many years and well knowing his manuscripts. They were Published in 1623 in Folio thus giving away their Private Rights therein. What they did was priceless, for the whole of his manuscripts with almost all those of the Dramas of the Period have perished.

Below the graven face we read from the title and introductions to the First Folio of the plays, as inscribed by the compilers:

Mr. William Shakespeares Comedies, Histories, Tragedies. Published according to the True Originall Copies.

And then from the first Introduction to the First Folio, addressed:

*To the most noble and incomparable paire of brethren,
William, Earle of Pembroke, etc., and Philip, Earle of
Montgomery, etc.* [That "etc." holds a rare vitality.]
    *We have but collected them and done an office to the
dead . . . without ambition either of selfe-profit or fame, only
to keep the memory of so worthy a Friend, & Fellow alive, as
was our SHAKESPEARE . . .*

JOHN HEMINGE

HENRY CONDELL

Then follows a passage from Heminge and Condell's
second Introduction to the First Folio, which is addressed
to us all, under the heading

TO THE GREAT VARIETY OF READERS

*It had bene a thing, we confesse, worthie to have been
wished, that the Author himselfe had liv'd, to have set forth,
and overseene his own writings; but since it hath bin ordain'd
otherwise, and he by death departed from that right, we pray
you do not envie his Friends the office of their care, and
paine, to have collected and published them; . . . absolute in
their numbers, as he conceived them, who as he was a happie
imitator of Nature, was a most gentle expreser of it, his Mind
and Hand went together; and what he thought he uttered with
that easinesse, that we have scarce received from him a blot
in his papers.*

There is beauty and felicity in the words and cadences
of these two actors of Shakespeare's company – of his
company also of friends. The living Shakespeare is there,
the man whose "mind and hand went together; and what
he thought, he uttered with . . . easinesse," and his friends
Heminge and Condell, his perpetuators, are there.
    "We cannot go beyond our owne power," they wrote;
and so, in the prosecution of their enormous untaught
task ("the faults," they said, "ours, if any be committed"),
they made enough slips and errata to keep scholars in
happy commotion three hundred years later. Yet without

the labour of these two men of Aldermanbury, the whole body of Shakespeare's works would not have existed "absolute in their numbers, as he conceived them," either for the schoolmen or for the Great Variety of Readers who now pay their big or little money for lasting joy or an evening's magic, according to their Variety.

I like the advice that occurs in the latter part of their Introduction to the First Folio:

> ... *It is not our province, who only gather his works, and give them you, to praise him. It is yours that reade him. And there we hope, to your divers capacities, you will find enough, both to draw, and hold you: for his wit can no more lie hid, than it could be lost. Reade him, therefore; and againe, and againe: And if you doe not like him, surely you are in some manifest danger, not to understand him.*

TWELVE

Fog

FOR SEVEN days fog settled down upon Vancouver. It crept in from the ocean, advancing in its mysterious way in billowing banks which swallowed up the land. In the Bay and the Inlet and False Creek, agitated voices spoke one to another. Small tugs that were waylaid in the blankets of fog cried shrilly and sharply "Keep away! Keep away! I am here!" Fishing-boats lay inshore. Large freighters mooed continuously like monstrous cows. The foghorns at Point Atkinson and the Lions' Gate Bridge kept up their bellowings. Sometimes the fog quenched the sounds, sometimes the sounds were loud and near. If there had not been this continuous dense fog, all the piping and boo-hooing would have held a kind of beauty; but it signified danger and warning. People knew that when the fog lifted they would see great freighters looking disproportionately large riding at anchor in the Bay because passage through the Narrows into the harbour was not safe. Within the harbour, laden ships could not depart but remained lying fog-bound at great expense in the stream ... booo ... booo ... they warned, "I am here! Keep away!" All the ships listened. The C.P.R. boat from Victoria crashed into the dock. Gulls collided in the pathless air. Water traffic ceased and there was no movement anywhere offshore.

In the streets, cars crawled slowly. Drivers peered, Pedestrians emerged and vanished like smoke. Up the draw of False Creek, fog packed thick on the bridges. Planes were grounded. People cancelled parties. Everyone arrived late for everything.

Mrs. Bylow was an old woman who lived in a small old house which was more cabin than cottage in an unpleasant part of Mount Pleasant. For the fifth day she sat beside her window looking into the fog and cracking her knuckles because she had nothing else to do. If she had owned a telephone she would have talked all day for pastime, repeating herself and driving the party line mad.

Mrs. Bylow frequently sat alone and lonely. Her diurnal occupations had narrowed down to sleeping, waking to still another day, getting up, making and swallowing small meals, belching a little, cleaning up (a little), hoping, going to the bathroom, going to the Chinaman's corner store, reading the paper (and thank God for that, especially the advertisements), becoming suddenly aware again of the noise of the radio (and thank God for that, too), and forgetting again.

This, and not much more, was her life as she waited for the great dustman and the ultimate box. So Mrs. Bylow's days and months slid and slid away while age – taking advantage of her solitariness, her long unemployment of vestigial brain, her unawareness of a world beyond herself, her absence of preparation for the gray years – closed down upon her like a vice, no, more like a fog. There had been a time about ten years ago when Mrs. Bylow, sitting on her small porch, beckoned to the little neighbour children who played on the sidewalk. "Come," said Mrs. Bylow, smiling and nodding.

The children came, and they all went into the kitchen. There was Mrs. Bylow's batch of fresh cookies and the children ate, looking around them, rapacious. They ate and ran away and once or twice a child hovered and said "Thank you." Perhaps that was not the child who said "Thank you", but parents speaking through the child ("Say Thank you to Mrs. Bylow!") so the child said "Thank you" and Mrs. Bylow was pleased. Sometimes the children lingered around the little porch, not hungry, but happy, noisy and greedy. Then Mrs. Bylow rejoiced at the tokens of love and took the children into the kitchen. But perhaps she had only apples and the children did not care for apples. "Haven't you got any cookies?" asked a bold one, "we got lotsa apples at home."

"You come Tuesday," said Mrs. Bylow, nodding and smiling, but the children forgot.

So within Mrs. Bylow these small rainbows of life (children, cookies, laughing, and beckoning) faded, although two neighbours did sometimes stop on their way home and talk for a few minutes and thus light up her day. Miss Casey who worked at the People's Friendly Market and was a smart dresser with fine red hair, and Mrs. Merkle who was the managing type and had eyes like marbles and was President of the Ladies' Bowling Club dropped in from time to time and told Mrs. Bylow all about the illnesses of the neighbours which Mrs. Bylow enjoyed very much and could think about later. Mrs. Merkle told her about Mr. Galloway's broken hip and Miss Casey told her about her mother's diabetes and how she managed her injections, also about the woman who worked in her department when she didn't need to work and now her kid had gone wrong and was in the Juvenile Court. Mrs. Bylow was regaled by everything depressing that her two friends could assemble because she enjoyed bad news which was displayed to her chiefly against the backdrop of her own experience and old age. All these ailments, recalling memories of her own (" . . . well I remember my Uncle Ernest's . . . ") provided a drama, as did the neglect and irresponsibility of the young generations. Like an old sad avid stupid judge she sat, passing judgment without ill will. It is not hard to understand why Mrs. Merkle and Miss Casey, hastening past Mrs. Bylow's gate which swung on old hinges, often looked straight ahead, walking faster and thinking I *must* go in and see her tomorrow.

During long periods of bad weather, as now in this

unconquerable fog, time was a deep pit for Mrs. Bylow. Her hip was not very good. She should have belonged to a church (to such base uses can the humble and glorious act of worship come) or a club, to which she would at least look forward. Gone were the simple impossible joys of going to town, wandering through the shops, fingering and comparing cloth, cotton and silk. Gone was the joy of the running children. Life, which had been pinkish and blueish, was gray. And now this fog.

So it was that on the fifth day of fog, Mrs. Bylow sat beside her window in a sort of closed-up dry well of boredom, cracking her knuckles and looking into the relentless blank that pressed against her window panes and kept her from seeing any movement on the sidewalk. Mrs. Merkle and Miss Casey were as though they had never been. I'm not surprised they wouldn't drop in, thought Mrs. Bylow modestly and without rancour, it couldn't be expected, it'll be all they can do to get home; and she pictured Miss Casey, with her flaming hair, wearing her leopard coat, pushing through the fog home to her mother. Diabetes, thought Mrs. Bylow, and she was sorry for old Mrs. Casey. Her indulgence of sorrow spread to include Miss Casey hurrying home looking so smart. Not much in life for her, now, is there, really, she thought, rocking. Mrs. Bylow peered again. She was insulted by this everywhere fog, this preventing fog. She needed a cup of cocoa and she had no cocoa. She repeated aloud a useful phrase, "The fog is lifting"; but the fog was not lifting.

Mrs. Bylow creaked to her feet. She wrapped herself up well, took her walking stick and went unsteadily down her three steps. Then, not at all afraid, she turned to the left and, in a silence of velvet, she moved slowly along beside the picket fence which would guide her to Wong Kee's store. At her own corner a suggestion of sickly glow in the air told her that the street lamps were lighted. She moved on, screwing up her eyes against the grayish yellow fog that invaded eyes, nose, mouth. At last another pale high glimmer informed her that she was near Wong Kee's store and, gasping, leaning now and then against the outside wall of the store itself, she reached the door with the comfortable knowledge that, once inside, she would find light and warmth. She would ask Wong Kee for his chair or a box and would sit down and take her ease while the Chinaman went with shuffling steps to the shelf where he kept the tins of cocoa. Wong Kee was a charming old man with good cheek-bones and a sudden tired Oriental smile. After Mrs. Merkle and Miss Casey he was Mrs. Bylow's third friend. She pushed the door open and waddled in to where there was this desired light and warmth, puffing a little.

Something was happening inside the store, a small whirlwind and fury. Mrs. Bylow was roughly pushed by large rushing objects. She lost her balance and was thrown, no, hurled violently to the ground. The person or persons rushed on, out and into the fog. The door slammed.

The store was empty. Everything was still. The old woman lay in a heap, bewildered and in pain. Gradually she began to know that someone or some people had rushed out into the fog, knocking her down and hurting her because she happened to be in the way. She whimpered and she thought badly of Wong Kee because he did not come to help her. Her body gave her massive pain, and as she looked slowly about her in a stupefied way she saw that a number of heavy cans of food had rained down upon her and lay around her. As she tried clumsily to heave herself up (but that was not possible), a customer came in.

"Well well well!" said the customer bending over her, "whatever . . . " then he straightened himself and listened.

A faint sound as of a bubbling sigh came from behind the counter on which was the till. The till was open and empty. The customer went behind the counter and again bent down. Then he drew himself up quickly. Wong Kee lay like a bundle of old clothes from which blood seeped and spread. The sound that the customer had heard was the soft sound of the death of Wong Kee who was an honest man and innocent. He had worked all his life and had robbed no one. He had an old wife who loved him. In a way hard to explain they were seriously and simply happy together. This was now over.

The customer paid no further attention to Mrs. Bylow on the floor but, stepping round Wong Kee's body, reached the telephone.

A small woman parted the dingy curtains which separated the store from the home of Wong Kee and his wife. She held in her arms a bundle of stove wood and stood motionless like a wrinkled doll. Then the stove wood clattered to the ground and she dropped to her knees uttering high babbling noises. She rocked and prostrated herself beside the impossible sight of her husband's dead body and his blood. The customer regarded her as he talked into the telephone. Then he too knelt down and put his arm round her. He could find nothing to say but the immemorial "There there. . . . "

Mrs. Bylow, lying neglected on the floor, endeavoured to look behind her but she had to realize as people do in bombardment, flood and earthquake that she was at the mercy of whatever should happen to her and could not do anything about it, let alone look behind her.

"They're slow coming," said the customer. "It's the fog."

The old Chinese woman wrenched herself from him. "I tarryphome," she cried out, "I tarryphome my son. . . . "

The door opened and there seemed to be some policemen. The outside fog poured in with this entrance and some other kind of fog pressed down upon Mrs. Bylow's understanding and blurred it. "I'm a very old woman," she mumbled to a constable who had a little book, "and they knocked me down . . . they mighta killed me . . . they shouldn't a done that . . . they've broke my hip . . . aah . . . !"

"Yes lady, we'll look after you," said the constable, "who was it?"

"It was . . . " (well, who was it?) "I guess it was some man . . . no . . . " she breathed with difficulty, she should not have to suffer so, "I guess it was a boy . . . no, two boys . . . they knocked me down . . . "

A constable at the door said to a crowd which had gathered from somewhere in the fog and now pushed against the front of the store, "Now then, you can't come in here, there's been a robbery, see? You best go on home," but someone battered on the pane with both hands enough to break it, and Miss Casey burst in at the door, her red hair wet with fog.

"She's here! Yes there she is!" said Miss Casey talking to everyone in her loud voice and bringing into the muted shop a blazing of bright eyes and hair and leopard coat and humanity, " – that's what I thought! I thought right after I left the store I'd better go in and see was she O.K. because she shouldn't be out and the fog was just *aw*ful and I prett' near went past her gate but I kinda felt something was wrong and my goodness see what happened. . . . Mrs. Bylow honey, what happened you," and Miss Casey dropped on her knees and took Mrs. Bylow's hand in hers. "Say, what's been going on around here anyway?" she said, looking up at the constable, ready to accuse.

"She's not so good," said the constable in a low tone in Mrs. Bylow's dream and a high noise came into the night ("That's the syreen," said Miss Casey) and some men lifted her and took her somewhere on a bed. It did not occur to Mrs. Bylow that perhaps she had been killed inadvertently by two youths who had just killed her old friend, but if a policeman had said to her "Now you are dead," she would have accepted the information, so unfamiliar was the experience of boring horizontally through a fog at top speed very slowly in a high and unexplained swelling noise. She opened her eyes and saw a piece of Miss Casey's leopard coat and so she was not dead.

"Is it reel?" she whispered, because she had always wanted to know.

"Is what reel?" said Miss Casey bending her flaming

head. "Sure it's reel. The collar's reel anyway." Mrs. Bylow closed her eyes again for several years and said "But I never got my cocoa." Then she began to cry quietly because she felt old and helpless and the pain was something cruel but it was good to feel Miss Casey beside her in her leopard coat. She did not know that Wong Kee was dead – slugged on the head, pistol-whipped, stabbed again and again in the stomach with a long knife – all because he had summoned his small strength and fought like a cat and defended himself for his right to his thirty dollars and some loose change and a handful of cigarettes and his life. "Well, here we are," said Miss Casey, standing up, very cheerful.

In a week or two, while she was better and before she got worse, Mrs. Bylow began to remember the two boys whom she had never seen and, as she constructed their leather jackets and their faces, she said she would know them anywhere. Of course she would not, and the murderers of Wong Kee were never found but carried the knowledge of their murder into the fog with them on their way from the betrayal of their youth to whatever else they would soon violently undertake to do. When they arrived back, each at his own home, their parents said in pursuance of their habit of long years past "Where you bin?" and the hoodlums said in pursuance of their habit of long years past "Out." This satisfied the idiot parents. They said "My that fog's just terrible," and the hoodlums said "Sure is." They were excited and nervous because this was the first time they had killed, but they had the money. One of the young hoodlums did not go into the room where his parents were but went upstairs because he was pretty sure there was still some blood on his hands and so there was. Wong Kee's blood was on his parents' hands too but they, being irresponsible, did not know this. And on their hands was the blood of Mrs. Bylow who was soon to die, and of Mrs. Wong Kee who could no longer be said to live, and of their own hoodlum children.

Before Mrs. Bylow died, wiped out by forces quite outside herself like a moth in a storm (not much more and no less), she began to be a little proud of almost being present at a murder.

"It's not everyone who's been at a murder, Miss Casey, love, is it?"

"No honey," said Miss Casey, seeing again that sordid scene, "it isn't everyone."

"I always liked that coat of yours," said Mrs. Bylow.

"And then," said Miss Casey to Mrs. Merkle, "d'you know what she said? She said if ever I come to die – just like she wasn't ever going to – would you please wear your leopard coat. She's crazy about that coat. And then she said she often thought of those two boys that killed the storekeeper and knocked her down and she guessed it was more their parents' fault and not their fault. It made the tears come to your eyes," said Miss Casey who was kind as well as noisy and cherished a sense of personal drama.

"Sure," said Mrs. Merkle who had eyes like marbles that did not weep.

Mrs. Bylow's death was obscure and pitiful. Miss Casey got the afternoon off and so there were two people at her funeral. Miss Casey wore her leopard coat as promised.

THIRTEEN

Hurry, hurry

WHEN THE mountains beyond the city are covered with snow to their base, the late afternoon light falling obliquely from the west upon the long slopes discloses new contours. For a few moments of time the austerity vanishes, and the mountains appear innocently folded in furry white. Their daily look has gone. For these few moments the slanting rays curiously discover each separate tree behind each separate tree in the infinite white forests. Then the light fades, and the familiar mountains resume their daily look again. The light has gone, but those who have seen it will remember.

As Miriam stood at the far point of Sea Island, with the wind blowing in from the west, she looked back towards the city. There was a high ground fog at the base of the mountains, and so the white flanks and peaks seemed to lie unsupported in the clear spring sky. They seemed to be unattached to the earth. She wished that Allan were with her to see this sight of beauty which passed even as she looked upon it. But Allan was away, and she had come for a walk upon the dyke alone with their dogs.

It was the very day in spring that the soldier blackbirds had returned from Mexico to the marshes of the delta. Just a few had come, but in the stubble fields behind the high dyke, and in the salt marshes seawards from the dyke, and on the shallow sea, and over the sea there were thousands of other birds. No people anywhere. Just birds.

The salt wind blew softly from the sea, and the two terrier dogs ran this way and that, with and against the wind. A multitude of little sandpipers ran along the wet sands as if they were on wheels. They whispered and whimpered together as they ran, stabbing with their long bills into the wet sands and running on. There was a continuous small noise of birds in the air. The terriers bore down upon the little sandpipers. The terriers ran clumsily, sinking in the marshy blackish sand, encumbered as they ran and the little sandpipers rose and flew low together to a safer sandbank. They whispered and wept together as they fled in a cloud, animated by one enfolding spirit of motion. They settled on their safe sandbank, running and jabbing the wet sand with their bills. The terriers like little earnest monsters bore down upon them again in futile chase, and again the whispering cloud of birds arose. Miriam laughed at the silly hopeful dogs.

Farther out to sea were the duck and the brant and the seagulls. These strutted on the marsh-like sands, or lay upon the shallow water or flew idly above the water. Sometimes a great solitary heron arose from nowhere and flapped across the wet shore. The melancholy heron settled itself in a motionless hump, and again took its place in obscurity among stakes and rushes.

Behind the dyke where Miriam stood looking out to sea was a steep bank sloping to a shallow salt-water ditch, and beyond that again, inland, lay the stubble fields of Sea Island, crossed by rough hedges. From the fields arose the first song of the meadow lark, just one lark, how curious after winter to hear its authentic song again. Thousands of ducks showed themselves from the stubble fields, rising and flying without haste or fear to the sea.

Miriam called to the dogs and walked on along the narrow clay path at the top of the dyke. She delighted in the birds and the breeze and the featureless ocean. The dogs raced after her.

Clumps of bare twisted bushes where scattered along the edge of the path, sometimes obscuring the curving line of the dyke ahead. In a bush a few early soldier blackbirds talked to each other. Miriam stood still to listen. "Oh-kee-*ree*," called a blackbird. "Oh-kee-*ree*," answered his mate. "Oh-kee-*ree*," he said. "Oh-kee-*ree*," she answered. Then the male bird flew. His red patches shone finely. What a strange note, thought Miriam, there's something sweet and something very ugly. The soldier blackbird's cry began on a clear flute's note and ended in piercing sweetness. The middle sound grated like a rusty lock. As she walked on between the twisted black bushes more soldier black-birds called and flew. Oh-kee-*ree*! Oh-kee-*ree*! Sweet and very ugly.

Suddenly she saw a strange object. Below her on the left, at the edge of the salt-water ditch there was an unlikely heap of something. Miriam stopped and looked. This thing was about the size of a tremendous hunched cat, amorphous, of a rich reddish brown. It was the rich brown of a lump of rotted wood. Although it did not move, she had instant warning that this creature was alive and had some meaning for her. She called the dogs who came wagging. She leashed them, and they went forward together. The dogs tugged and tugged. Soon they too looked down the bank at the strange object. In the brown mass something now moved. Miriam saw that the brown object was a large wounded hawk. The hawk was intensely aware of the woman and the dogs. As they paused, and then as they passed along the high dyke path, the hawk's head turned slowly, very slowly, to observe them. Its body was motionless. Its eyes were bright with comprehension. Miriam was glad that she had leashed the dogs. In another minute they would have descended on the hawk. One brown wing lay trailed behind the big bird, but with its sharp beak and tearing claws it would have mauled the terriers, and they would have tormented it. The hawk stared brightly at her. She wished that she could save the hawk from its lingering death on the marshes, but there was nothing she could do. Motionless, save for the slowly turning head, the great bird followed them with intent gaze. Its eyes were bright with comprehension, but no fear. It was ready. The hawk made Miriam feel uneasy. She walked on faster, keeping the dogs still on the leash. She looked back. The hawk steadily watched her. She turned and walked on still faster.

One of the dogs growled and then both barked loudly. Round a thorn bush, hurrying towards her came a man. In all their walks upon the dyke before Allan went away, they had never met another human being. Miriam was startled. She was almost afraid. The strange hawk. The strange man. The man stopped. He was startled too. Then he hurried towards her. Crowded on the narrow clayey path of the dyke stood Miriam and the two dogs, uncertain. The man came close to her and stopped.

"Don't go on," he said urgently, "don't go on. It isn't safe. There's a cougar. I'm going to a farmhouse. To warn them. Perhaps I can get a gun. Turn back. And keep your dogs on the lead," he said sharply.

"Oh," said Miriam, "you must be mistaken. There's never been a cougar on these islands. No, of course I won't go on though. I'll turn back at once. But you *must* be mistaken. A dog or even a coyote, but not a cougar!"

"It *is* a cougar," said the man vehemently, "did you never hear of the cougar that swam across from the North Shore last year? Well – I can't stop to argue – there *is* a cougar, I saw it. Beside the dyke. It's driven in by hunger, starving, I expect. Well?"

He looked at her. He held her eyes with his eyes.

"Oh," said Miriam, "of course I won't go on. I should never have come! I'm so glad I met you. But it's extraordinary!" and she turned in haste.

The man paid her no further attention. He stepped down a bit from the path on to the steep grassy side of the dyke, and pushed past her and the restless dogs. He walked on very fast without another word. Miriam hurried after him along the narrow dyke path, the dogs impeding her as she hurried. This was like a bad dream. Hurry, hurry! I can't hurry.

She nearly ran along the slippery bumpy dyke path,
past the brown heap of the wounded hawk whose bright
eyes watched her, and past the straggly bushes where the
soldier blackbirds flew from tree to tree and sang. She
hurried along until she turned the curve of the dyke and
saw again the mountains behind the city. The peaks now
hung pink and gold in the cold spring sky. To the farthest
range of the Golden Ears the sunset caught them. Miriam
fled on. The leashed dogs ran too, bounding and hinder-
ing her as she ran. She crossed the little footbridge that led
to the lane that led to her car.

She had lost sight of the man a long time ago. He had
hurried on to give the alarm. She had seen him stumbling
down the steep dyke side and splashing across the salt-
water ditch to the stubble fields.

Far behind them along the dyke the body of the young
woman who had just been murdered lay humped beside
the salt-water ditch.

The man who had killed her reached the cover of the
hedge, out of sight of that woman with the dogs. When he
reached the cover of the hedge he began to run across the
tussocky field, stumbling, half blind, sobbing, crying out
loud.

FOURTEEN

Truth and Mrs. Forrester

I

"I DON'T OBJECT to truth being stranger than fiction," said Mrs. Forrester to Laura who was young and dark and beautiful and sitting in the corner of the couch across the room, "what I object to is that truth is so hard to tell, while fiction is the easiest thing in the world. It is rarely," she confessed without shame, "that I find myself speaking truthfully. I do not say 'quite' truthfully, because there again one begins to dodge about, with one's 'quites', and 'absolutelys', and 'virtuallys', and all the nonsensical adverbs (are they adverbs? you ought to know, Laura), that people use in order to shy away from truth. Another thing is that truth is often very uncomfortable. It is quite (there I go!) easy for me to tell you truthfully that I enjoy sitting in this armchair talking to you or being silent because you are able to enjoy silence, and also you are an admirable listener at the times when I wish to hear my own voice, and I can listen, too, but not so much, and because I admire your large dark eyes like an odalisque's (no, not by Cézanne or is it Matisse), but your hair is at this moment untidy enough to spoil your beauty and you should do something about it, and you should reduce. But when it comes to some people . . . "

"It is remarkable," said Laura smiling gloriously at her adopted aunt, "c'est tout à fait remarquable que si . . . "

"Stop being French and talk English," said Mrs. Forrester. "We'll save our French till Miss Riley comes in and use it for defence. What is remarkable?"

"It is remarkable," said Laura in her English voice that always retained her mother's R's, "that although I am young and you are . . . "

"Yes, old, say it; old," said Mrs. Forrester vehemently.

"Yes, old but not old, we do understand what each other means, and what is true, and what is false, and what is terribly" (how her R's rolled and rolled) "ridiculously funny. And it is formidable how if Cousin Max – for example I say Cousin Max *or* Miss Riley – should come in and talk and talk as they do, that you and I would both act our parts as though they had been written for us, without prompting, and each of us would know it. That is truth. Or is it lying?"

"I'm an amateur and you are nearly a professional, but I understand what you mean," said Mrs. Forrester, "and it is strange (still talking about truth) how in the presence of Cousin Max, or Miss Riley, or Lee Lorimer Smith – all of them nice people – in order to preserve one's integrity – that is, truth – one proceeds to act, which is to lie. At least I find it so. I don't know if they also act, but I don't seem to think so. I think their integrity is more consistent than mine. But at any rate it seems to be always I – we – who try to conform."

"So, Aunt Fanny," said Laura, who was smoking too much, "can one wonder if, since the presence, of – for example – Cousin Max, or Miss Riley, or Mrs. Lorimer Smith, changes one's identity just a little," ("No, a lot," said her aunt) "that Moscow – why do I put Moscow first? – and London and Washington when they are reduced to actual people talking to each other change their identities, and complicate issues, and make things very hard for my generation – and also for yours of course," she added generously. "This matter of truth is really difficult and important."

"One thing that I always adore about your Uncle

Mark," said Mrs. Forrester, "and one of the reasons why I cannot endure his still being in China, and life is not life without him, is that truth is never distorted between your Uncle Mark and me, whether we talk or whether – I assure you – we stay whole days silent like male and female happy Trappists. There is nothing that intervenes. There is just truth. Tell me, do you think you are going to let Johnny Watt propose to you, and do you know what you want to do about him? Don't forget about his alarming mother; you'd have to marry her too."

"I think that is Cousin Max," said Laura, getting up off the foot she was sitting on, and looking out of the window. "He begins talking the minute he gets out of the taxi. Probably before; he rehearses in the taxi."

"Oh, dear, what can we do," exclaimed Mrs. Forrester. "That's another of the unendurable things about Mark being away. He always manages Max and everybody else so well, and I can always look at Mark being handsome and kind and himself and not pretending, and Cousin Max play-acting and living up to himself and therefore being consistently himself. You go Laura – no you go and tidy your hair and do look a bit more beautiful if you please and I'll go to the door because I don't matter."

The door bell rang, and because Miss Riley had made them have short rapid dinner at six so that she could go out (and had gone out) before seven, Mrs. Forrester went to the door and there stood Cousin Max wearing a smart hat on the side back of his head and a smart top coat and pale yellow chamois gloves turned back at the wrists – thus – and thus –

"Fanny my dear!" said Cousin Max, lifting the hat high, revealing the polished dome, and standing back as if to look adequately at Mrs. Forrester because she dazzled him. "My *dear* Fanny! As beautiful as ever! No, *more* beautiful than ever!"

You old ass, thought Mrs. Forrester and said gushingly, "Cousin Max, *are*n't you sweet! How nice of you to come! I was longing to show you the new flat and you must tell me whether Mark will like it when he comes back and yes, you see, we have a hall cupboard. Very small but a hall cupboard – give me your things!" (Is there any whiskey – Scotch Scotch, Max must specially have Scotch, oh dear, it's on my hat shelf or is it?)

Cousin Max wheeled round, taking in with slow revolving gaze the carpets, the ceilings, the walls, the furniture, the books, patronizing them, permitting them, possessing them, discarding them.

"Quite admirable," he announced. "You have done very well, Fanny. I have seen apartments even in Paris with which this could be compared most favourably." (Mrs. Forrester tried to sound pleased.) "Thank you my dear – a cigarette lighted for one by a pretty woman . . . one of the little pleasures! One of the little pleasures!"

Cousin Max settled himself in an armchair, cast himself back, pinched his tie, and looked this way and that over his collar. The apartment was approved, accepted. I wish it would get up and kick him thought Mrs. Forrester. There we were, Laura and I, having a nice time, discussing truth. And now, where is it?

"And what news from the good Mark?" asked Cousin Max loftily, blowing a spiral.

Well, darn you, thought Mrs. Forrester . . . "the good Mark" indeed! and she answered sweetly with a pang in her heart, "Mark? Oh his return is delayed again . . . negotiations are difficult . . . delayed . . . the people I think aren't easy . . . there are complications . . . " She faltered, she could not tell him that Mark was ill, obscurely ill, oceans away, worlds away, inside China. She could not face with equanimity the fuss, the patronage, the "told you so," the – with an air – "Of course it is ridiculous that Mark should work so hard . . . this trip to China . . . such a place . . . the fact is, my dear Fanny, he has brought this upon himself . . . I always said . . . " So she smiled and lied and said, "Well, Cousin Max, *you* know the Chinese, or perhaps you don't, but Mark does, and he is more patient than I. He's just being patient.

Now. Will you have some Scotch?" and she stood, smiling down at him.

Cousin Max was pleased. There he sat, a bachelor, a diner-out, a man of the world on his way to a party at Lee Lorimer Smith's; a pretty woman – not so young now it was true, but still she *had* been a pretty woman even if only a cousin – was standing near him. He raised his hand, gesticulating silently, and the cigarette smoke curled upwards; the lamps were mellow and yellow; his complete and shining baldness was redeemed and complimented by his small improbably dark moustache bristling all but fiercely. In the evening Max was a trifle splendid in his own way. His shirt front gleamed; he would drink one small Scotch; he would tell one or two of his stories; he would impress, cheer, and excite; and then he would go and, departing, leave a pleasant flutter behind him.

"Ah, since you ask me!" deprecatingly, "just a little *little* Scotch!"

Mrs. Forrester went into the bedroom. She slipped through the door and closed it behind her. She went to her hat shelf. Laura was talking softly to the telephone and gave her a quick dark look, her fine eyebrows showed distress on her white brow.

"Johnny," she said . . . and Mrs. Forrester went out with the Scotch and closed the door.

"Johnny," Laura said into the telephone, "it's no good trying to *make* me. It was all right when it didn't matter . . . yes . . . yes . . . yes, I loved it . . . I told you . . . but now . . . it's different when you're trying to force me . . . Why? . . . oh Johnny . . . how can I say . . . over the telephone . . . the truth is . . . the truth is . . . "

(Well, what is the truth? The truth is that you can't tell him the truth. The truth is that you're not quite what I want, Johnny Watt. The truth is that I'd like to marry you if I loved you well enough, and I don't. The truth is that I knew the minute I saw your mother that I didn't like her, and I knew that she wouldn't like me, and then very soon you wouldn't either. I suppose the truth is that you're not

the man for me, Johnny, and you want to know why, and
I can't tell you the truth.)

"All right then Johnny. Tomorrow. But don't let's discuss and discuss. Yes. For dinner. I must go. We have
Cousin Max in full force. Good-bye Johnny." And Laura
went out of the bedroom, shining.

Cousin Max rose from his chair. He stepped forwards
and then leaned backwards as though adequately to
behold Laura who stood there laughing, eyes soft and
laughing, modest, teasing, not quite Canadian, rather
French, rather English; welcoming Cousin Max; flattering
him; telling him just by standing there and looking at him
that he was male and experienced and a man of the world
and . . . oh Laura, thought Mrs. Forrester, you do go too
far.

"Laura!" exclaimed Cousin Max as if smitten with
amaze. "More beautiful than ever . . . quite dazzling!"

All right. I'll oblige. I'll play. I'll dazzle. And Laura
looked at him with her odalisque eyes and gave him a nice
time, and he sat down again, crossed his legs, leaned back,
blew smoke into the air, and regarded Laura meditatively.
He said, "You remind me, Laura, of someone I knew in
Naples." Laura listened, attentive. "There were some very
lovely women in Naples that winter, but there was one
girl . . . we young fellows at the Consulate were very much
enamoured of this girl . . . amazingly like you if you don't
mind my saying so my dear Laura . . . engaged to a young
Italian of good family . . . but she was mad about Ned
Forman (*you* remember Ned Forman, Fanny, the For-
mans of Brock Street) . . . Ned was a ve–ry good-looking
fellow and at first we chaffed Ned you understand, and
were a leetle envious . . . and then pon my word the thing
got serious . . . she would elude her chaperon, to encounter Ned, you understand – a very serious matter with a
good Italian family and a young chap in the Consulate –
she even (*with* her maid) came down to the Consulate! . . .
the thing became very serious . . . Ned never travelled
alone . . . always one of us with him . . . she was ravishing,

ravishing but a bit of an ass . . . and if Ned hadn't been engaged to a nice girl in Toronto he might have lost his head . . . as it was he nearly lost his job. I was with Ned when she at last appeared in his room . . . *gorgeous*, absolutely *gorgeous* I assure you my dear child . . . and it was I, I who took the weapon from her hand . . . " Coolly, magnificently, Cousin Max removed an invisible weapon from an invisible Italian beauty.

"How marvellous of you! How clever! How brave! *Do* go on!" breathed Laura.

Cousin Max's face had assumed a worldliness and knowingness that Mrs. Forrester was forced to admire. Where did he learn it? How does he do it? She began to like him all over again as she sometimes did, because, of his own type he was perfection, and how rare perfection is. She knew well his type, orchid amongst our plain field flowers. She had heard the story of the Italian girl before and so, as it was being told for the benefit of Laura whose dark eyes and cream eyelids had recalled the affair, she gave herself up idly to watching Cousin Max doing his stuff. How perfect the timing, the word, the lifting of the eyebrow (one), the tone, how well he told his story. One saw, one heard the swish of long skirts over small buttoned boots as this exciting dangerous girl pursued Ned Forman round corners, up forbidden places, and to the futile culmination when, urbane, prepared, cruel only to be kind, Cousin Max himself, it appeared, disposed with indulgence and adroitness of that last passionate episode . . . Oh Mark . . . who is caring for you . . . who is looking after you . . . what strangers put their hands on you . . . I can't bear it . . . I cannot endure this any longer and yet I have to. And the truthful deceiving tears welled up and she looked at Max through the tears she dared not raise her hand to wipe away, and saw no more the Italian beauty.

"So," said Cousin Max in an accomplished manner, "I tossed it out of the window and it fell into the pond, a miniature lake, actually. It was a beautiful little revolver,

pearl-handled. Frankly, I should like to have kept it, not as
a souvenir of course (poor girl!) but for its intrinsic
charm ... She became the wife of ... well ... well ...
perhaps not ... stormy, I admit ... I must go, or Lee
Lorimer Smith will not be pleased ... dinner at eight ...
her guest from Ottawa ... charming woman, a little odd,
but charming ... Tell Mark to come home soon."

"Oh I will," said Mrs. Forrester humbly.

She had only at intervals heard Max talking. Her heart
was, as always now, consumed with its anguish yet not
consumed. She had seemed to attend with customary
politeness. ("Onlie the body's busy and pretends.") She
rose, and the partings were made with almost Chinese
elaboration. She knew that Max was kind. She knew that
he had come in order to "cheer her up". She picked up his
gloves from the cupboard floor as retribution. Poor Max, I
treat him badly in my heart. I am not fair to him. I am
suffering and I am bad-tempered and I am not fair to
people.

"You see. We acted," said Laura when the departure
was achieved. "What did I tell you."

"Yes, I know," said Mrs. Forrester, and went into her
bedroom for a while.

II

When Mrs. Forrester came out of her bedroom she sat
down in her accustomed chair opposite Laura who was
knitting, and proceeded to talk with unusual vivacity.

(Cousin Max having conferred distinction on the apartment by his appearance and by his manner of leaving it
and of entering the taxi-cab which was by arrangement
awaiting him, directed the taxi driver with a pale gloved
hand and then leaned backward at his ease. He would not
say at dinner time to his partner, "I dropped in to see my
poor cousin, Fanny, whose husband, unfortunately, is so
long at some extraordinary place in China, and that good-
looking English girl who has been visiting her." He would

say with secrecy and implication, "I have spent the last hour with two very pretty women." The note is struck. The tone is established.

The kindly feeling that he felt for Fanny remained with him, also the faint re-echoing success that he had undoubtedly had with Laura; but as the taxi sped on he was aware, as often now, of an ennui; the aridity of his small club bedroom and of his stepping forth dismayed him again . . . This feeling he banished, temporarily, with an unpleasant effort as the taxi drew up and stopped outside the Lorimer Smith's house where in the rather spacious driveway other cars were standing. The spaciousness of the driveway in itself benevolently raised Cousin Max's spirits and comforted him and so did the small white apron of the maid who opened the door. The potency of symbols is astonishing. The pleasant warmth and light and the laughter of eleven pleasant people about to be fed at Lee Lorimer Smith's dinner party reached him at once and he hastened into his natural heaven and was soon saying to Lee Lorimer Smith who advanced towards him with her practised and petite hostess gaiety, "Forgive me, but I have just . . . " Here was a room full of well-dressed well-mannered people about to be well-fed, and at present drinking cocktails and exchanging – what? Nothing could be more congenial to Max, and his ennui was now as though it had not been. It would return.)

Because Mrs. Forrester knew that if Laura wished to speak about the problem presented by Johnny Watt and augmented by his mother, she would do so; and because Laura knew that if her Aunt Fanny wished to speak about her own inner grief, she would do so, neither spoke of these things, but Mrs. Forrester began speaking French for pleasure. She spoke fluently and fearlessly, with a good accent and atrocious grammar, lapsing into English when the impetuous need of a word demanded it. Laura spoke beautifully and flowingly and the very speaking of her mother's tongue sometimes transformed her and she became extremely Gallic in thought, appearance and gesture, which entertained her aunt as well as anything, at the moment, could.

"Your letter from your godmother," said Mrs. Forrester in her good bad French, "you said it was amusing? Is it news?"

"No," said Laura, "not unless you could call *seins* news. The French seem often to be preoccupied about *seins*."

"Dear me," said her aunt, "I should have thought that everyone knows everything about *seins* by this time without having to write about them from Paris. Whose *seins*. Yours or hers?"

"Oh, in a general sense, but as applied to 'young girls' (that's me)," said Laura. "Mme. Duhamel likes to write in English just as you like to talk French and, darling Aunt Fanny, she does it equally well and equally badly. She says 'I feel a great concern, my dear, that you shall be at this Canadian university learning about these poultries and these cows. Poultries are not for a young girl *bien élevée* and also that you should employ your spare time in learning to play that dreadful flute. Why my dear child do you occupy yourself with such infeminine matters as flutes and poultries? There are other things for *la jeune fille*. And in chief because the flute will destroy *absolument* the beauty of your mouth, all these grimaces, and because the poultries will destroy your figure. And for the young girl, believe me my dear child, you may not know, but the mouth and *les seins* are the most important.' So you see!"

Mrs. Forrester and Laura derived a great deal of pleasure from Laura's godmother's advice which they regarded as peculiarly French and, as they were Anglo-Saxons in thought, they appreciated the advice in an Anglo-Saxon way.

"The French seem to do a lot of delicious things which Balzac describes so well and which seem to promote *l'amour* and involve them a lot. Things seem to be on another plane with them and more exciting than with us. It may be more *spirituel* but it all strikes me as being fairly physical," said Mrs. Forrester. "I want to talk about Lee Lorimer Smith, idle chatter, because I did a very silly thing about three weeks ago, before I had that first cable about your Uncle Mark – it got me nowhere. I had often wished to do it, but it was silly, pointless."

"What did you do to Mrs. Lorimer Smith?" asked Laura.

"I sat beside her at lunch. I became through three courses so involved in Lee's parties, and guests, and in people who seemed to Lee to be 'news' but had done nothing to deserve being 'news' except to be relatives or accredited friends of people whom Lee knows – and I suddenly revolted. I revolted in the middle of the pudding. I eventually found myself smirking politely, you know Laura, in that false way, acting (as we said earlier this evening), and so I thought instead of me being Lee Lorimer Smith all lunch time, she can, just for fun, be me during the pudding, and I said a terribly stupid thing. I said, 'Do you like Dylan Thomas?' And Lee stopped short and said 'Do I like what, who?' and I said, 'Dylan Thomas,' and Lee said 'Does he live in town?' and she was terribly upset and thought that there was someone I knew and she didn't, and she said 'For goodness sake Fanny, if this Thomas man is nice, do bring him to dinner. Your cousin Max is a dear of course, but living in the club he's always out when I want him, and sometimes I *do* need an extra man so badly.' And then she said to Margaret Fensom, 'What do you suppose, Fanny has a stray man up her sleeve, some Mr. Thomas,' and I said 'Oh he wasn't really in town but . . . ' 'Well,' she said, 'if he doesn't live here he's no good to me,' and then she forgot all about him and was off on something else. It was very silly of me, because you can't make worlds mix, not at luncheons anyway; you've got to move into one or the other. I think 'social life,' Laura, is a most peculiar erection built of imponderables and invisibles . . . "

"*And* solids, don't you forget," said Laura.

The door of the apartment opened. Too many lights

were put on, and Miss Riley came in with her waterproof and umbrella and dripped on to the carpet. She advanced into the middle of the room bringing into the room with her some kind of dislocation or perhaps some kind of re-adjustment. Miss Riley lived in the country, but came to town every Friday morning and shopped for her family household at the farm, then she cooked Mrs. Forrester's dinner rapidly and then went with some friends to a show; she did some cleaning and cooking on Saturday and, encumbered with parcels, left on Sunday morning, arriving at the farm fresh and invigorated by her exciting and profitable trip to the city and full of continuous conversation.

But Mrs. Forrester paid more than wages to Miss Riley. She paid ear-service. Miss Riley, like Cousin Max and Lee Lorimer Smith, was a talker by profession but, unlike Cousin Max and Lee Lorimer Smith, she could not be smiled with, and responded to, and lost (as is done at parties) with impunity, because Mrs. Forrester was in thrall to her.

On entering the room Miss Riley became at once the principal character in it, and Laura and Mrs. Forrester soon lost their identities as two women conversing as they pleased in a slightly superior and literary and independent manner; they became as two spaniels, sitting and gazing upon Miss Riley while she spun her cocoon of words – two cigarette-smoking spaniels.

"Well say," said Miss Riley who dripped onto the carpet, "bull-eeve me, you've never seen such a night! Talk of cats and dogs (my brother always says cats and dogs) it sure is raining outside! And was I glad I never went to a show! Just before I left here my sister Bertha telephoned me – that was the telephone call I had when you and Laura was eating – and she said Let's not go to a show because George's – that's my second brother's – dotter (that's my niece) came into town yesterday she lives in Noo Westminister and her husband's in the drug business not right in Westminister but just a ways out and they haven't their own home yet but his father – he's an old-timer in Westminister – is going to build them a home and my sister-in-law – that's George's wife'll give them the drapes and she said don't you be dictated to, you *say*, if you want a split level home the trouble about these gift horses (that's what my brother calls them) is you can't choose but they're pretty smart she used to sing in the choir till the baby came and now she can't but she certny has a lovely voice it's real high she took vocal for six months and her teacher said Give me that girl for five years and I'll make her an opera star that's the kind of voice she has and she and the baby came in yesterday from Noo Westminister and Bertha said for us to go over and see the baby and bull-eeve me that is the kee-ootest baby you'd ever see. I'll bet you never saw such a kee-oot baby it's not talking yet but say is she smart it's a girl she doesn't take after our family but Hazel says she's the living image of Bert's grandmother she was Scotch and they have a picture of her in one of those old albums – and she sure is, they're calling her Darlean and . . . "

The cocoon continued to spin and spin. The two cigarette-smoking spaniels gazed receptively upon Miss Riley. Mrs. Forrester wondered why is it that babies are so good to look at and so awful to hear about. Miss Riley continued, "Guess I'll take off this rain-coat it's real wet," which she did, and sat down.

"My niece Hazel," she said. "Will you bull-eeve me . . . " and so inept were these two clever women who had made fun of Cousin Max (who was much too skilful to tolerate such weekly tyranny as this), and of Lee Lorimer Smith (who wouldn't have tolerated it either), and had talked French to each other – so inept were they that Miss Riley continued to dominate them unchecked for twenty minutes. They became supine.

It was true that under this domination (as slaves must) Mrs. Forrester's mind reverted to the private anguish which monopolized her waking life. If I don't have another cable tomorrow I shall fly there somehow . . .

immediately . . . I shall find a way, I have waited too long now . . . and Laura revolved her own private thoughts. In their minds they lived, but as spaniels they gazed on Miss Riley because Laura knew that her aunt was in thrall to Miss Riley and this was part of her socage. And just as Miss Riley said, "My family was always smart at figures it came natural to all my brothers and sisters and the teacher said if I hadn't been so smart at other things I certny shoulda taken commerce . . . " the doorbell rang.

"Well say," said Miss Riley, "if that isn't the bell! At this time of night! What do you suppose? Was you expecting callers? Whenever I hear a bell like that last thing at night I always think of telegrams and that time my eldest brother was in Quee-bec and . . . "

She turned towards the door. Laura had risen to her feet but Mrs. Forrester was before her. She was at the door – it seemed to her – without moving there.

"Cable for Mrs. Forrester," said the telegraph boy in a god-like way. "Sign here," said the boy nonchalantly. Her fingers shook as she signed. She took the envelope and walked past Miss Riley who was saying, "My goodness whenever I see a telegram I always . . . ", and past Laura, and into the bedroom.

Miss Riley continued to talk about telegrams but Laura did not hear her. She stood waiting. It seemed to her a long time.

"Laura," her aunt called to her in a strange voice.

Laura went quickly and greatly fearing into the bedroom. She saw the true Mrs. Forrester standing there, holding the telegram in her hand. Something had dropped away from her. Something had changed her into herself. Something had caused her face to shine even though she wept as she laughed for joy.

"Look, Laura, look!" she said, shining, holding out the piece of paper.

Miss Riley, standing at the door, saw with much interest the woman and the girl – embracing, laughing, liberated, no longer in thrall to her, guards all down.

"Well say," said Miss Riley, expanding the obvious, "looks to me like it musta been good nooz . . . " and louder, "I said it looks to me like it musta been good nooz!" but nobody listened now. Nobody heard her.

FIFTEEN

Mr. Sleepwalker

D URING THE time that Mary Manly's husband was in
Australia, Mrs. Manly had an experience that was
peculiar. I should like to say that up to the time that her
husband went to the war, Mrs. Manly had never shown
any tendency to undue imagination, nervousness, hyste-
ria, nor to any of those weaknesses which are supposed to
be the prerogative of her sex, but are not – any of which
might have been considered responsible for the mounting
episodes which culminated in her nearly killing Mr. Sleepwalker. Let us begin with Mary Manly, because we do not
know very much about the past of Mr. Sleepwalker. It
would be provocative, but not fair, to speculate about Mr.
Sleepwalker's past, but unless we knew something about
his origin and his history, the speculations would be use-
less, and disturbing.

Mary Davidson married Hugh Manly who was a for-
ester in the government service of British Columbia, and
so able a man was Hugh Manly in the matter of conserva-
tion of forests, marketing of lumber – especially as these
things applied to the Province of British Columbia whose
forests are among her noblest treasures – that his government began to send him on long journeys to foreign coun-
tries where export trade might be developed, and it
became no great surprise – but a source of something like
grief – to Mary when Hugh walked in for dinner, and said
later on in the evening as he often did, "Well, it looks as

though I'm off again," and Mary would learn that Hugh was being sent by his government to South Africa, or to the United Kingdom, or to Sweden, and so it was that Mary had to gear herself – as they say – to these absences which became to her a mounting sorrow, because she loved her husband beyond expression, and he loved only her. Each time that Hugh left he said something like this, "Next time, darling, we'll see if you can't come too," and Mary would say, "Yes, next time, Hugh." But next time Hugh might go to Hyderabad, and how can a young wife whimsically accompany her husband to Hyderabad, when there is a future to look to. I mention all this because it is possible that the unhappiness of repeated separation in a world whose essential limit is bounded by the life and love of two people closely united, may have done something to Mary's otherwise calm and extroverted nature, and may have made her susceptible to outside influence of an eso-teric, supra-human, or even sub-human kind.

Just at the time when it seemed that Hugh had approached the point in his chosen profession at which he could say, "Come with me and be damned to everything and hang the expense," there came the war. Hugh went to the war, and Mary's sense of separation became exacer-bated to the point where it was anguish. Are we who love each other so dearly, she said to herself, always to be deprived of our greatest joy, and have I to accustom myself to the theory that we belong to each other *in absentia* only, for it is an actual fact that the woman in the next apartment and I have lived for seven years with only one wall dividing us, and we do not belong to each other; while Hugh and I, who belong to each other, have lived for seven years with half the world between us most of the time. And now this war!

She busied herself at once, but in spite of being daily involved in responsibility and detail, her other life – that is to say her absent life with Hugh – gradually became more real to her than the life of meetings, administration, billet-ing, in which her body was engaged, especially after Hugh

left for overseas. ("Onlie the body's busy, and pretends.")
Again I say that this other-worldness, which developed in
Mary, and in many other young women like her during
those years, but more in Mary Manly, because absence
and frustration had already made some mark on her
before the war began, may have been responsible for
many queer things, one way and another. Directly the war
was over, Hugh came home (fortunately) and was placed
at once at the head of his department; and before the two
had spent a month together, Hugh was sent to Australia.
"You're coming this time, Mary, and no nonsense about
it," said Hugh, and Mary with rapture prepared to go,
broke her left elbow, and Hugh went without her.

To go now to Mr. Sleepwalker.

Before Hugh went overseas he was stationed for a while
in Winnipeg. Mary camp-followed him to Winnipeg, and
it was in Winnipeg that she first saw Mr. Sleepwalker. It
was in a street car. The street car swinging along Portage
Avenue was full, and Mary stood, holding onto a strap.
She looked idly about her, and the swaying of the street
car so determined that her eyes fell upon this person and
that sitting in the row of seats immediately beside the
entrance to the street car. She saw a small slim man sitting
in this seat, with people on either side of him. Mary's
whole attention was taken by this man, although no one
else seemed to observe him, and as the body of someone
swaying beside her interposed between her and the small
man seated, she did not see him, and then she saw him
again.

She became violently curious about the small man, and
began to speculate about him. He appeared unaware of
people around him, and certainly unaware of Mary's
occasional scrutiny. If I were accustomed to menservants,
thought Mary, or if we lived in a different age, I should
think that this little man is, or has been, a "gentleman's
gentleman". He is drilled in some precision of thought
and action, and he hides behind that soft and deferential
pose and immobility some definite and different entity.

The small man sat erect, looking straight ahead of him, servile yet proud, his hands – in worn black gloves – folded on the head of his walking stick which rested between his knees. His hat was a kind of square obsolete bowler. He wore a wing collar, and a small black tie of the kind known as a string tie. His black suit was old, worn and very neat. Below the anachronistic hat was the face that so attracted and repelled Mary Manly. The features were neat and of a prissy femininity. The eyes were a warm stealthy reddish brown. His hair descended in reddish brown sideburns; otherwise he was clean-shaven. The hair was soft and unlike the hair of a man; in fact it resembled a soft fur. His mouth was set – so, with gentility. He is a mixture, thought Mary, as she watched the little man, now and again obscured from her, of gentility – a fake product of civilization – and of something feral, I do not know what. I seem to have seen those russet eyes, she continued to herself, in some animal. Is it a fox? No, I know no more about foxes than about gentlemen's gentlemen, and yet it seems like a fox. Or a watching hawk. Or some red-eyed rodent. And why is he in the middle of Canada, in Winnipeg, new city of grain, utility and railroads, looking like this, dressed like this? He is as much a phenomenon in his dreadful respectability, riding on an unlikely street car in the city of Winnipeg as if he wore a crown, or a gray topper, or a sarong. What life does he lead, and why is he here? The small man sat alone, it appeared, in his personal and genteel world, politely apart from those who rubbed shoulders with him or crowded his neatly-brushed worn buttoned boots, and he looked straight ahead of him. Mary now avoided looking at the small man, because, so lively had been her interest in his peculiarities, she was afraid that he might become aware of her, and she did not want this to happen; so she turned her back, and faced in the other direction. Then she got off the street car and, for the moment, forgot him.

On the next evening, Hugh came in from barracks, and they had dinner together. Mary tried to tell Hugh about the small man on the street car, but found that she was unable to describe him in such a way as would interest Hugh; and when Hugh told her, as he did, that he was ordered east and that he thought that embarkation would be the next step, this drove other thoughts from Mary's mind and she determined at once to move east also, because, as she said, "We may as well continue living together, Hugh, in our own peculiar haphazard fashion. I have really loved it in Winnipeg, and who knows but that they may keep you in the east longer than you think. So I shall not go back to Vancouver. I shall go east, too." Mary then prepared to go east, following Hugh, who left at a day's notice.

She had by this time attained (she thought) a fairly philosophic regard for things as they have to be, realizing of course that she was only one of the millions of persons – friends and enemies – whose lives were dislocated by war; that she could expect no special privilege because she was Mary Manly, wife of Hugh Manly (usually *in absentia*); and that she could and must assume the matter-of-factness which is necessary in the successful conduct of life, which other people achieve so admirably, and which passes very well for courage. So she took life as it came, allowing herself to hope, as was natural, that her husband would be kept in Canada, although a part of each of them wished that he would be sent away and would see action, but safely, with everybody else, and no favours sought or granted. Mary said good-bye to her friends in Winnipeg, many of whom, like herself, were also in motion one way or another, and then, late one night, she boarded the east-bound train.

Because Mary was what is called a good train traveller, she soon bestowed her things neatly away and settled down for the remainder of the night in her lower berth. She slept at once, and only in a half-conscious and comfortable way was she aware of the stopping, starting, moaning, creaking of the great train. Suddenly she was awakened by a quiet. The train was standing still, perhaps in a siding, because there seemed to be no noise, or it may have been in the night-time stillness of the railway station of a town. Mary was half awake, and did not care. She was sleepily aware of stillness, of time and place suspended – and then of persons passing quietly, almost stealthily, in the aisle outside her curtain . . . the porter . . . perhaps . . . passenger . . . porter . . . a murmur . . . a smell . . . earth . . . rotted wood . . . an animal . . . in the sleeping-car . . . impossible . . . a smell . . . earth . . . rotted wood . . . an animal . . . it passed. She fell asleep.

When day broke, the train had left Manitoba and was speeding into the vast western wooded lake-strewn regions of Ontario. The train stopped at Chapleau for twenty minutes. Mary got out, and wandered, as she always did at Chapleau station, to the small stone memorial that bears the name of Louis Hémon. Why, she wondered, did Louis Hémon come to Canada, write his book which, although unknown to most young Canadians, had already dimmed to a reputation faintly classic, and die. And why did Louis Hémon die, still young, at Chapleau, straggling rawly beside its railway station and its forests. A young man stood beside her and studied the carved words. Mary looked up at him and spoke tentatively. "Do you know why Louis Hémon came here?" she asked

"Sawry," said the young man awkwardly, "I never heard of him. I was kinda wondering myself who he was," and he strolled away.

Mary turned and walked briskly up and down the platform, with the breeze and against the breeze that blew refreshingly through Chapleau. She heard the cry "All aboard". She turned towards her own porter at her own car. As she waited to mount the steps, she saw walking down the platform the small man in black whom she had seen in the Winnipeg street car. She was startled to see the small figure in motion. He walked, one might say, with as much stillness as he sat, regarding no one. He walked with his arms at his sides, guarded, genteel, like a black-suited doll. She climbed on the train, entered her car, and found her seat. She did not see him again.

When she rejoined Hugh in Halifax, there were many urgent things to think about without recalling to mind the small man whose hair was like fur, and so it seemed that he had never been. Hugh's convoy sailed, and Mary Manly went back to Vancouver and put herself at once to work.

It was months later that Mary Manly and Thérèse Leduc went to a movie together. At the end of the first picture, the two people who were sitting beside Mary went out, and, in the dark, another occupant took the seat beside her. Suddenly Mary's attention was taken from the screen by the scent, slight at first, then stronger, of, perhaps, an animal, or, perhaps, rotted wood, thick and dank (but how could it be rotted wood?). This smell was not at first heavy, but pervasive, and was very unpleasant to her. It became at last heavy in the air, and made her uneasy. It recalled to her a journey . . . a what? . . . some smell . . . not train smell . . . something that passed by. She tried to look at the person next to her without appearing to do so. This was difficult. She murmured to Thérèse Leduc, "Do you smell anything queer?"

"No," whispered Thérèse. "What kind of thing?"

"I don't know," answered Mary.

"I smell nothing," said Thérèse.

The smell persisted. Suddenly the skin on the back of Mary's neck seemed to prickle. The man (it was a man) who sat beside her, was small, and sat very still. Mary sat still too, and thought, "I want to get up and leave. I can't. That is unreasonable." But at last she whispered to Thérèse, "I'm sorry, Terry, but the man beside me *does* smell. Let's get out . . . perhaps we can move. Let's go your way."

The two women got up and shuffled out of the long end of the row.

"How disgusting!" expostulated Thérèse.

"Yes, wasn't it? It really *was*," said Mary, but she did

not explain that the smell was not what Terry thought it was. Not dirt. Nothing like dirt. Something animal. Something wild. They found other seats, but Mary could not give her attention to the play. After the movie, she discovered also that she could not tell Thérèse about the small man, and about this animal smell which she had begun to associate with him. The thing was fanciful, and Mary did not like to be thought fanciful. Most of all, she did not like to admit to herself that she was fanciful. But there it was. She put her mind to other things, and that was not very difficult.

Some time later, as Mary rose from her knees in church, she did not need to look in order to see who it was that had come into the pew and had now dropped on his knees beside her. The feral scent wafted and then hung heavy. The small man in black drew himself up to his seat, and sat, doll-like, prim, just as (Mary knew) she had seen him sit in the street car on Portage Avenue. She saw him as plainly now as though her physical eyes observed the genteel shape, the russet fur of the sideburns, the prissy set of the mouth. He sat beside her, she knew, correct, genteel, yet vulpine, if it was vulpine. Mary's head began to spin. My imagination plays tricks, or does it? she asked herself . . . Soon, of course, I shall see the two people in front of me move, turn slightly, disturbed by the smell that disturbs me. It cannot be to me, me alone, that it comes. He carries it round with him. Others *must* smell it – always. He is horrible, horrible. But now I can't leave . . . I must stay . . . he can never have observed me (for we never think, do we, that we are the observed ones; always we are the observers), I shall sit here. I shall stay for the service, and out-stay him. But he is horrible. And a revulsion at the proximity of this small being almost overcame her, and she felt faint.

The little man sat still; his worn-gloved hands were on his knees, she could see. He took his Prayer Book and found his place, following the service respectfully, and in an accustomed manner. Mary's mind worked obliquely, directed, in spite of herself, towards the small man.

But the two people in front of her did not turn round, disturbed by the alien smell of rotted wood, of something animal, unknown.

Mary out-sat the service. Then, with elaborate negligence, while the small man was leaving and after he had left, she put on her gloves, leaned back in her pew and awaited the end of the slowly-drifting columns of church goers moving with slightly rocking inhibited motion down the aisles. Then she joined the departing stream at its end, went out into the open air, felt refreshed and, by a foolishly roundabout way, returned home.

I shall tell Hugh, she thought. It's very silly. I take this too seriously, and if I tell Hugh, I'll get rid of it. The thing bothers me out of all proportion. What concerns me is the war, and Hugh, and my jobs of work to do, and my life that I have always had; and a small being that smells like – perhaps – a weasel or a musk-rat has no part and does not matter. So she wrote, but when she read the letter that she had written to Hugh, her story seemed idiotic. She tore the letter up, and wrote again and did not mention the small man. Hugh, she thought, would not in any case be amused. She could not make the story amusing. She could just make it sound silly. Hugh might be interested in a man that smelled like an animal (she had seldom smelled an animal), but she would not be able to conceal from him the fact that something was being established that affected her unreasonably and unpleasantly; it seemed to her that the small man, in spite of his apparent immobility and unawareness, was in some peculiar way, aware of her also. This, of course, was possible, yet unlikely and very unpleasant. She neither saw the small man, nor did the strange scent reach her, for a long time.

One night it rained. Mary drove carefully in her little car. She picked up her cousin, Cora Wilmot, and drove through the lashing rain, and through the lights and reflections of lights, cross-hatched in the early dark in splashing pools and pavements, lighted by and left behind by the beams of her own headlights, onto Granville Street Bridge. She drove carefully in the late dinner-time traffic, peering through the rainstorm. She drove rather slowly. Cora, beside her, peered too. Then the thing nearly happened.

Just before Mary reached the narrow span of the bridge, Cora cried out, and stifled her cry. Off the slightly raised platform-like sidewalk of the bridge, into the light of the headlights of Mary's slowly-moving car, stepped a small man. He faced the lights of the car, and seemed to look through the windshield of the car and at, or into, the occupants. The lights showed all in one flash the white face (and Mary could see the lighted russet eyes), the intolerable propriety of mouth and chin, dark lines of hair framing the almost rectangular face. The man threw up his arms with the stiff gesture of a marionette. Mary swerved sharply to the left into whatever cars there might be, into the span, if need be, rather than touch, or become involved in any way with the man who had stepped in front of her car. She did not touch him. She touched neither cars nor span. She did not speak. She drove to the end of the bridge, up Granville Street hill, through lights, darkness and rain, and then she pulled up at the side of the road. She was trembling violently. Cora was voluble.

"That horrible little man!" she said, "*What* was he doing? *Why* did he do it? He did it on purpose! No one crosses the bridge there! There's nothing to cross for! Oh Mary, what a narrow shave! Let's sit here a while. What a face! He looked as if he could see us, as if he was looking at us! I'll never forget him, will you? Do you feel like driving now? Let's get there, and then they'll give us a drink before dinner, and that will help us both."

"Yes," said Mary, and she drove on. He saw me, she thought, as I drove so slowly in the lights, and then he stepped out.

Before the end of the year, Hugh came home, the war

being incredibly over. And then, as I said, Hugh went to Australia, and Mary, with the complicated fracture of her left arm in a sling, stayed at home.

Many and many a time, towards the end of the war, and now, when alone, when sleeping, and at waking, she seemed to see the doll-like figure of the small man with her motor lights full on his white face. She saw a marionette's gesture – two dark arms flung stiffly upwards, she swerved, she drove on in her dream. And then, the obsession became less frequent. Nevertheless, within herself, she knew that she had begun to be afraid of something.

Hugh wrote from Melbourne, "I'm going to be here longer than we thought. Just as soon as that elbow is better enough cable me. I'll advise you, and you get a passage by air. And at last . . . " The load of aggravation lifted from Mary, and she began to lie about her elbow in order to get away and to join Hugh in Australia. However, their friend the doctor, Johnny Weston, put her off for a week.

One afternoon she returned from John's surgery with the permission that she might now make arrangements for her flight to Australia, and so she cabled to Hugh. Such a thing as this had never happened to Mary Manly before. She went home, and in her ecstasy, her rapture, she telephoned Thérèse Leduc and Cora, and anybody else that came to mind, to tell them that she was flying to Australia to join Hugh.

There came a ring at the door of the flat. Still careful of her clumsy left arm, Mary went lightly to the door and opened it. A feral smell entered the apartment, followed by the small respectable man who had stood outside Mary's door and had rung her doorbell. The man was dressed as usual in black. As he stepped humbly but without question into the hall, he took off his obsolete square-shaped bowler hat, laid it upon a table, turned and shut the door in a serviceable manner, and then advanced obsequiously on Mary. In his hand he carried a small black valise. Scent hung heavy and it was the smell of fear.

Mary was aghast. Her right hand flew to her mouth. She

pressed the back of her hand to her mouth and gazed at the small man over her hand. She did not think, I am alone in this apartment with this unpleasant little creature. She did not think at all. The air was full of the dank wild earthy smell of something old and unknown. She backed, and obsequiously the small man advanced upon her. She saw the russet animal eyes, the reddish animal fur. She saw the prissy gentility of the lips. She smelled the smell.

"Sleepwalker," said the man softly, looking at her.

Mary snatched up a small bronze vase, and hit the man hard upon the side of the head. He looked at her with infinite surprise and reproach, swayed, and sank to the floor. He lay there like a large black-garbed doll, and blood began to flow from the wound on his head. His eyes were closed and he was very pale.

Mary stood looking down upon him, and tried to measure what she had done. "Three minutes ago," she thought, "I was mad with joy because I was going to Hugh, and now perhaps I have killed a man who is a stranger." She now felt curiously hard and not at all frightened. She went to the telephone and called John Weston at his surgery.

"John," she said, "this is Mary Manly. I am at home. I think I have killed a man. Please come." And she hung up the telephone and went back to the small man who lay as she had left him.

I am very stupid, thought Mary, because I do not know whether he is unconscious or whether he is dead, and I don't know how to find out such things. At least I will bathe his head, and perhaps if he is unconscious he will rally a bit. She got water and a cloth, and although it was repugnant to her, she knelt down and bathed the wound which she had inflicted on the small respectable man. He stirred. He opened his eyes and looked steadily at her. She rose to her feet and looked down at him.

"Dear lady," whispered the man, still prostrate on the

floor, "whatever made you do that to me?" and his eyes were indeed the eyes of an animal.

Well, thought Mary, I can see that this is going to be a very odd conversation. She could not answer his question, and so she said, "I am very, very sorry that I have done this to you, but why are you here? And why did you walk into my flat like that? And what was that you said to me when you came in?" It gave her satisfaction that John Weston would soon come, and would act as some kind of a solvent to this situation.

The man sat up slowly, and felt his head. He looked at his red hand with surprise, and again looked up at Mrs. Manly.

"Name of Sleepwalker," he said, "carrying a line of ladies' underwear samples of special buys in rayon, silk, crêpe, also ladies' hosiery put out by the Silki-Silk Company with agents in all major cities of Canada," and he looked at the black valise which lay where it had fallen.

"Oh," said Mary, feeling very silly indeed. "And do you really mean that your name is Sleepwalker?"

"Name of Handel Sleepwalker," said Mr. Sleepwalker, and subsided again into a faint on the floor.

The doorbell rang, and Mary opened the door to Dr. Weston. Because Dr. Weston was ruffled, and had – unwillingly – left his patients when Mary summoned him so imperatively and strangely, he had, since leaving his consulting-room, built up a genuine and justified annoyance mixed with real uneasiness, and because he could find no other object for his annoyance, he had hung it upon Mary Manly. Therefore by the time Dr. Weston arrived at Mary's apartment he was very angry indeed with her for having killed a man at a quarter-past five in the afternoon, for having taken him forcibly from his consultations and for having chosen to do this at a time when Hugh was not at home and therefore was unable to take the matter in hand. Although a very good friend of Hugh and Mary, Dr. Weston was not at that moment in

the frame of mind to shoulder the results of murder. This
is why, when Mary opened the door with a sense of relief,
John Weston dismayed her by a complete absence of sympathy; he turned on her an angry face, and roared at her
in an injured manner, "What on Earth *have* you been
doing?" as if she were guilty. Well, so she was.

Mary, aware of all that had gone before that was so
ridiculously unexplainable at that very instant, realized
that she had to cope with her own emotions to attend – in
the first place – to Mr. Sleepwalker who lay inert on the
living-room floor, and to manage Dr. Weston either by
returning anger for anger, innocence for anger, or by disre-
garding anger. This latter she decided to do.

"Come," she said. She turned and indicated Mr. Sleepwalker with an air quite sublime. "You see!"

When Dr. Weston saw the actual body of Mr. Sleepwalker lying on the floor of the room in which Dr. Weston
and his wife had so often enjoyed a cocktail, and saw Mr.
Sleepwalker's blood upon the carpet, and saw Mary standing there pale, helpless, bandaged and gentle, other feelings began to take possession of him. He kneeled down
and examined the prostrate one. Then he looked up and
said to Mary in a fretful tone, "He's not dead at all!"

Well, really, thought Mary, this is too much! Does John
expect that one should make sure of *killing* someone
before disturbing him! John is going to be aggravating, I
can see. But she said simply, "Oh, John, I am so thankful.
This has been very alarming."

"Did *you* hit him?" asked Dr. Weston, scrambling to his
feet.

"Oh yes, I hit him."

"Why . . . ?"

"He *terrified* me," said Mary. "He stole into the room
when I opened the door, and followed me up, and did not
explain his business, and then he said something that
frightened me very much. And here I was with my bad
arm and alone, and before I realized what I was doing,
John, I hit him with that little vase."

"What did he say to you?" asked Dr. Weston.

Mr. Sleepwalker spoke from the floor. His eyes were closed. He said softly, "I did not indeed desire to frighten the dear lady; I merely told the dear lady my name."

Dr. Weston shot a very baleful look at Mary; he became suspicious of her again (and there were all those patients in the waiting-room).

"And what *is* your name?" asked Dr. Weston.

"Sleepwalker," said Mr. Sleepwalker, opening his eyes.

"And where do you live?" asked Dr. Weston.

Mr. Sleepwalker closed his eyes again. "I am afraid," he said, "that for the moment I am unable to remember."

"Well, where would you like us to take you?" asked the doctor.

"Yes, where would you like us to take you?" asked Mary, eagerly.

Mr. Sleepwalker paused for a moment. Then, "I would like to stay ere," he said.

"That is impossible, quite impossible," said Dr. Weston crossly. "You can take him to the hospital, Mary. He's all right to move, and a day or two will be all that's needed."

"John," said Mary, taking the doctor aside, "do you notice a very queer smell in this room?"

"No, I don't," said the doctor. "Do you?"

She did not answer. "I will get an ambulance if you will arrange with the hospital," she said.

"I would much prefer," said a silky voice from the floor, "if the dear lady would take me to the ospital erself. Far be it indeed to go in an ambulance."

Mary scowled at the doctor, who said at once, "No, we'll get an ambulance. See if you can sit up now."

Mr. Sleepwalker obediently sat up, a little black figure with legs outstretched on the floor. The doctor supported him.

"Now into this chair."

"I am a poor man," said Mr. Sleepwalker, sitting up straight and stiff in the chair, with his disfigured head.

"I will pay for your ambulance, Mr. Sleepwalker, and I

will pay for your days in the hospital as long as Dr. Weston
says that you must stay," said Mary.

"Oh, ow kind, dear lady," said Mr. Sleepwalker humbly,
and Mary thought, What a brute I am, I've never abased
myself and really apologized for hitting him! "I shall get
you some tea," she said. Meanwhile, the doctor was busy
at the telephone. He looked at his watch. "Don't leave
me!" murmured Mary as she brushed past him in the hall,
and Dr. Weston gave her an un-affectionate look. She
took a tray in to Mr. Sleepwalker, who gazed round the
room as though he were memorizing it.

"I shall burn this tray, break the cup and saucer, give
away the chair, and send the carpet to the cleaners, or we
can sell it – in fact, we might leave the flat. I can't bear to
have had this little horror in the room," Mary said to
herself unfairly, forgetting that she was very lucky.

Mr. Sleepwalker coughed. "One thing may I hask," he
said.

"What," said Mary.

"I should like to hask," he said, "that the dear lady will
visit me in the ospital."

Mary considered. That was the very least she could do.

"Yes, of course I will," she said, trying to sound hearty.

"Oh, thank you, *thank* you," said Mr. Sleepwalker. The
doctor came out of the hall.

"I have arranged for the bed and the ambulance," he
said, looking again at his watch. "Some time I will hear
more about this." He had one leg out of the door.

"You will stay!" besought Mary with agitation, seizing
his arm.

The doctor put down his overcoat again. "Very well, I
will stay," he said irritably, and thought of his waiting-
room. He did not like Mary Manly at all just now,
whether because she had or had not killed Mr. Sleepwalker (although on the whole he was relieved that she
had not); but chiefly he disliked Mary because she had
behaved in an irrational manner – he disapproved of people being irrational – and had called him away from his

surgery in the middle of the afternoon. He whirled to the telephone, and Mary heard him say brusquely, "I'll be back. Keep Mrs. Jenkins, and tell Mr. Howe I'll see him tomorrow, and explain to the two others that I'll see them tomorrow, and give them a time, and tell Mrs. Boniface that I'll drop in on the way home, and don't let the Jackson boy go home till I've seen him, and . . . "

"Oh Lord," thought Mary, contrite, "what have I done to all these people! Poor Johnny!" and she tried to look pathetic, but it was no good.

The ambulance arrived, and Dr. Weston sped away. Two burly ambulance men helped Mr. Sleepwalker; he walked between them in his still fashion. One big man carried his absurdly small valise. The other one took charge of the obsolete hat. Mary stood.

At the door Mr. Sleepwalker made as if to turn.

"I do hask, dear lady, that you will recollect your promise?" he said, with a question.

"I will indeed," said Mary heartily and with the greatest repugnance.

She heard the door close. She turned and opened all the windows, and did what she could to the room. Then she telephoned Cora. "Cora," she said, "a very peculiar thing has happened. I won't tell you over the telephone, but here, but for the grace of God, sits your cousin, the famous murderess . . . " a thought checked her, "or," and she laughed, "the famous huntress."

"What *do* you mean!" asked Cora.

"Well," said Mary slowly, "you remember the night we nearly ran that man down on the bridge?"

"Yes, yes," said Cora.

"Well," continued Mary slowly, "it's the same man. Coincidence, of course, of the most extraordinary kind" (was it coincidence?) "and it's left me rather shaken."

"Too much happens to you. Come at once and have dinner," said Cora.

"I will," said Mary gratefully.

As Mary Manly went to her cousin's house, she asked

herself some questions. If I wished to go to the bottom of the queerness of this, if I had any scientific curiosity and not just a detestation of the whole affair, I would take up a notebook and pencil, and question that . . . that . . . person (she avoided even his name). I would say to him, Was your aunt a fox, or was your grandmother a weasel, and of course, he would say no, and where should I find myself then? I could ask him if he seeks me in particular, and how, and why. But I am such a coward that I don't want to know. Then I would say, My good sir, do you know that you smell? And if he said yes, I should have to ask him, Do some people (such as I) and not other people, recognize this animal (yes, I should have to say "animal") scent? I can see how totally impossible such a conversation is, and so I shall leave it alone, and shall admit, to myself, and not to others, only the fact that this man frightens me. . . .

When Mary left Cora the next morning (for Cora easily persuaded her to stay the night), she knew that the talk of her attack upon Mr. Sleepwalker would spread among her friends and acquaintances, and that it would be well and properly launched by Cora. She realized that she would be the object of universal pity ("Poor Mrs. Manly, wasn't it dreadful for her! The man, my dear, walked straight into the flat, and there was Mary all alone, with a broken arm . . . I think she's very good not to prosecute! And so brave. The most extraordinary coincidence, my dear! Cora Wilmot says . . . ") and that this was not quite fair to Mr. Sleepwalker who, after all, was the one who had been hit on the temple with a bronze vase and was now in hospital. She knew that she would be decried as soft, foolish, and too kind because she had provided the ambulance and was about to pay the hospital bill. However, she had to choose between all or nothing, and the section of the story which was in Cora's possession and which Cora would launch on all their acquaintances with her well-known energy, approximated to nothing, and that was best.

The following afternoon Mary said to herself as she alighted clumsily with parcels at the hospital, This (calling on this man, I mean) is the most unpleasant thing that I have deliberately done in my whole life. I don't call hitting . . . Mr. Sleepwalker . . . deliberate. It was instinctive. If only Hugh were with me it would be easier. However, as she had that afternoon received a cable from Hugh which read: "Cheers and cheers take first passage and cable me," she felt more carefree than she would have thought possible. I can tell this . . . individual . . . she thought, that I am going to Australia (that seems far enough away) – which is true – that I'm going tomorrow, which is not true, but it is true enough. And she entered the hospital.

She found Mr. Sleepwalker propped up a little on his pillows, looking very pale. His head was bandaged, and when she saw the bandage, she felt much more guilty than when, in the storm of terror, she had struck down Mr. Sleepwalker and had seen him lying on the floor, with blood flowing upon the carpet.

Patients in the adjacent beds regarded her apathetically. Mr. Sleepwalker looked earnestly, too earnestly, at her. I should, of course, give him my hand, she said to herself, this hand which has struck him down. But she did not wish to do so. She found that her feelings were strangely involved. In order to avoid touching Mr. Sleepwalker's hand, and for no more altruistic reason, Mary had filled her good hand with flowers, and carried magazines and a box of chocolates under her arm. As she disposed these articles awkwardly about Mr. Sleepwalker's bed, the handshaking moment passed, as she had intended it should. A nurse, seeing her arm in a sling, brought forward a chair. Mary smiled at her, thanked her, and sat down.

"I hope you are not too uncomfortable," she said.

"Oh, no, thank you, dear lady," said Mr. Sleepwalker. "This is a very nice ospital, nicer than what I was in in England that time the dogs bit me."

"Dogs . . . !" said Mary.

"Ounds," said Mr. Sleepwalker.

Mr. Sleepwalker's bandages really afflicted Mary. They made her feel more guilty even than her own conscience. However, she could not afford to get soft about Mr. Sleepwalker, even though she had hit him with a vase.

"I am sorry that I cannot have a nice long chat," she said untruthfully, "but the fact is that I am flying to Australia tomorrow to join my husband."

"Come a little closer, dear lady," said Mr. Sleepwalker. His reddish eyes were fixed upon her. Mary made hitching noises with her chair, but she was near enough. She began to feel faint. "I should like to go to Australia," he said. "Oh, ow I should like!"

"Australia is, I am sure, a very nice country," replied Mary with considerable idiocy. I must keep this impersonal, she thought, and proceeded to talk about Australia, of which she knew very little. "So you see I cannot stay any longer; in fact, I must go. Everything will be arranged, the bill, you know. I am so very sorry for what I did to you. It was really some terrible misunderstanding."

The little man in the bed continued to look earnestly at her.

"It as been a pleasure indeed to meet you, dear lady," he said in his soft voice. (What an extraordinary statement! thought Mary.) "May I thank you indeed for your kindness, and may I tell you, dear lady, ow grateful I ave always been to you, and ow I ave frequently and in oh ever so many places enjoyed your delicious smell . . . fragrance, I *should* say."

"My . . . ! my . . . !" stammered Mary, and sprang to her feet. She stood for one moment looking down at Mr. Sleepwalker. Then she turned and the patients saw her running like a hare out of the ward.

SIXTEEN

Beware the Jabberwock, my son . . .

beware the Jubjub Bird

I

THOMAS KRISPIN and his wife Dolly drove through the late-summer-shining valley of the Fraser River. Golden sheaves shone, green hops glowed, emerald grass gleamed and ripened for a new crop of scientific cutting, poplars grouped themselves in the right places, nature improved upon art, the folded hills revealed and withdrew themselves in summer haze with the utmost charm and Tom Krispin was, as usual now, savage and gloomy.

Dolly said: " . . . and you know when I looked at her I said to myself Mercy I've seen you somewhere before and then I thought you remember Tommy that time we were at La Jolla and there was that woman named Nolan no Johnson no was it Finnegan and she had those two dear little children and stayed at that auto court where they sent coffee in first thing and you said she was dumb but I thought she was cute like one of those models oh I do love those models but I always wonder if they've got any Ideas in their heads I wouldn't be surprised if they had and I said to this woman Oh excuse me but didn't we meet at La Jolla and she said No she'd never been there and I said Oh but we *must* have met at La Jolla and I said Well perhaps it wasn't La Jolla but it might have been Santa Barbara and she said she'd never been there either and I said Well that's the most extraordinary thing and then after she'd gone out of the store I remembered after all it was Banff but really though you wouldn't call her old I do think when a woman's got to that age she shouldn't do her hair like that though kiddies and some girls do look really cute with ... oh look at all those cows what a lot of cows I suppose they're Herefords or are those brown I do think it's heavenly and so peaceful driving through this valley with those lovely cows don't you think it's lovely Tommy if only there wasn't so much traffic on the road it would be utterly peaceful but we'll get there early I hope they're not entertaining people Melody always has so many ... "

Tom drove on. He looked gloomily ahead and did not speak.

"Oh I don't think I told you about that book *The Legacy* ... "

"Don't tell me don't tell me," said Thomas who could not endure to have stories told him of novels or plays or television. When Dolly began to tell him the story of the last novel she had read, as she often did, or the story of the last movie she had seen, he suffered and seemed to shrivel up inside. It became a conflict of which Dolly was not aware. "Don't tell me!" Thomas would warn her, almost shouting, "I hate hearing stories of novels," and Dolly would protest, "But this is a *good* novel Tom, everyone says so ... " and Tom would say rudely "I don't care how good it is, *don't tell me*, I'll read it if I want to and not unless ... I may come to it but I won't be pushed ... I *don't want* to hear that story!" Then Dolly would reply almost tenderly, "But Tommy don't be so cross, you'd love this novel because the man in it is simply ... " and the waves of frustration would rise softly and submerge him again.

So, driving up the Fraser Valley (the sky had become darker, for clouds had begun to creep up over the edge of the hills and were invading the whole saucer of sky that capped the glowing valley which now had a different aspect) Dolly continued to tell Tom the story of *The Legacy* which she found difficult to tell, and Tom gave up because Dolly would do this, and he endeavoured to close his ears to the story of *The Legacy*. He fixed his eyes on the road ahead and on the whizzing traffic. His profile which was inclined to be handsome was bad tempered. Some day he would hit her.

Dolly continued, "It's an awfully hard book to tell the story of because first the story is here and first it's there and sometimes in a room but you can just hear them talking it's so real and sometimes in a castle or fields and a most terrible thing happens at the beginning of the story – oh here we are at the Vedder Canal! – and then when everyone's life has gone on and on and they're awfully queer people some of them Tommy the sort of people you couldn't rely on some of them and very different if you know what I mean" (Oh God, said Thomas and he tightened his lips until they could not be seen) "well, oh what was I saying – as everybody's life goes on chickens come home to roost if you know what I mean and the climax or maybe it's climaxes are just terrible and . . . "

At that moment the sky which had become darkest gray was split. Zag! went fork lightning that seemed to enter the car . . . the whole heavens broke open and crashed with thunder immediately over their heads . . . "Oh Mercy!" cried Dolly cowering, "I thought we were struck! Is it safest in the car or should we get under a hedge or right out in the open and not under a tree at all because trees get struck oh look at those poor cows right under that tree I suppose they don't know!"

Zag! went the lightning again into the car, coming in somewhere and out through the floor, Dolly thought. "Oh Mercy!" she exclaimed and closed the window as the thunder roared and crashed above them and the splitting thunder and lightning released from the skies a torrent of rain that hit the car and obscured the road. Dolly was silent, and Thomas drove on in a comfortable pleased soundless quiet, unalloyed by thunder, lightning and rain. They turned off the highway, splashed down a country road, down a lane, and drew up at a farmhouse surrounded by gloomy trees which an hour ago had stood green and dustily golden in the sunshine.

Dolly pulled her coat round her, bowed her head and sprang out. She ran to the door of the house which was opened by her younger sister Melody.

"Oh Melody!" she cried, "I simply can't tell you . . . " and proceeded to tell her. Dolly talked all afternoon but Tom had the relief of the presence of his brother-in-law Jed. They went out to the barn and said practically nothing, wet as it was. Weather moderated, but Tom and Dolly left early for home. Melody was about to have another baby and showed her sister the room and the crib, so Dolly had to tell Thomas on the way home and afterwards many things in which he was not interested. He thought, I believe I have a temperature.

"Oh Tommy," she said, "Melody made the cutest . . . "

Years and years later (it seemed to Tom) they went to bed and, at last, to sleep.

II

Young Felix Krispin who later became known as old Mr. Krispin, established a small bookshop on a side street in Vancouver about sixty years ago. Nobody in Vancouver except a few eccentric individuals bought books at that time and it is hard to see how Felix Krispin remained solvent; but by some alchemy the bookshop prospered and was moved to fairly handsome premises on a main business thoroughfare. By this time young Felix Krispin had become Mr. Krispin and the proprietor of a well-known bookshop ("new and secondhand") and on the window was the name F. KRISPIN, BOOKSELLER. Late in life his small dark silent wife bore him a son. A light lit up inside the bookseller as he looked at the crumpled infant and he saw before him a sign; the sign read F. KRISPIN & SON, BOOKSELLERS. Mrs. Krispin's quality of silence did not preclude thought on her part but she was prevented from uttering these thoughts by a great deal of reserve so she kept her hopes to herself. The two men of her family loved her but were accustomed to her as men of families become accustomed. Nevertheless they recognized sometimes her rather sardonic and latent humour. She lived for them and remained a silent woman.

When the infant grew to be a boy named Thomas (somewhat spoiled), his father held in front of him the duty and privilege of attending a university. Thomas attended the university dutifully and alarmed his father by becoming involved (in turn) in football, fraternities, dances, delayed concentration on work, delayed flirtations with law, the Players Club, girls, very amateur journalism, and the social sciences – everything but books. He was lazy, agreeable, a dilettante, a doodler. Then Tom Krispin came under the influence of the distinguished and sarcastic Head of the English Department and discovered that books (his father's stock-in-trade) were not commodities like tinned soup and cosmetics. Tom Krispin became a reader in spite of himself and books took on another dimension. Within five years the sign on Mr. Krispin's window was, in actual fact, F. KRISPIN & SON, BOOKSELLERS.

One summer Tom met a girl called Dolly Morgan and married her. This marriage was the result of a summer's propinquity chiefly on the water at weekends and in the evenings, the very blue gray-blue eyes (darkly fringed) of Dolly Morgan, and a prattling sweetness possessed by her. Her eyelids were so formed as to give Dolly's eyes a look of tenderness that continued to be beguiling, even under provocation, to Tom Krispin.

Dolly was ingenuous and had already become a prattler. In her great desire to enchant and subjugate Tom Krispin she prattled more than ever. Sometimes Tom did not even hear what she said as he looked at her beautiful eyelids, upper and lower, but that did not matter, because she said nothing. Jub-jub, said Dolly, tirra-lirra tweet-tweet jub-jub-jub, or something of the kind as she looked up at Thomas and he looked down at her, fatuous, hypnotized by that particularly radiant summer and Dolly's eyelids. From being a cool lover he became ardent and smothered her into silence. Some time after their marriage, he became aware that sweet Dolly was stupid. She talked far too much. She could and did bore him almost daily. But she loved him.

Tom's mother, that small dark silent woman, was of the opinion that Shakespeare and the writer of *Through the Looking Glass* had said, between them, all there is to say; so it should not have surprised her husband that on her deathbed she whispered to him feebly, "And he married a jubjub bird." Mr. Krispin sat by his wife's bedside with her thin hand in his. He looked with anguish into her beloved face and saw the whole of life receding and taken away from him. Nothing would remain. It was his own death that he witnessed as he held her hand. He was deaf and could not hear what she had said. It did not seem possible that she had said what he thought she had said. He turned in his desolation to Tom who stood at his mother's side, awkward and silent.

"What did she say?" he murmured to his son, thinking She is wandering.

"Nothing, nothing," whispered Tom *navré*.

Mrs. Krispin slowly moved her head a little and looked with a lifetime of the offering of love upon her only son. It seemed to him that she smiled. Then she died.

A few months later Mr. Krispin also died, and with great satisfaction. Sweet Dolly comforted her husband as best she could.

Gradually Thomas and Dolly jelled to a married life that was fairly happy and – later – fairly unhappy. One evening Tom said to his wife rather uneasily, "Doll, I never said anything to you before about it but would you like to adopt a child . . . I mean, some women feel that . . . I mean, I'd like you to do whatever you'd like to do . . . I mean . . . "

Dolly put down her cigarette and looked at him with the habitual tenderness of her lower lids and said, "Oh Tommy how hard that makes it! Do you mean you *would* like to adopt a child or do you mean you *wouldn't* like to . . . or do you mean for me to do what I like?" and Tom said, "If you put it that way, I mean do what you like. I don't care one way or another."

"Oh Tommy," said Dolly, sounding shocked. "I don't think it would be right to adopt a dear baby with . . . well . . . no more strength of feeling than that, do you? It wouldn't be fair to the dear little baby. And, speaking personally, I'd just as soon not if it's all the same to you."

"Okay," said Tom and went on reading.

"What's that you're reading?" asked Dolly.

"This," said Tom not raising his eyes from his book.

"I always think Tommy that if you're going to adopt a little baby . . . " said Dolly and continued to develop the theme of adoptions while her husband continued to appear to read without being able to read. He had cultivated a churlish habit of inattention and of positive rudeness when needed, but had never conquered the feeling of a rising temperature.

Tom had turned the matter of adoption over in his mind and had decided that if Dolly really had something to talk about she might not talk so much, or at least she might be more worth listening to, or things might cancel each other out and break even. He was rather spoiled and selfish and would be the last to admit it. His passion for reading in the evenings had grown upon him and he wished to read all the new books as they came in from the publishers and as many reviews as possible, but he could not settle to this reading if the radio were on, nor if someone was talking talking. He could move away from the radio, but if he moved away from Dolly she followed him except to the bathroom where he sometimes went to read. She followed him there eventually and said at the door, "Are you quite sure you're all right?" He lived with too great concentration throughout the week except for Wednesday afternoons and Sundays which he always took off for golf or Dolly. Sometimes at home he retreated to a sort of carpenter's workshop that he had set up in the basement although he was not good with tools. This was a retreat that he did not particularly care for as, being clumsy, he sometimes cut his thumbs, but that was preferable to suffering upstairs.

As the years passed, talking had become as natural and continuous to Dolly as breathing, but more consciously enjoyable. Tom had become nervous, and then very highly nervous indeed, not to say bad-tempered. No stratagem succeeded in keeping Dolly quiet. He remembered his quiet mother. He remembered her words, but what can you do when you have married a jubjub bird. Sometimes he nearly hated sweet Dolly whom he had loved, but because of the gentle and tender look of her eyelids he could not be continuously harsh with her. He enjoyed the evenings when Dolly went to her Creative Writing Classes but ah, they passed so soon. He could have wished Dolly to be more intelligent. He did not think of enlarging that wish to include himself and it did not occur to him that love and intelligence – or their lack – might have any relation to each other.

So poor Tom whose charm expanded profitably in the daytime to all the customers and contracted to hostility in the evenings had become in the last years an unhappy man and did not acknowledge it. He was no longer conscious of the unique and lasting pleasure of seeing again (although parting was only that morning) before his very eyes the person he had guaranteed in public to love and to cherish and still desired to see; for when he arrived home each evening his spirits rushed rapidly downhill and he was frighteningly and expectantly bored. What is the second worst calamity that can befall a man? That second worst calamity is to be consistently and expectantly bored.

III

(We should all be happy and hardly ever bored, like that family of five beautiful children who live at Blue Lake Mountain in the heart and heights of British Columbia. They are so happy that they do not know they are happy.

They say, "Oh do we have to go away? Do we *haf*to?"
They are busy all the year round, and are never bored,
these beautiful Renoir children and their young parents.
What enviable bliss. Their voices and laughter trill like
birds and bells beside the capricious mountain lake. They
run hand in hand in the open spaces between the ponderosa pines. They walk entwined and their happiness is
un-marred and beautiful to look at. Nothing is planned or
arranged for them any more than for birds except when
their mother rings a bell for lessons or supper. They run
after each other calling and laughing and silent. They do
not cry. Was it like this in Arcady? Their childhood should
never end but it must – look, it is ending even now! Yet
perhaps they will carry it with them; perhaps the green
and gold happiness among the pines with the loons uttering their mournful laughter in the silence on the lake will
stay with them when they are grown-up people, and the
city will not quite quench as cities often do. Among the
advantages of cities there lie lurking massive areas of boredom waiting for inexpert dodgers. In cities there are no
ponderosa pines with the children running calling
between and the place so quiet that the loons' laughing
and crying ejaculations sound clearly even from far up the
lake. There are no dangers of any kind for these children
on that mountain except bears and the occasional cougar
which cannot compare with the dangers of cities. There
are no traffic jams, no tall or squat buildings staring with
nothing but right angles not even an inferred curve, no
mass meetings, no mass appeals, no mass advertisement,
no mass uglification, perhaps no mass destruction, no
mass anything, no . . .)

IV

Upon a dull Wednesday, at noon, Tom Krispin reached
some climax or nadir. He took a turn among the
bookshelves. He thoughtfully touched a switch and some
of the lights went out. The store, like a woman, looked still

more handsome. He went into his small office and closed the door. The departmental reports lay upon his desk – Mullett on the main floor, Miss Van der Velde in the paper backs and magazines, and young McIntyre in the basement. Tom sat down and looked at his watch. He wrote a few lines to Mr. Mullett saying "I shall not be down tomorrow but . . . " He then wrote and addressed a letter. This is what he wrote:

"My dear Dolly, I may not get home until tomorrow or later. Something has arisen. If I don't get home tomorrow will telephone Mullett. Don't worry. In haste, Tom."

He did not seem to know that this was a needlessly stupid letter. He was sure he had a temperature. He said to himself I am a coward, sealed the envelope and stamped it. He continued sitting, looking into space and sometimes tapping with his fingers. Time passed. The telephone rang and rang. You can go to hell, he said pleasantly to the telephone as though it were a person. At last the telephone stopped ringing.

This short conversation between the telephone and himself gave him a disproportionate pleasure and a sickening awareness of his cowardice. He was due, now, to be at home early to lunch and the telephone was the voice of Dolly which he could not hear. He was due immediately after lunch to drive Dolly to Chilliwack to see Melody's new baby and then, in the late evening, they would drive home. Although reasonably brave, he could not face it today. Dolly would talk all the way through lunch, all the way to Chilliwack, all the time there, all the way home and until she slept. She would talk about nothing. And then in the morning she would begin talking again. And tomorrow night when Tom tried to read the paper in all its detail, she would talk.

During the last few months all the frustration of these many years had culminated and he was aware that something shocking was likely to happen. Either he would put his head into the gas oven and keep it there some night when Dolly was at her Creative Writing Class, or he would take too many tranquillizers, or he might some evening throttle sweet Dolly. Each Wednesday afternoon lately he had decided to act and he had not acted, but continued to hear Dolly talk until he had sunk into such a sink of misery because he was a peaceful man in a trap and could not gag her or poison himself with any lasting pleasure.

So here was Tom, still a good-looking man in a post-athletic way, gazing upon the letter in his hand. The telephone rang again and he leapt up, put on his raincoat and hat and went out of the back door into the lane, locking the door behind him.

V

He said to himself, First I will mail this letter Special Delivery and then I will walk at random. After he had mailed the letter at the Post Office, he walked at random.

How beautiful was the day and the air so fresh and fair! Actually, people going about their normal affairs would have stated that the day was lousy. Drizzling rain fell. Dust had, where possible, become mud. People hurried to be gone on their Wednesdays out of all this rain. What was only a wet Wednesday afternoon to other people was a fresh free day for Tom Krispin when the bottom had at last fallen clean out of his mind, and his memory (which would at some time stir and re-assert itself) had succumbed to the assaults of misery; conscience had fainted. He turned up his collar from the rain and walked with a current of hurrying people, down Hastings Street, along Water Street, onto the ferry amongst all the other wet people.

In spite of the rain Tom climbed the stairs of the ferry and chose to stand in this fine free wet air which had never before seemed to him as admirable. He looked at the gray receding city which included Dolly Krispin in a state somewhere, but his irresponsible thoughts – vague as clouds – did not include Dolly. The ferry cautiously arrived and slowed into the North Vancouver wharf. He

looked down at the cataract of people funnelling together
onto the slipway, hot foot wet foot for home. He turned
and walked to the stern of the ferry which had now
become the bow, and looked across the lightly tossing
water. He was as in a foolish pleasant dream, riding forwards and backwards on a ferry.

On the fourth ferry journey Tom was joined by other
passengers who moved lethargically or stomping up to the
deck because rain had for the moment stopped falling.
There was a commotion at the stern. He rose in a leisurely
way and joined the clot of people at the stern. Engines
were reversed, the ferry stopped in a thrash and froth of
waters. Two small fishboats deflected their courses and
raced towards the ferry. Tom, leaning out of his dream,
saw a dark object emerge from the gray waters, and then
disappear. The fishboats – near to the point of collision –
manoeuvred, and a great rope and hook, cast into the
slate-gray sea, caught at what must have been a body. Two
young men who had leapt overboard caused a turmoil of
water and seized – between them – an unpleasant lumpish
object which they hauled to a fishboat and succeeded in
raising to the deck. They toppled it in. A third man knelt
and began to pummel the figure of a young woman who –
for some reason that must have been good, and terrible, to
herself – had jumped from the stern of the ferry into the
deep water.

Why had she done this thing? No one knew. Suicide,
suicide, said the passengers sibilantly. However, now she
was in the fishboat. There was a good deal of hanging
about and coming and going and then a seaman gave the
ferry captain a reassuring wave and the boats chugged
away from each other to the opposite shores.

Thomas Krispin was shaken by this incident. Will she
be glad she did not die? Will she be sorry? Whatever (he
thought) goes on in people's minds on ferry-boats? His
dream had freed him from gas ovens as applied to himself,
but now he was removed into a general awareness extend-
ing (he knew) to his home in Kerrisdale, to Chinatown, to

Africa both north and south, to Washington D.C., to London, to Russia, to a member or members of every crowd that walks or drives anywhere up and down a street. It is universal. People may (he thought) even be unhappy in the Arctic. He thought it unlikely that people would commit suicide there; they are at a too near remove from death. Even a leap is not required. His release of spirit was gone now that someone had jumped into the deep water because of unhappiness. He became sententious in his thoughts, assisted by such fine phrases as "Man's Inhumanity to Man," as he contemplated the lot of this poor leaping woman. He felt noble, until he was brought up suddenly against the thought of Dolly and then he no longer felt noble but immediately became lacerated by an identification of this poor leaping woman with Dolly whom he had wantonly left for an afternoon or forever, he did not know which.

I must go back! he thought, seeing in his mind that wet tossing figure. She will be unhappy and bewildered and if there is anything worse than being unhappy it is being unhappy and bewildered. He did not know how he guessed that but he knew it must be true. Yet here he was, and when the ferry touched the shore he did not land.

Next time the ticket man collected a fare from Tom he said (disturbed that a woman had jumped off his ferry and that the incident would be reported in tomorrow's papers – one suicide enhanced his ferry's prestige, two would be regarded unfavourably) – he said "You okay?" and gave Tom a searching and splendidly official nosey unfavourable look so as to recognize him next time. What next time? Who could say. He did not think there was anything wrong with this passenger but one must be sure, and ten thousand guesses would not have told him that this passenger's wife talked too much. He was relieved when the passenger – a good-looking well-dressed guy – said coolly "Certainly I'm okay. Why not?" The ticket collector said "Well you needn't get mad, you bin riding up and down this ferry which is not customary except under unusual circumstances on a wet day, and what with that young woman . . . "

The passenger smiled and said in a superior way, "I'm not going to jump off your damn ferry." The ticket man looked at the passenger again to make sure and strolled away. He said to himself I'll tell you what, I bet you he's a deteckative looking for someone, and the ticket collector's day lit up again.

Three more trips on the ferry (the day was now dark) had so far emancipated Tom from responsibility that it seemed natural, indeed necessary, that he should land at the North Vancouver end of the run. He did not know what he would do there. He looked at the passenger who sat beside him. The man was bearded and, Tom saw, blind. The white cane which he held easily was not clearly white and no effort had been made to re-paint it. He held on his knee a canvas bag with handles.

When the ferry touched shore, everyone rose – there were not many people now on board. The blind man rose easily enough but seemed momentarily at a loss. Tom Krispin moved beside him and in the special manner that had recommended many good books said, "May I help you at all?"

The blind man replied shortly "No," and then as he stepped carefully forward turned and added, as if with apology "Thank you." He then walked fairly briskly on to dry, or rather, wet land and mounted a bus as if he could see it. This surprised Tom who followed him as by some random compulsion. He sat down in the bus behind this man and observed him.

The blind man sat motionless. He wore an old raincoat that might have belonged to a millionaire or a bum and he wore an old and shapeless hat but Tom found his appearance impressive. Tom in his business life made instinctive appraisals of men and women partly according to how they wore their clothes and, in part also, according to what clothes they wore. He would have denied this, but undoubtedly he was not alone. People do this, whatever

they may say. He was not entirely superficial in his obser-
vations and was vaguely aware of the acceptance of being
a clothes snob, or even a beard snob. He approved the rear
view of the man in front of him although the hat and coat
were old. Tom had often noticed the obscure forms taken
by snobbery. Some people, he thought, are snobs about
the people they know, or the people they don't know –
some are snobs about wearing the right clothes – some are
snobs who like wearing the wrong clothes (are clothes
right and wrong?) – increasing thousands of people are car
snobs – some people are whiskey snobs, book snobs, art
snobs, music snobs, house snobs – I'd like you to tell me
how many different kinds there are, he was saying to
himself, and now he was aware again of the man in front
of him. There was a nobility in his stillness. He might
know both the right people and the wrong people, he
might be well connected or not connected at all, faithless,
a philosopher, a murderer, a saint, but he would not be a
snob. He wore a beard because it was convenient for him.
All this Tom inferred from his back. And so the bus
trembled and travelled and stopped on its journey in the
dark up the road following the North Arm of Burrard
Inlet and he thought about snobs to take his mind off
himself. He remembered that as he and Dolly on their
annual holiday had driven their car about the North
American continent (Dolly forever talking) he had
become aware, all of a sudden, of a new inversion which
seemed to have taken over the motoring public – particularly the public in search of holiday. From unnecessarily
long handsome cars which loudly proclaimed the solvency
of their owners emerged men hoboes, women hoboes,
baby hoboes dressed in deliberately unflattering and rad-
dled garments, a new race of universal travellers, no treat
to the eye, a new snobbism . . . but the bus he was riding
in had stopped. The driver turned and said "Mr. Olsen!"
and the blind man, who had sat motionless all this time,
arose. So did Tom.

Mr. Olsen stepped out into the night and into the now

pouring rain and slippery mud and was at once charged by a heavy object. He slipped in the mud and fell while a large dog, an Airedale perhaps, welcomed him with whinnying ecstasy. Tom jumped down from the bus. "Can I help you?" he said, and did.

Together they went down a muddy path, accompanied by the bounding dog, each one leading the other, their heads bent to the rain, and entered a small dark house, a shack it seemed. Mr. Olsen, to whom daylight and dark were the same, did not turn on a light. His companion stood helpless. At last he said diffidently, "Is there a light and anyway, may I come in?"

A switch clicked and there was a light. Tom now saw Mr. Olsen full face and covered with mud. The cabin was small and ill-lit, with a cot in one corner, a small sink beneath a window, a stove beside which was a large box containing firewood, an electric ring, there were two chairs, some shelves of tinned foods, and a pile of boxes. A glass door seemed to lead to a rough porch or balcony and through this glass Tom had momentarily seen the black waters of Burrard Inlet spangled with the lights of boats, fishing-boats he supposed. The big Airedale stood before his master, quivering, springing and whinnying with joy.

"Down Pluto down . . . " said Mr. Olsen. "Well, I suppose I'm in a mess."

"If you will allow me," said Tom, nearly saying the "Sir" of the army, such was the effect of Mr. Olsen upon him. He took off the muddy coat and hung it across two pegs near the stove. "That'll dry by morning and brushing will do the rest."

Mr. Olsen went slowly but unerringly to the sink and sluiced his hands and face. As he dried himself, Tom looked at him.

The man was above middle height. His face was dark and although Tom would not have spoken the word saturnine, he would have thought the face was saturnine but not harsh. It was deeply lined. Very fine bones of his face now he's washed off, thought the observant Tom, and not too much beard.

"Stay and have a drink," said Mr. Olsen.

"Well thank you," said Tom.

"What's your name?" asked Mr. Olsen, and that was all. Not "Who are you?" "What do you want?" "Why are you here?"

"Krispin," said Tom.

"Well Krispin, make yourself at home, here's the bottle, there are some glasses somewhere, there's the tap."

Tom should have felt like an intruder but no such idea seemed to be present in the cabin. He found two glasses and sat down, as that seemed to be the idea. Mr. Olsen paid him no more attention and went – moving deliberately – onto the porch, returning with kindling. You would not have supposed him blind as he bent down to make a fire. Warmth quickly pervaded the shack and, as Tom sat waiting, sensations of complete luxury and a comfortable languor and freedom filled him. The silence, with the crackling of the kindling fire, was in itself luxurious. The Airedale dog lay behind the stove and watched his master. Mr. Olsen talked to him, not to Tom. He mixed a bowl of food carefully and took it out to the porch. The dog followed, wagging. The man returned, and Tom noticed that although his motions were slow and premeditated, they were accurate and it seemed as though all his faculties of touch and the faculty of thought were employed without distraction, the distraction of speech, for example.

Mr. Olsen touched a chair. He pulled it from the table and sat down. "Pour the drinks Krispin," he said. "And fill her up at the tap," he said. "Well, cheerio."

When Tom sat down again, Mr. Olsen had begun to pack his pipe with tobacco.

"Sausages?" he asked.

"Are you asking me to stay to supper?"

"I am. One thing though," said Mr. Olsen, "you don't

need to talk unless you have to. I don't much like the sound of the human voice myself."

"You don't *what*! Well I'll be . . . " said Tom, and then unnecessarily loudly, "I hate the sound of the human voice!"

Mr. Olsen paid no attention to this statement which Tom believed to be true and in this he was inconsistent. So far from hating the voices of Mr. Mullett, Miss Van der Velde, young McIntyre, and all the customers, Tom did not hate them at all, but he derived pleasure and a sense of justification from making this simple, violent, and incorrect statement. He also struck at Dolly as with an open hand, but she did not know that. Tom then settled down quietly. Together they smoked and drank their drinks. The timeless placeless feeling of the evening was acceptable, medicinal. The dog lay beside his master. Mr. Olsen seemed unconscious of his incidental guest but he was not, for when he finished his drinks he put two plates and two cups on the table.

"Tea?" he asked.

"Yes," said Tom. "Can I do anything?" but Mr. Olsen paid him no attention.

Tom watched with increased but nervous admiration the practised activities of Mr. Olsen. They sat down in silence to the sausages which Tom ate like a sacrament with his fingers because there was no fork.

At last Tom said awkwardly, "I'd better go. That was . . . that was very kind . . . thank you . . . if there's ever anything . . . " and he took down his coat from one of the many nails around the walls, looking around him with the feeling of farewell. Everything a man really needs is here, he thought. He did not know where he would go. There was some curious transmission in the cabin. The blind man puffed his pipe.

"Is something wrong?" asked Mr. Olsen.

"Yes," said his visitor.

"Do you want to stay here? There's bed and blankets in

the lean-to. You go out and then in. Goodnight," and he began to prod his pipe again.

Tom looked earnestly at the dark and enigmatic person who was Mr. Olsen and felt towards him the rise of a feeling that was too warm for liking and could only be love. He wanted to say, "But you don't know me. Can you trust . . . " but that was obvious and did not require saying. Mr. Olsen was a man without fear. A watcher might have thought that Tom was acting some part, for the enormity of the kindnesses – this day, at this hour – touched and overcame him. All he said was, "Well . . . I will. Goodnight," and he went out and went in.

Fumbling inside the door of the lean-to he found a light. The poverty of the lean-to was welcome. He took off his outer clothes, lay down and pulled up the blankets.

Into the mysterious benediction of chance and the blind man and this place came the certain knowledge of a bill to be paid. He knew without doubt that at home his wife lay awake, frightened, hurt, bewildered. He saw her very presence, small and crumpled in the bed. Pity invaded him and he tried to push pity away. He must go back, but he would hold this night against such invaders as right, or wrong, or love, or hate, or pity. Through the broken pane of window came the sound of water lapping. Through the partition came the sounds of movements, which at last ceased. Here was an oasis which was only a mirage. Before dawn he slept.

VI

Dolly stood by the window on that day. Her first concern was that lunch was ready, that they were to leave early and Tom had not come home. This concern was to spread until, as far as her mind could reach, her world would consist of one fact alone – that Tom had not come home. She thought she would not telephone to the store about so trifling a matter but time was passing and so she walked resolutely to the telephone . . . but there was no answer. She could not see Tom sitting at his desk, leaning back and regarding the ringing telephone with a certain look.

He must have left, she said, he's on his way, and she went into the kitchen again. At last her concern about the delayed afternoon spread as a cloud spreads and darkened as a cloud darkens to include too-lateness in leaving for Chilliwack. She telephoned again with some irritation, but there was no answer. The cloud now included some kind of foolish fear that Tom had left the store as planned and had met with an accident ("City man in car collision." "City man killed in crash.") Drumming drumming on the window-sill, Dolly saw clearly the speeding car, the crash, the tangle of cabs, the police, and heard the ambulance scream. Who had struck whom? By this time she would settle gladly for Tom being only a little hurt as long as he had not killed a man. His lateness made the house too quiet.

Dolly then disciplined herself and summoned the images of her friends and relatives, none of whom would be as seriously apprehensive because George or Rod or Gordy was (by this time) an hour and a half late for lunch on Wednesday afternoon with plans already made. The images of her friends despised her and she despised herself. I haven't much sense, she thought humbly, but then I never did have. There were steps mounting. The doorbell rang. "Krispin?" said a mysteriously contemptuous boy in a slovenly uniform. He handed her a letter marked Special Delivery and clattered down the steps. Oh thank you, she said, surprised, to the contemptuous boy. But why didn't Tom just telephone.

"My dear Dolly" (but he always writes "Hello Kid"!). "I may not get home till tomorrow or later" (tomorrow or later! tomorrow or *later*!). "Something has arisen." (Something? What something? If it's business why can't he say? What does he mean "arisen"?). "If I don't get home tonight will telephone Mullett tomorrow." (*Mullett? Tomorrow?* What is it?). "Don't worry." (Oh Tommy, how can you say that?). "In haste." (What is it what is it, "in haste"?).

Is it a trap? Is it a secret? Is it danger? Is it . . . ? and nearly all her mind rose up and said No, but a small remaining whisper said Is it a woman?

No, said Dolly firmly and frightened, it is not a woman but why would he telephone Mullett tomorrow, but not me? Why has Tommy been queer and silent? Her mind showed her husband dark, unresponsive, looking away. This letter – and she turned the paper over and over in her hands – is not about a woman yet, even as she thought this, something gave within her, just below her soft bosom. Has he been driven to something? she thought shrewdly, and her eyes so wide and tender looked blankly at the wall. Is it me? and again something gave within her. What should I do that I don't do or what shouldn't I do that I do? Why couldn't he tell me not Mullett? She saw nothing now as she looked at the wall but Tom morose, silent, touchy, dark with irritation – not just this week only but for time long past. It is me? Is it money troubles? Oh Tom, if it's money I don't mind anything (and she looked round the comfortable familiar room already taking on a new aspect, ready to leave it, ready for hardship, happy in hardship) if you'll only be more happy.

Time went on, which is all that time can do in the way of assuagement or cruelty. She must telephone Melody.

"Is that you Jed? How is she . . . ? Good, and the baby? . . . good. Oh Jed, I'm *so* sorry, I just had a message from Tom, he can't get away . . . no, I say he can't get away . . . yes it's too bad . . . I'll telephone . . . yes maybe Sunday . . . what? Oh no, nothing wrong, nothing wrong at all, just he can't get away. Give her my love . . . "

She hung up the receiver and felt herself helpless in spite of the reassurance of the sound of her own voice as the sound of a voice of a reasonable person alone in a house. People never can tell from what we say, only from how we say it, she thought. The sight persisted of Tom's face like a violin player looking down, averted, morose, dark, different indeed she must admit from what Tom used to be. What troubles you, Tommy, why couldn't you tell me these things? You wouldn't be in despair and go and jump off anything would you? Is this the way people act who do these things? – because people do. And thoughts like these spread and consumed gentle silly Dolly and she dared not telephone her friends, talking and talking to pass the time or for comfort, or shop or sleep or sew and certainly not read, because she was too proud to say to her aunt (for example, giving out information to be quoted widely when the time came, "Yes we were going but . . . ") nor could she give her stupidly ravaged mind to a shop or to flowers or a book while Tom looked down and away from her like that angry violin player that she had once, somewhere, seen.

I will make a cake, she said, and was aware of evening coming on. Then she laughed out loud. The sound of the laugh was strange and did not belong to the silent house. Oh she said, shaking her head, it's just me being silly. There is nothing, nothing – as if a man can't send his wife a note without her thinking he's going to sh-shoot himself! But why has he looked so strange? That night when we came back from Melody's I was frightened but I'm sure I never showed it; I just talked and talked as if nothing was wrong, just talked right along, but he frightened me.

I will sing. I'll make that cake. Come now . . . . page 100 . . . four eggs . . .

The evening passed slowly and the darkness which was now complete held the house down and surrounded it and the house became changed – the furniture became hostile because Dolly did not know why her husband had not come home and so the aspect of life was altered. She was a hostage and there was no one near her. There seemed no reason to turn a light on, the radio on, just to turn them off again before going up to bed, as people do, but when the cake was out of the oven she turned the lights out and up the strange stairs she went to the strange room where

Tom was not coming. Shadows attended her. I will have a bath, she said and began to undress. The telephone rang.

"Oh!" she breathed at the telephone, "Who is it? Is it . . . " and stopped.

"Is that you, Dolly? I mean is that Mrs. Krispin?" said her aunt's voice. "Oh, it *is* you Dolly? You didn't sound a bit like you! How did you find Melody"

"We didn't go," said Dolly. "Tommy couldn't get away and we'll go next week . . . no, he didn't . . . he couldn't get home and I'm just going to have a bath and go to bed . . . yes I have, a bit of a chill so it's just as well we didn't . . . "

"You *sound* hoarse," said her aunt. "I'll come round in the morning."

"Oh no no," said Dolly, "I'm going to take a day off in bed tomorrow, I mean I have a 9 o'clock appointment at the dentist's or else I'll stay in bed so don't ring, I won't be here or I'll be in bed . . . oh no don't come around . . . "

"Well, if you say so," said her aunt rather crossly, and rang off.

I can't endure the telephone, said Dolly, and I certainly can't endure Aunt Liz coming over and finding . . . I must be alone until it's Tom . . . but where is he? . . . and she got into the bath and lay there. But when she had had her bath she had had her bath and the night of sleep or waking still to come. For the first time in life Dolly was one with the women who are unwillingly alone in the evening and the night and she knew what they sometimes know except that she assured herself that she was so lucky, with nothing, nothing at all to worry about, and she looked round the room. Life will never be the same after this, she thought with unusual wisdom.

I will get into bed. I will read. That will help time to pass till morning . . . I can't read. Something somewhere is wrong for Tommy and me. She turned out the light, curved herself into the habitual curve that followed Tom's body, and in the dark she began to cry.

VII

By six o'clock Tom was awake again and washed by sleep. He was shocked to discover by the morning light of a new day what an unpremeditated fool he was, for he despised fools; but however much he despised fools he could not return to yesterday.

There had been sounds on the other side of the partition. Tom ran his hand over his chin. He got up, went out, and went in.

"Good morning," said Mr. Olsen at the sink.

"You must let me talk, sir," said Tom, "You must let me thank you. I'm not going to explain – don't worry – why I'm here. The way you'd look at it I've done a damnfool thing and yet I had to do it. Perhaps it's final . . . I don't know. It was provoked by . . . well, an innocent person, incurably innocent I do think." ("Your wife of course. I know about innocence . . . innocence is hell," murmured Mr. Olsen wiping his beard). " . . . and now I've done it and nothing can change it. She'll never forget. There'll be no question of forgetting. I have to get a telephone at once," he said urgently.

"Cruel . . . " said the blind man as though pondering. "When you're finished telephoning come back here. I shall tell you something about cruelty and innocence . . . yes, I think you should know. Come back here."

"Certainly certainly," said Tom with both legs out of the door, "certainly," he called back.

He walked to the village in the morning sunshine of a day washed by yesterday. All around him were the coloured trees. He walked so fast that he nearly ran, approaching the telephone with the excitement of the dog Pluto. This is a funny damn thing, he thought, but I can't do without her.

He heard her voice.

"Darling," said Tom unexpectedly.

"Tommy oh Tommy!" cried Dolly and she was too frightened to sob, "where are you and what is it all about

oh Tommy how could you . . . why didn't you tell me
what it is . . . are you all right . . . have I done something
oh what have I done I wondered all night because oh
darling you've been so cross you've been cross for years
now . . . and these last weeks terribly cross I felt something was going to happen . . . I almost felt you were going
to jump off something . . . people do . . . oh are you all
right it's been terrible Tommy . . . tell me quickly don't
keep me waiting . . . are you there . . . "

"Dolly," said Tom, "stop talking and I'll tell you but
only if you stop talking," and he thought, surprised, I'll
tell her now! "You talk too much Dolly and you have for
years and it nearly kills me." ("Oh!") "I get bad tempered.
I can't stand it – talk talk talk. I'll be back this afternoon
and you must practise holding your tongue still." (He saw
Dolly's blue eyes very tender but filled now with tears, red
rimmed and plain from a night's weeping.) "And I'll practice being good tempered – but if you go on talking all the
time I can't – and I won't come home, or if I do I won't
stay." He was vehement.

"Oh! Over the telephone too! Do you think anyone's
listening? It sounds so peculiar! Is it really only that, is it
really? I'll practise oh I will . . . but tell me do you love me
and when are you coming home? Oh how could you do
this to me, Tommykins!"

"I love you and I can't come home now but I'm coming
this afternoon," he needed to put his arms round her in
spite of her saying that hated name.

"Not now this minute? What are you doing? . . . oh, oh,
all right, I'll try so hard my darling!"

"Goodbye." He was about to put up the receiver.

"Goodbye . . . "

"Goodbye."

"Oh but Tommykins just a minute, do you *really* love
me?"

"*Yes*! And don't call me that!" A prophetic wave of
frustration rose and broke softly over him with familiar
competence and his future lay clear without delusion.

VIII

The two men sat beside the window, light to Tom but dark to Mr. Olsen.

"The last thing I ever remember seeing at all clearly," said Mr. Olsen with his hand on Pluto the dog, "was a stand of aspen trees that reached down to the water's edge and stood quivering, like a green screen. I've been told that the aspen leaf is set on its very thin tough stem at an angle and so it's subject to a sort of imbalance and trembles in every breeze or wind . . . I don't know whether that is so but I remember quite well these aspen leaves were all shivering together as aspens do but as I looked at them the pain in my eyes was very bad and it seemed sometimes as if the aspen leaves were red or even purple and then they became green again. Sitting here now I can see them looking green and then I see them looking purple . . . "

Mr. Olsen stopped for so long that Tom began to think that he was only going to speak about aspen trees and had forgotten the cruelty. But that was the way he told Tom his story. He would stop, and seem to forget, not like an old man for Mr. Olsen was still young, but as one who looks at something unseen. Tom could not tell whether he was seeing that moment's picture or whether he was thinking of the cruelty. That was the way he told the story and the listener watched his face for he had never seen anyone like him. Mr. Olsen seemed to gather himself together, and went on:

"I'd had these headaches and eyeaches for some time, getting worse, before the day at home that I spoke to her as I did, the night I accused her, but they were only part of the way I felt and I didn't really consider them at all, these headaches. So the night I spoke to Janet," (Tom heard the name and was aware that Mr. Olsen had perhaps already forgotten him – he sat so still – or perhaps Tom was one within Mr. Olsen. He seemed to speak out of darkness and only to himself). " . . . and when I accused her the pain in my eyes was bad but I didn't think of that, only of what I believed about her . . . and she didn't say anything. She wouldn't say a word but I knew she was very angry, but I didn't care what she felt, I was a devil . . . I believe now and I have believed for a long time that I hurt her beyond everything on earth . . . " He waited. "When she wouldn't speak and just looked at me I said again she was a damn obstinate woman. I went out of the room and got a bag and threw some things into the bag and went out and banged the door. I got hold of Joe Gibson that I'd known overseas. Joe was going back to San Francisco and I told Joe that I was going west and to come along and we'd go to British Columbia and maybe have some fishing and he could go back that way just as well. My father was a timber cruiser on the coast but mostly in the interior and when I was a kid I went with him in the summers . . . all my holidays . . . all over the upper country. I didn't tell Joe a thing about what had happened and I know I was poor company for him. My headaches were pretty bad but what with the things I was thinking about – well, it was all mixed up together and the thinking was worst but Joe was a nice guy to travel with and I threw the thing off in a way. I hadn't begun to feel like a heel then, I was just angry with her for what she'd done and because she was stubborn and wouldn't say a word and I thought – I absolutely thought I was justified. I said to Joe to bring his brother's fishing gear and if he'd got two fishing-rods to bring them or we'd get one in Kamloops. We took the CNR through Jasper and down the North Thompson and got off at Clearwater and went in to the Clearwater River. We were travelling light and sometimes we'd get a lift or we'd walk or there was a chap with horses and we packed in. Weather was good and fishing was fine but not easy to get to so after we'd fished the Clearwater a bit we went back to the North Thompson because otherwise we couldn't get through very well to the Cariboo. We went up to Taweel for a couple of days and then we took the train again and got off at Ashcroft. We drove up to Hundred Mile and stuck around and did nothing for a bit and Joe said "This'll do your headaches good" and I was inclined to think it did. So then we went into Canim Lake and Mahood and fished there but I wanted to push on to somewhere right off the highway on the west side so went out and back to the Cariboo and up past Hundred and Seventeen Mile and bore west and into a small lake where an Indian had a flat bottom boat cached in the reeds. The Indian took us into that lake. We drove right through tall bear grass. I never saw anything like it. Cast with one fly and the fish would rush at it. We'd put on two flies and then three flies just to see and we'd be playing three fish at the same time and if we'd had four flies on it would have been the same. We stopped that and took to using barbless hooks and putting the fish back. The fishing in that lake was too good to be good but I'll never forget it. I can see it now . . . all those fish, it was murder. All this time we'd been going about in the Clearwater and Canim Lake country and at night I'd begun feeling not so angry and sorry for myself and begun feeling uneasy and I was looking back all the time at that night when I'd accused her and she never answered me and just looked at me . . . just looking straight at me and not a word or any crying. I must have been mad the things I'd said to her, trying to hurt her – I did hurt her and that's what I wanted to do. And it began to seem as though I was looking at the other side of a globe now and the picture was different. I began to know that *if* she never had, and *if* what I'd said to her was all . . . wrong . . . and a mistake and a lie (and I was sure it was now), I had hurt her beyond anything any women'd been hurt and she would never in all her life get over it . . . this happening between her and me . . . doing that to any woman was bad enough but doing it to her . . . I began to want to crawl back and tell her – and would she listen. I wouldn't if it was me. The pain in my head got worse and Joe had to move on to San Francisco and I remember he said Was it all right to leave me like that and I said Yes it was fine because if it got unbearable I'd go to the doctor in Kamloops. I remember telling him that there were good doctors in Kamloops and he needn't worry. But Joe persisted Why didn't I go home, but he didn't push it too much because though I'd never said a word about the trouble he must have known there was something. I thought when Joe left me I'd go up to Lac le Jeune which is just about my favourite fishing lake, sizeable but not too big and the people are nice people and then I would absolutely make up my mind there whether to crawl home though I didn't think Janet would see me – I don't know why she would – *I* wouldn't – or if this blasted pain got worse I'd go to the doctor – and then, well it would all depend. It was one of those times when you can't make up your mind neat and easy and I had to wait and see. I got a fellow to drive me up to Lac le Jeune and when I got there, I tell you my heart rose up the way it does when you see your favourite lake away up in the hills all shining and saying Come on, Come on, and the sky all blue and the reflections of the forest upside down in the water and everything as innocent as a kitten. That lake is nearly forty-five hundred feet up and even in summer after hot days it can be cold and you can have storms like winter but there's a smell of the pines there and especially when the sun's on them and even when the rain's been on them, and all the way up there's the smell of the sage too. And right away when you see the fish jumping and hear the loons crying on the big lake or Little Lac le Jeune Lake you know – well, it's heart's desire, that's what it is. The cry of the loon is the finest sound I know," said the blind man. "There's nothing, nothing, like the cry of the loon. I got a room for a day or two but I told them that I might have to go. I was going to make my decision and, as far as I could see, the thing was to go home and prostrate myself and get kicked all over as I deserved and then maybe have some peace of a kind inside myself but I was sure Janet would send me away why wouldn't she, and that would have to be okay because how could things ever be right again between us after what I said, and she believing that I believed it, as I did then . . . but I wasn't wanting to open the subject again, all I wanted was to get back, and then see her. . . . Weather on these mountain lakes is very capricious and you can look at the sky and look at it but you can't tell. The sky can be all blue the same blue as a mountain bluebird, bluer in fact, and as innocent as can be and then round the rim of the hills and behind the smaller lake the weather breaks up and the clouds come rolling in very surreptitious and in less than half an hour the clouds are there in every shade and shape of gray and black and the wind moving them all in the wrong direction and thunder all around you in the hills. All mountain lakes are the same. I had a pretty good idea that the weather wasn't settled but I had a pretty good idea too that I was going to take the road to Kamloops that night. I figured it out like this: I'd go to the doctor the next day and if he said my headaches and the pain in my eyes were just nerves caused by – the kind of things doctors say, well, I'd head for Calgary and fly home and try to see her. But if the doctor said there was something radically wrong and I was – well maybe going blind – but I didn't believe that, no one ever does, then just like the black clouds coming over the lake, up came this new thing that if he said I was losing my sight then I couldn't go back to Janet after what I'd said to her and put her on the spot, me not having my eyesight and she being the kind of woman she is . . . I said to myself I'll row up to the head of the lake and fish the far reeds and then I'll go back and fix up with Johnny Wilson and telephone to Kamloops for a car to come up and take me in. So I headed for the top end of the lake and as I passed the aspens I say they looked queer but very good. First they were shivering green the way they really are, and then they were all colours and then they were shivering black. And perhaps they were blackish too, because the clouds had come up dark all over the lake and as I rowed and got out of sight of the lodge and round that bend I thought it was foolish to try to reach the far reeds after all and maybe I'd better turn back because I heard a queer sound in the hills but somehow I didn't take any recognition of it at first. The sound got louder and louder like a drumming or a roaring or a whole lot of aeroplanes and did it come from the sky or from the ground, and still I hadn't the sense to know what was happening but I turned my boat and began to row back towards the bend, I thought. I couldn't see the surface of the water at any distance at all but whether that was because I didn't seem able to see or whether there was something queer about the water I didn't know. Both, I guess. The roaring came nearer till it was all round me and it wasn't until the hailstones hit me that I understood the roaring and drumming in the hills and the roaring down on the lake and sweeping onto the lake. I guess the hailstones were hitting the lake surface and the water bouncing up in millions. The hail hit very hard like marbles shot from a gun and the hailstones hammered down and stung my head and my face and my hands when I tried to row. I think I rowed and then stopped because it wasn't much good, I couldn't see which way to go and the hail must have been like a steel curtain coming down. It seemed as though it would never stop. I suppose all the boats had gone off the lake and so everyone was inside. I shipped my oars and sat there in the rowboat somewhere round the bend and in the middle of the lake and the hailstones hitting and stinging, and inside myself I knew that sometime this must stop and someone must come out when it was fine to go fishing again because fishermen always do that the minute the weather seems to turn fine, and someone would find me. So I sat there like a target and this pain in my head . . . I remember I sat on my hands because of the hail stinging. I don't know how long it was before the storm swept off the lake or stopped but it seemed like forever. Then someone saw me just sitting and called out. I looked up but I couldn't see, and they towed me in and Johnny Wilson fixed me up and took me right into town. They tried to find out where I lived but I didn't say. When I'd been travelling with Joe he always put San Francisco and that was that. When they let me go from hospital in Kamloops at last they sent me down to Vancouver for training and there's a man here that's helped me a lot and he's done a bit of business for me and he found this place for me that was about what I wanted and here I am and, as far as I know, here I'll stay and I may as well accept that fact because I can't see any other."

Thomas Krispin had nothing to say. He scrutinized the dark profile earnestly as if he could not stop looking. Mr. Olsen turned his face in the general direction of where Tom sat, and spoke in a different tone of authority. He spoke as another man. He said, coldly, as if he might regret having revealed himself, as if Tom had forced him in some way, "I take it you understand, Mr. Krispin, you will not be tempted to speak of this to anyone. I do not know who you are. I have told you because perhaps . . . it may be of use to you and then there'll be only one fool instead of two of us. Goodbye," and he turned his head again towards the window and Tom was dismissed.

Tom does not know if he said "I promise not to speak"; he thinks he did; he does not know whether he thanked the blind man or whether he said nothing and went away, closing the door behind him.

IX

Tom is as gentle with Dolly as he knows how to be and Dolly who has had a severe shock of discovery (one does not enjoy the discovery of one's own stupidity) tries not to be ostentatiously silent but finds it difficult because habit is strong. But there they are, together again, two as one.

Because Tom Krispin and Dolly are people of good will, and have been frightened, and are fallible, the stars give warning that their mutual future happiness is likely, but not assured. The stars, taking refuge in cliché, say It all depends. On what? asks Tom, and the stars reply It all depends.

In the evenings and when Tom woke in the mornings he thought of Mr. Olsen and what he would continue to experience in the dark with only Pluto. Sometimes when his employees assumed that he was thinking about business – no, he was suddenly thinking of Mr. Olsen. He wished to go to the cabin and he did not wish to go. Chiefly he did not wish to go because he thought he would be unwelcome as a stranger who would remind Mr. Olsen by his presence of what he had – perhaps inadvertently – said, and such an intrusion would be outrageous after his dismissal; but still he wanted to go – and yet he was a stranger.

On the Wednesday afternoon following the Wednesday when he had travelled on the ferry boat and the woman had thrown herself into the sea (why did she throw herself into the sea? But he no longer cared, and his mind flickered past her) he nearly told Dolly that he had to go and see someone, and go alone, but his feelings were complicated on behalf of Mr. Olsen for whom he felt this deep respect, and he did not go.

But the next Wednesday he said to Dolly, "Now today I have to go and see someone. I can't take anyone with me – it's nothing to do with you and me so don't worry."

Dolly said that anyway it was time she had her aunts in to tea so that was all right and she asked no questions. But she felt fear come over her and suspension of breathing and living.

Tom crossed to North Vancouver on the ferry and drove along the road that runs by the shore of the North Arm of the Inlet. He did not know how he would be received but he had to go to the cabin. He stopped the car and got out. Nailed to the door of the cabin was a piece of cardboard and on it in hand-scrawled printing the words TO RENT. Tom walked round the cabin and the lean-to and looked in at the windows. He tried the doors. He saw through a window that there was confusion in the room as if someone had left in haste and had not minded that the room was disorderly. He was angry with himself that he had not come to see Mr. Olsen before, which he had so much wished to do. And now Mr. Olsen had gone, and if he ever thought of Tom whom he had befriended, he would think of a man who was insensitive and ungrateful. Tom did not wish to be thought insensitive and ungrateful by Mr. Olsen who – more likely, though – might have forgotten him. But, more than that, what had happened to him? Could he be ill. Tom would go to all the hospitals. He would do anything for him not only because Mr. Olsen had befriended him but on account of something within Mr. Olsen, and on account of the look on his face which was as strong as a tree in Tom's mind.

He walked back along the road to a small house very superior to Mr. Olsen's cabin, and knocked at the door. A woman in blue jeans and spectacles came to the door. Two children looked from behind her.

Tom said, "Could you tell me what became of Mr. Olsen the blind man who lived down the road? Do you know where he is?"

"Where he is I couldn't say I'm sure," said the woman. "I can't say as I knew him very good, he was kinda reserved. But I *do* know there wuz a woman came because I seen her, me and the kids happened to be passing."

"A woman?" said Tom.

"Yair, she jumped out of a cab and ran into the cabin and she was there quite a while and kept the cab waiting pretty near an hour but me and the kids stuck around nearby and then we seen the two of them come out and she had his arm and they had the dog and they got into the cab and went away. I couldn't say where they went I'm sure."

"The lady was crying," piped one of the children.

"Yair, and she was laughing too, I seen her," said the other child.

"Wuz you wanting anything?" asked the woman, who liked to know.

"No no, nothing at all," said Tom laughing, "oh thank you no, nothing at all, nothing at all," and he turned away, repeating himself out loud with the joy bursting out of him.

"He must be nuts, that fella," said the woman, staring after him, "see him walking along laughing like crazy with nothing to laugh at."

SEVENTEEN

Till death us do part

I HAVE A friend, well I should say an acquaintance, well anyway someone who works with me in the wool shop that is, and she is a very interesting girl not because she says anything, oh no. She is very silent and I don't know whether she is bad tempered or just silent. I think she is proud. Her name is Kate and she is very efficient in the wool shop. If her expression was happier I would say she is beautiful. She is small with a natural golden coiffure or is it coiffeur, well what I mean hair-do and a very clear complexion but I wish she would respond a bit. She silences me. We never laugh and I am used to laughing when I feel like it.

Kate seems to have got a queer defensive thing, I can't imagine why. Perhaps she *has* to defend herself in some way. Me being older than she is although I am junior in the shop, I've had to knock about a bit and I know things happen sometimes so you *have* to defend yourself but she doesn't need to defend herself against me, I'm not going to do her any harm, or is she jealous? oh surely no. I'd like to like her but as it is she won't let me. I think she's scared of intimacy but heavens I don't want to be intimate. Probably she just doesn't like me. Oh well, you can't like everyone.

If I say, Good morning isn't it a lovely day, she says it's going to rain. And if I say, Did you see that warship come into harbour this morning, she says, That wasn't a warship. At first I used to argue a little but that was silly and got nowhere. She'd be better to say just Yes and No. It would save argument and be pleasanter. And better still I'd be wiser not to make a remark of any kind. However.

The result is that neither of us speaks because it is no fun speaking, except to the customers and we are both lovely to the customers. The owner and manager is away sick and I sure hope she comes back soon and sweetens the atmosphere a little. Perhaps Kate has a secret sorrow. Well so have I.

I began to go home at night pretty ruffled. I knew I was being put in my place and supposed to stay there but couldn't see why this should be. I'm a human being too, aren't I.

Today I was very pleased at a good order of wool to a new customer for bed jackets and I thought why not say so.

Yes, said Kate, I saw you. You didn't sell her enough wool for those bed jackets. I could of told you. Then we'll be out of wool when she wants it.

I was really annoyed and said, I always sell that amount for bed jackets and in my experience – and then I thought, This isn't intelligent, and I said no more.

Then I thought What shall I do about this. Shall I

Sit on a stile and continue to smile
That should soften the heart of this cow

but it did not soften the heart. However I had to speak to Kate because the telephone rang and someone asked if Mrs. Physick was there. I said I was sorry but Mrs. Physick was away ill and could I take a message. And the lady said, Oh dear, well I'll get in touch, but say her aunty called.

I said to Kate, That was Mrs. Physick's aunty and I was to say she called.

Kate said, Mrs. Physick hasn't got an aunty.

Well really that attitude made me mad if people have to

feed their ego that much, so when I got home at night I rang up Mrs. Physick's place although I didn't really know her and I said to the person who came to the phone, Oh it's Muriel Brown from the shop, and please would you kindly tell Mrs. Physick that her aunty rang up today.

And the person said, Her aunty? Mrs. Physick hasn't got an aunty. Oh you must mean Mrs. Bonaventure, she always calls her aunty. Was there any message?

I felt very small and said, Oh no, she only rang up and will get in touch, and the lady said, Yes she did.

I sat still on the telephone stool and thought So she's right and there isn't any aunty and I can't win.

I had begun to be very introspective because there were ever so many more silly little things like that and I started not sleeping at night. I've got troubles of my own.

One morning Kate came in late to the shop with her right hand bandaged and began to fumble among the boxes. She didn't seem to want to speak about her hand nor about being so late but turned her face away from me and then she dropped a box because she only had her left hand, and the balls of wool rolled all over the floor.

Oh I said, don't try to pick them up! and I began to pick them up. I looked up at her from where I was on my knees and I saw that her face was scarlet and I knew that Kate's pride was hurt to an absurd degree that she should have to be indebted to me, picking up the balls of wool off the floor.

When I had finished I straightened up and looked right at her. I said with authority (a trembling sort of authority I'll tell you, because I had become frightened of Kate and what snub might lie in wait for me), I said, You are not used to letting people do things for you or letting them co-operate with you, but you must let me help you all I can with the boxes and things. It will be a pleasure I assure you except I'm sorry about your hand. Oh what is wrong with your hand?

My hand . . . said Kate turning deathly white, and she

had been so scarlet, my hand . . . my hand . . . and a customer came in.

July 7.

I began writing this about Kate's hand and her strangeness and then I was much busier for some days and I hadn't time to write down about it. A story has to end and this story hasn't ended yet and I don't know what the end will be.

Kate tried to ignore her hand as much as possible and went back again into her silent way and I went back into my silent way except that I did watch to make things easier if possible, lifting, and boiling the kettle for tea and so on. I do think the shop had the unpleasantest feeling that ever I knew in a place but I decided to go on with it. There's always something.

I got a letter from my sister in Portage la Prairie and she said that when their busy season was over she and Frank would put the boys at his mother's and they might drive to the coast and see how I was getting along, and oh how my heart warmed up under these circumstances. She wrote about Peterborough Edwards too and that was the first time she had mentioned Peterborough Edwards and I found that I didn't mind at all because although it was all on account of Peterborough I had left Portage la Prairie and at first I had felt really badly about it, I found that by this time I was relieved about Peterborough rather than feeling badly. You can go on and on and on with a person till you get past the disappointment point, and then they begin to bore you. I was really just a habit with Peterborough although to my surprise he was awfully shocked when I decided to go off. You never can tell. I like it here in Vancouver except for Kate, it's a change but then I might like to go back to Portage la Prairie some time but no more Peterborough unless he can make up his mind. It seems that he had rung up my sister to see was there any news from me but she was very airy fairy with him she said and she said I was having a wonderful time in Vancouver.

Ha ha.

After a week Kate had the bandage off her hand and it was really very nasty looking. There were still plasters on it as if there were cuts and it was evidently painful, so I helped all I could but not what you'd call ostentatious. There was once that Kate turned to me with such lovely sweetness and gratitude and her pretty customer smile and oh how my heart warmed as it does, foolishly I expect.

That sweetness did not last only long enough for me to think how lovely it would be, because then Mrs. Physick rang me up.

All my arrangements with Mrs. Physick had been made by mail and so I had not seen her because the doctor said she must have this operation.

But now Mrs. Physick asked me to go and see her in the evening if convenient and take the order book and the old order book too, to compare stocks for ordering. She sounded quite young, I was surprised.

After I hung up I said to Kate, Is Mrs. Physick old or young? She sounds quite young to me.

Kate said coldly, It all depends on what you call young.

Kate was uneasy. At last she said, Why did she ring you not me? Why did she tell *you* to take the order books?

Well really how silly! Mrs. Physick probably wanted to give me the once-over but it was no good entering on a silly argument so I said snappishly Better ask her yourself, and we were quits but the atmosphere was nearly unbearable again.

July 10.

I took the order books to Mrs. Physick's flat were she lived with a woman friend who Mrs. Physick told me had a hat shop. Mrs. Physick was lying on a couch and said she was still taking it easy after the operation. She was pleasant looking, youngish but her hair going gray. She had the nice kind of face with some lines on. We went through the order books and she told me to leave them and she'd run through them again and then Kate or I could come and get them. She looked at me and said, How do you get along with Kate?

I said, Oh I get along. And then I said, But I don't think she likes me.

Mrs. Physick looked worried and she put out her hand. I know, she said, it's not easy. Don't take it personally.

I was afraid of beginning to discuss Kate which would be a disloyal thing to do and anyway I did not think Mrs. Physick would do such a thing, Kate being the senior employee.

Just the same I said, Oh yes it is personal. It would be impossible not to feel that – but I don't take it too seriously. I'll be going now Mrs. Physick, is there anything else?

Mrs. Physick did not speak for a moment and then she looked down and almost whispered, Kate is a very unhappy young woman.

I was standing up to go. I wondered whether I ought to tell her about Kate's right hand or was even that talking too much. However, I blurted out, She hurt her right hand, I think she had an accident, she didn't say, the bandage is off now and it looks nasty but she can manage more easily.

Mrs. Physick stared at me. An accident? she said, an accident to her right hand? It seems to me people always have accidents to their left hand! What kind of accident?

I said, I don't know. She didn't say. It looked to me as if something had hit it.

Mrs. Physick was silent and then spoke sort of unhappily, Oh do be good to her, she said, and I said I'll try. I began to think that Mrs. Physick might be the whole world to Kate and she couldn't bear to have her friendly to any new person.

July 17.

It must have been a few days after I wrote last time and I had been doing what Mrs. Physick said, making every allowance and paying no attention and I thought that perhaps Kate seemed happier and I remember feeling happier myself, and easier, when one day I saw a woman in black standing very still outside the door of the shop. Kate was serving a customer at the back of the shop where the new stock of children's small foreign toys are and I was in the front with a customer who wanted to make some baby outfits. There was the wool and there was the pattern book. The customer was taking a long time looking and making little remarks to herself, and in between I happened to look at the glass front door.

The woman began to peer closely this way and that through the glass as though she was looking for someone. She saw me but paid me no attention. I had to attend to my customer and so I could not keep looking at the woman as I wanted to. But I did see that now she was bending down and gazing in and then it seemed to me that she saw what she was looking for. She looked fixedly and with a very unpleasant expression deep into the shop. Between pleasing my customer and advising with her and looking at the woman and looking to see if Kate had seen her, it was all difficult, but the woman (I could see) remained bent down nearly double and peering in.

Next time I could look away from my customer I saw the woman had gone, and I saw that Kate was moving up the shop with her customer who had in her hand one of those little music boxes that seem so funny in a wool shop.

Oh the woman wore a shabby black coat and had her head tied up like an old peasant woman. Her face was sallow, almost yellow, but although I did not know her, there was something familiar about her face and then I knew that if you can have someone ugly look like someone pretty, this woman looked like Kate.

I was very horrified because I thought could this ever be the mother of Kate who is so pretty and so clean and proud and refined and tension-full and – as Mrs. Physick said – so unhappy. And I thought Oh how terrible, Kate going home every night to perhaps such a mother in a small place and coming back in the morning full of the feeling of it. How terrible! Next day the woman came again and I found myself watching each day for her and each day she came and bent down to peer through the glass but if Kate was in full view, or on the approach of Kate, she always vanished.

I began to make up stories in my head and I think that Kate had forbidden the mother ever to come near the shop, and so shame her who was so proud, but that in order to annoy her the woman came every day and watched, and that was the kind of woman she was.

Sometimes either Kate or I go into the little back place and get out new stock or paper bags or something, and one of these times when Kate was in the back, the woman came to the door. This time she was bolder. She put her hand on the latch and pushed the door open and stood and I saw more clearly her yellow face which seemed to me terrible and without, well, without humanity. I went up to her (and I felt ready to defend Kate) and said, Can I do anything for you? and the sour smell of cheap whiskey came strong right at me. I did not know what to do. She gave me a look only, and then with a kind of derision she looked slowly round the shop, up and down the shelves, as if to fix in her mind the kind of heaven her daughter came to every day.

I said again, Can I do anything for you? and I wondered Is she foreign or what because she doesn't answer, and all the time the reek of whiskey was on her, when Kate came out from the back and suddenly stopped. The peculiar bright scarlet came up her neck and over her face and then the whiteness and she looked like a frozen woman.

I did not know what was the best thing to do. Everything rushed through my mind in a turmoil about Kate's pride and tension and the hurt right hand and Mrs. Physick saying She is unhappy and there was a kind of yawning terribleness of how unhappy she must be to act like she does. There was also this at the same moment, that I must do something at once and that I must not let Kate think in all her pride that I knew that this woman (a hag if ever I saw one) could be her mother, or the sight of me would always be unbearable to her. So I stepped between them and took the evil-smelling woman gently but firmly by the shoulder and said Let's ... let's go outside, and I walked her out of the door and shut it.

She was surprised at my action and looked angrily into my face and tried to shake me off.

I got a perfect right, she said, to go into your old shop, and I said, Oh no, you've been drinking, we can't have you in our shop, and she said, I have not so been drinking, and she looked very vicious. Then she spat at me and that made me really mad, a little short and sharp spit.

So I said, You certainly have been drinking and I'll have to get a policeman if you try to come into our shop, there's a policeman at the Bank at the corner, and the woman looked at me like a snake and slipped out of my hand and was gone. There's nothing like the word policeman.

I stood outside in the fresh air for a minute. I felt awful, not just because of this woman but because of Kate. Then I went into the shop but I left the door wide open because it seemed to me the whole place smelled of the stench of that woman. It was lucky there was no customer there, but it would have been just the same if there had been a customer.

Kate was not in the shop. So I wondered What do I do now? It isn't natural for me ever to go to the back and talk to Kate about anything but I'd better do it, casual like, and now. So I went into the back and I think Kate had had her head on the desk but she straightened up and looked at me quite wild.

I didn't seem to notice, I hope, and said, Did you see that woman in the store? She'd been drinking so I took her

out and told her not to come in. She said she'd come in if
she liked but I said No, not when she'd been drinking, in
fact I'd have to call a constable if she came in again and
she beat it. I kind of hated to speak to an old wom . . . an
old lady like that but what could I do. I hope that was all
right? I said, anxious like.

Kate nodded her head, still looking at me in that wild
way, and I went back into the shop. When the time came
to close up I could not bear to think of Kate going home
to what she was going home to, but what can you do?

July 25.

This has been an uncomfortable week. If it weren't for the
fact that business is good and us busy (I think those little
foreign dolls and houses and things in the window attract
people) I don't think I could stick it. Things seem out of
control. Kate is the silentest person I ever did see, but
more than that she is so unhappy. It would be no good
trying to horn in with a little comfort and what's more she
looks ill, in herself, I mean. Her hand was very inflamed
this morning and she had it bandaged all over again, but
badly. Could I help you fix that, I said, and she said, Well
just a bit tighter here, and pin it, and then she actually said
Thank you.

I'm not one to tell tales but I just felt that it was too
much responsibility and I must go and talk to Mrs. Physick after supper. Mrs. Physick came to the door herself
and she looked better but she moved slowly and we went
into the room and sat down.

I said, I'm very worried Mrs. Physick about Kate, and I
told her about the woman and about Kate's reaction to
the woman (all out of proportion, I thought, though it
sure was bad enough) and how her hand was infected and
red and swollen up her arm and what could we do. I said,
I am very willing to go and do things up for her at her
home but I don't know where she lives.

No no, said Mrs. Physick. That would never never do.

Kate is very very proud (I said, I'll say she's proud) and it would spoil your relations together for always if you went into that house and saw it – she'd never forget it. I know it. I'll go. I can drive the car now. You go home. I'll phone later. So I went home.

It was midnight before Mrs. Physick phoned and she didn't waste words.

She said, Can you carry on alone tomorrow? Maybe I'll be down for a bit some time. I got Kate into hospital. She's running a fever. When I got there the mother let me in but Kate's bedroom door was closed. Yes it was locked and I had to knock and knock and call but she was suspicious and it was some time before she'd let me in. To think of her barricaded against that woman! I don't blame her. The place was a dirty shambles. Well goodnight Muriel. Do you know my belief? My belief is that bitch hit her on the hand with a bottle.

July 29.

I'm carrying on at the shop with Mrs. Physick down half days. Kate's been up to the O.R. and they've taken splinters of glass out of her hand. I don't know how I can bear it when Kate comes back, and she will come back, to think of her and that mother going on for ever and ever together and no escape till death comes for one of them, whatever way it comes, but some way death will part them.

There was a letter from Peterborough Edwards tonight when I got home, addressed care of my sister. Peterborough wants to come down to Vancouver on his holiday. He seems upset. I won't answer right away. Do him good to be upset. But my mind turns to Peterborough Edwards as a comfort when I think of Kate and her mother going on until death parts them. I don't say I'd really choose Peterborough Edwards and I never thought I'd turn to Peterborough on account of these circumstances but he might be a comfort and anyway, what can you do.

EIGHTEEN

The Window

THE GREAT big window must have been at least twenty-five feet wide and ten feet high. It was constructed in sections divided by segments of something that did not interfere with the view; in fact the eye by-passed these divisions and looked only at the entrancing scenes beyond. The window, together with a glass door at the western end, composed a bland shallow curve and formed the entire transparent north-west (but chiefly north) wall of Mr. Willy's living-room.

Upon his arrival from England Mr. Willy had surveyed the various prospects of living in the quickly growing city of Vancouver with the selective and discarding characteristics which had enabled him to make a fortune and retire all of a sudden from business and his country in his advanced middle age. He settled immediately upon the very house. It was a small old house overlooking the sea between Spanish Banks and English Bay. He knocked out the north wall and made the window. There was nothing particular to commend the house except that it faced immediately on the sea-shore and the view. Mr. Willy had left his wife and her three sisters to play bridge together until death should overtake them in England. He now paced from end to end of his living-room, that is to say from east to west, with his hands in his pockets, admiring the northern view. Sometimes he stood with his hands behind him looking through the great glass window, seeing the wrinkled or placid sea and the ships almost at his feet and beyond the sea the mountains, and seeing sometimes his emancipation. His emancipation drove him into a dream, and sea sky mountains swam before him, vanished, and he saw with immense release his wife in still another more repulsive hat. He did not know, nor would he have cared, that much discussion went on in her world, chiefly in the afternoons, and that he was there alleged to have deserted her. So he had, after providing well for her physical needs which were all the needs of which she was capable. Mrs. Willy went on saying " . . . and he would come home my dear and never speak a word I can't tell you my dear how *frightful* it was night after night I might say for *years* I simply can't tell you . . . " No, she could not tell but she did, by day and night. Here he was at peace, seeing out of the window the crimped and wrinkled sea and the ships which passed and passed each other, the seabirds and the dream-inducing sky.

At the extreme left curve of the window an island appeared to slope into the sea. Behind this island and to the north, the mountains rose very high. In the summer time the mountains were soft, deceptive in their innocency, full of crags and crevasses and arêtes and danger. In the winter they lay magnificent, white and much higher, it seemed, than in the summer time. They tossed, static, in almost visible motion against the sky, inhabited only by eagles and – so a man had told Mr. Willy, but he didn't believe the man – by mountain sheep and some cougars, bears, wild cats and, certainly, on the lower slopes, deer, and now a ski camp far out of sight. Mr. Willy looked at the mountains and regretted his past youth and his present wealth. How could he endure to be old and rich and able only to look at these mountains which in his youth he had not known and did not climb. Nothing, now, no remnant of his youth would come and enable him to climb these mountains. This he found hard to believe, as old people do. He was shocked at the newly realized decline of his physical powers which had proved good enough on the whole for his years of success, and by the fact that now he had, at last, time and could not swim (heart), climb mountains (heart and legs), row a boat in a rough enticing sea (call that old age). These things have happened to other people, though Mr. Willy, but not to us, now, who have been so young, and yet it will happen to those who now are young.

Immediately across the water were less spectacular mountains, pleasant slopes which in winter time were covered with invisible skiers. Up the dark mountain at night sprang the lights of the ski-lift, and ceased. The shores of these mountains were strung with lights, littered with lights, spangled with lights, necklaces, bracelets, constellations, far more beautiful as seen through this window across the dark water than if Mr. Willy had driven his car across the Lions' Gate Bridge and westwards among those constellations which would have disclosed only a shopping centre, people walking in the streets, street lights, innumerable cars and car lights like anywhere else and, up the slopes, people's houses. Then, looking back to the south across the dark water towards his own home and the great lighted window which he would not have been able to distinguish so far away, Mr. Willy would have seen lights again, a carpet of glitter thrown over the slopes of the city.

Fly from one shore to the other, fly and fly back again, fly to a continent or to an island, but you are no better off than if you stayed all day at your own window (and such a window), thought Mr. Willy pacing back and forth, then into the kitchen to put the kettle on for a cup of tea which he will drink beside the window, back for a glass of whisky, returning in time to see a cormorant flying level with the water, not an inch too high not an inch too low, flying out of sight. See the small ducks lying on the water, one behind the other, like beads on a string. In the mornings Mr. Willy drove into town to see his investment broker and perhaps to the bank or round the park. He lunched, but not at a club. He then drove home. On certain days a woman called Mrs. Ogden came in to "do" for him. This was his daily life, very simple, and a routine was formed whose pattern could at last be discerned by an interested observer outside the window.

One night Mr. Willy beheld a vast glow arise behind the mountains. The Arctic world was obviously on fire – but no, the glow was not fire glow, flame glow. The great invasion of colour that spread up and up the sky was not red, was not rose, but of a synthetic cyclamen colour. This cyclamen glow remained steady from mountain to zenith and caused Mr. Willy, who had never seen the Northern Lights, to believe that these were not Northern Lights but that something had occurred for which one must be prepared. After about an hour, flanges of green as of putrefaction, and a melodious yellow arose and spread. An hour later the Northern Lights faded, leaving Mr. Willy small and alone.

Sometimes as, sitting beside the window, he drank his tea, Mr. Willy thought that nevertheless it is given to few people to be as happy (or contented, he would say), as he was, at his age, too. In his life of decisions, men, pressures, more men, antagonisms, fusions, fissions and Mrs. Willy, in his life of hard success, that is, he had sometimes looked forward but so vaguely and rarely to a time when he would not only put this life down; he would leave it. Now he had left it and here he was by his window. As time went on, though, he had to make an effort to summon this happiness, for it seemed to elude him. Sometimes a thought or a shape (was it?), gray, like wood ash that falls in pieces when it is touched, seemed to be behind his chair, and this shape teased him and communicated to him that he had left humanity behind, that a man needs humanity and that if he ceases to be in touch with man and is not in touch with God, he does not matter. "You do not matter any more," said the spectre like wood ash before it fell to pieces, "because you are no longer in touch with any one and so you do not exist. You are in a vacuum and so you are nothing." Then Mr. Willy, at first uneasy, became satisfied again for a time after being made uneasy by the spectre. A storm would get up and the wind, howling well, would lash the window sometimes carrying the salt spray from a very high tide which it flung against the great panes of glass. That was a satisfaction to Mr. Willy and within him something stirred and rose and met the storm and effaced the spectre and other phantoms which were really vague regrets. But the worst that happened against the window was that from time to time a little bird, sometimes but not often a seabird, flung itself like a stone against the strong glass of the window and fell, killed by the passion of its flight. This grieved Mr. Willy, and he could not sit unmoved when the bird flew at the clear glass and was met by death. When this happened, he arose from his chair, opened the glass door at the far end of the window, descended three or four steps and sought in the grasses for the body of the bird. But the bird was dead, or it was dying, its small bones were smashed, its head was broken, its beak split, it was killed by the rapture of its flight. Only once Mr. Willy found the bird a little stunned and picked it up. He cupped the bird's body in his hands and carried it into the house.

Looking up through the grasses at the edge of the rough terrace that descended to the beach, a man watched him return into the house, carrying the bird. Still looking obliquely through the grasses the man watched Mr. Willy enter the room and vanish from view. Then Mr. Willy came again to the door, pushed it open, and released the bird which flew away, who knows where. He closed the door, locked it, and sat down on the chair facing east beside the window and began to read his newspaper. Looking over his paper he saw, to the east, the city of Vancouver deployed over rising ground with low roofs and high buildings and at the apex the tall Electric Building which at night shone like a broad shaft of golden light.

This time, as evening drew on, the man outside went away because he had other business.

Mr. Willy's investment broker was named Gerald

Wardho. After a time he said to Mr. Willy in a friendly but respectful way, "Will you have lunch with me at the Club tomorrow?" and Mr. Willy said he would. Some time later Gerald Wardho said, "Would you like me to put you up at the Club?"

Mr. Willy considered a little the life which he had left and did not want to re-enter and also the fact that he had only last year resigned his membership in three clubs, so he said, "That's very good of you, Wardho, but I think not. I'm enjoying things as they are. It's a novelty, living in a vacuum . . . I like it, for a time anyway."

"Yes, but," said Gerald Wardho, "you'd be some time on the waiting list. It wouldn't hurt – "

"No," said Mr. Willy, "no."

Mr. Willy had, Wardho thought, a distinguished appearance or perhaps it was an affable accustomed air, and so he had. When Mrs. Wardho said to her husband, "Gerry, there's not an extra man in this town and I need a man for Saturday," Gerald Wardho said, "I know a man. There's Willy."

Mrs. Wardho said doubtfully, "Willy? Willy who? Who's Willy?"

Her husband said, "He's fine, he's okay, I'll ask Willy."

"How old is he?"

"About a hundred . . . but he's okay."

"Oh-h-h," said Mrs. Wardho, "isn't there anyone anywhere unattached young any more? Does he play bridge?"

"I'll invite him, I'll find out," said her husband, and Mr. Willy said he'd like to come to dinner.

"Do you care for a game of bridge, Mr. Willy?" asked Gerald Wardho.

"I'm afraid not," said Mr. Willy kindly but firmly. He played a good game of bridge but had no intention of entering servitude again just yet, losing his freedom, and being enrolled as what is called a fourth. Perhaps later; not yet. "If you're having bridge I'll come another time. Very kind of you, Wardho."

"No no no," said Gerald Wardho, "there'll only be

maybe a table of bridge for anyone who wants to play. My wife would be disappointed."

"Well thank you very much. Black tie?"

"Yes. Black tie," said Gerald Wardho.

And so, whether he would or no, Mr. Willy found himself invited to the kind of evening parties to which he had been accustomed and which he had left behind, given by people younger and more animated than himself, and he realized that he was on his way to becoming old odd man out. There was a good deal of wood ash at these parties – that is, behind him the spectre arose, falling to pieces when he looked at it, and said "So this is what you came to find out on this coast, so far from home, is it, or is there something else. What else is there?" The spectre was not always present at these parties but sometimes awaited him at home and said these things.

One night Mr. Willy came home from an evening spent at Gerald Wardho's brother-in-law's house, a very fine house indeed. He had left lights burning and began to turn out the lights before he went upstairs. He went into the living-room and before turning out the last light gave a glance at the window which had in the course of the evening behaved in its accustomed manner. During the day the view through the window was clear or cloudy, according to the weather or the light or absence of light in the sky; but there it was – the view – never quite the same though, and that is owing to the character of oceans or of any water, great or small, and of light. Both water and light have so great an effect on land observed on any scene, rural urban or wilderness, that one begins to think that life, that a scene, is an illusion produced by influences such as water and light. At all events, by day the window held this fine view as in a frame, and the view was enhanced by ships at sea of all kinds, but never was the sea crowded, and by birds, clouds, and even aeroplanes in the sky – no people to spoil this fine view. But as evening approached, and moonless night, all the view (illusion again) vanished slowly. The window, which was not illusion, only the purveyor of illusion, did not vanish, but became a mirror which reflected against the blackness every detail of the shallow living-room. Through this clear reflection of the whole room, distant lights from across the water intruded, and so chains of light were thrown across the reflected mantel-piece, or a picture, or a human face, enhancing it. When Mr. Willy had left his house to dine at Gerald Wardho's brother-in-law's house the view through the window was placidly clear, but when he returned at 11.30 the window was dark and the room was reflected from floor to ceiling against the blackness. Mr. Willy saw himself entering the room like a stranger, looking at first debonair with such a gleaming shirt front and then – as he approached himself – a little shabby, his hair perhaps. He advanced to the window and stood looking at himself with the room in all its detail behind him.

Mr. Willy was too often alone, and spent far too much time in that space which lies between the last page of the paper or the turning-off of the radio in surfeit, and sleep. Now as he stood at the end of the evening and the beginning of the night, looking at himself and the room behind him, he admitted that the arid feeling which he had so often experienced lately was probably what is called loneliness. And yet he did not want another woman in his life. It was a long time since he had seen a woman whom he wanted to take home or even to see again. Too much smiling. Men were all right, you talked to them about the market, the emergence of the Liberal Party, the impossibility of arriving anywhere with those people while that fellow was in office, nuclear war (instant hells opened deep in everyone's mind and closed again), South Africa where Mr. Willy was born, the Argentine where Mr. Wardho's brother-in-law had spent many years – and then everyone went home.

Mr. Willy, as the months passed by, was dismayed to find that he had entered an area of depression unknown before, like a tundra, and he was a little frightened of this tundra. Returning from the dinner party he did not at once turn out the single last light and go upstairs. He sat down on a chair beside the window and at last bowed his head upon his hands. As he sat there, bowed, his thoughts went very stiffly (for they had not had much exercise in that direction throughout his life), to some area that was not tundra but that area where there might be some meaning in creation which Mr. Willy supposed must be the place where some people seemed to find a God, and perhaps a personal God at that. Such theories, or ideas, or passions had never been of interest to him, and if he had thought of such theories, or ideas, or passions he would have dismissed them as invalid and having no bearing on life as it is lived, especially when one is too busy. He had formed the general opinion that people who hold such beliefs were either slaves to an inherited convention, hypocrites, or nitwits. He regarded such people without interest, or at least he thought them negligible as he returned to the exacting life in hand. On the whole, though, he did not like them. It is not easy to say why Mr. Willy thought these people were hypocrites or nit-wits because some of them, not all, had a strong religious faith, and why he was not a hypocrite or nit-wit because he had not a strong religious faith; but there it was.

As he sat on and on looking down at the carpet with his head in his hands he did not think of these people, but he underwent a strong shock of recognition. He found himself looking this way and that way out of his aridity for some explanation or belief beyond the non-explanation and non-belief that had always been sufficient and had always been his, but in doing this he came up against a high and solid almost visible wall of concrete or granite, set up between him and a religious belief. This wall had, he thought, been built by him through the period of his long life, or perhaps he was congenitally unable to have a belief; in that case it was no fault of his and there was no religious belief possible to him. As he sat there he came to have the conviction that the absence of a belief which extended beyond the visible world had something to do with his malaise; yet the malaise might possibly be cirrhosis of the liver or a sort of delayed male menopause. He recognized calmly that death was as inevitable as tomorrow morning or even tonight and he had a rational absence of fear of death. Nevertheless his death (he knew) had begun, and had begun – what with his awareness of age and this malaise of his – to assume a certainty that it had not had before. His death did not trouble him as much as the increasing tastelessness of living in this tundra of mind into which a belief did not enter.

The man outside the window had crept up through the grasses and was now watching Mr. Willy from a point rather behind him. He was a morose man and strong. He had served two terms for robbery with violence. When he worked, he worked up the coast. Then he came to town and if he did not get into trouble it was through no fault of his own. Last summer he had lain there and, rolling over, had looked up through the grasses and into – only just into – the room where this guy was who seemed to live alone. He seemed to be a rich guy because he wore good clothes and hadn't he got this great big window and – later, he discovered – a high-price car. He had lain in the grasses and because his thoughts always turned that way, he tried to figger out how he could get in there. Money was the only thing that was any good to him and maybe the old guy didn't keep money or even carry it but he likely did. The man thought quite a bit about Mr. Willy and then went up the coast and when he came down again he remembered the great big window and one or two nights he went around and about the place and figgered how he'd work it. The doors was all locked, even that glass door. That was easy enough to break but he guessed he'd go in without warning when the old guy was there so's he'd have a better chance of getting something off of him as well. Anyways he wouldn't break in, not that night, but if nothing else offered he'd do it some time soon.

Suddenly Mr. Willy got up, turned the light out, and went upstairs to bed. That was Wednesday.

On Sunday he had his first small party. It seemed inevitable if only for politeness. Later he would have a dinner
party if he still felt sociable and inclined. He invited the
Wardhos and their in-laws and some other couples. A
Mrs. Lessways asked if she might bring her aunt and he
said yes. Mrs. Wardho said might she bring her niece who
was arriving on Saturday to meet her fiancé who was due
next week from Hong Kong, and the Wardhos were going
to give the two young people a quiet wedding, and Mr.
Willy said "Please do." Another couple asked if they could
bring another couple.

Mr. Willy, surveying his table, thought that Mrs. Ogden
had done well. "Oh I'm so glad you think so," said Mrs.
Ogden, pleased. People began to arrive. "Oh!" they
exclaimed without fail, as they arrived, "what a beautiful
view!" Mrs. Lessways' aunt who had blue hair fell delight-
edly into the room, turning this way and that way,
acknowledging smiles and tripping to the window. "Oh,"
she cried turning to Mr. Willy in a fascinating manner,
"isn't that just lovely! Edna says you're quite a recluse! I'm
sure I don't blame you! Don't you think that's the loveliest
view Edna . . . oh how d'you do how d'you do, isn't that
the loveliest view? . . . " Having paid her tribute to the
view she turned away from the window and did not see it
again. The Aunt twirled a little bag covered with iridescent
beads on her wrist. "Oh!" and "Oh!" she exclaimed, turning, "My dear how *lovely* to see you! I didn't even know
you were back! Did you have a good time?" She reminded
Mr. Willy uneasily of his wife. Mr. and Mrs. Wardho
arrived accompanied by their niece Sylvia.

A golden girl, thought Mr. Willy taking her hand, but
her young face surrounded by sunny curls was stern. She
stood, looking from one to another, not speaking, for
people spoke busily to each other and the young girl stood
apart, smiling only when need be and wishing that she had
not had to come to the party. She drifted to the window
and seemed (and was) forgotten. She looked at the view as
at something seen for the first and last time. She inscribed

those notable hills on her mind because had she not arrived only yesterday? And in two days Ian would be here and she would not see them again.

A freighter very low laden emerged from behind a forest and moved slowly into the scene. So low it was that it lay like an elegant black line upon the water with great bulkheads below. Like an iceberg, thought Sylvia, and her mind moved along with the freighter bound for foreign parts. Someone spoke to her and she turned. "Oh thank you!" she said for her cup of tea.

Mr. Willy opened the glass door and took with him some of the men who had expressed a desire to see how far his property ran. "You see, just a few feet, no distance," he said.

After a while day receded and night came imperceptibly on. There was not any violence of reflected sunset tonight and mist settled down on the view with only distant dim lights aligning the north shore. Sylvia, stopping to respond to ones and twos, went to the back of the shallow room and sat down behind the out-jut of the fireplace where a wood fire was burning. Her mind was on two levels. One was all Ian and the week coming, and one – no thicker than a crust on the surface – was this party and all these people talking, the Aunt talking so busily that one might think there was a race on, or news to tell. Sylvia, sitting in the shadow of the corner and thinking about her approaching lover, lost herself in this reverie, and her lips, which had been so stern, opened slightly in a tender smile. Mr. Willy who was serving drinks from the dining-room where Mrs. Ogden had left things ready, came upon her and, struck by her beauty, saw a different sunny girl. She looked up at him. She took her drink from him with a soft and tender smile that was grateful and happy and was only partly for him. He left her, with a feeling of beauty seen.

Sylvia held her glass and looked towards the window. She saw, to her surprise, so quickly had black night come, that the end of the room which had been a view was now a large black mirror which reflected the glowing fire, the

few lights, and the people unaware of the view, its departure, and its replacement by their own reflections behav-
ing to each other like people at a party. Sylvia watched Mr.
Willy who moved amongst them, taking a glass and bringing a glass. He was removed from the necessities, now, of
conversation, and looked very sad. Why does he look sad,
she wondered and was young enough to think, he
shouldn't look sad, he is well off. She took time off to like
Mr. Willy and to feel sorry that he seemed melancholy.

People began to look at their watches and say good-bye.
The Aunt redoubled her vivacity. The women all thanked
Mr. Willy for his tea party and for the beautiful beautiful
view. They gave glances at the window but there was no
view.

When all his guests had gone, Mr. Willy, who was an
orderly man, began to collect glasses and take them into
the kitchen. In an armchair lay the bag covered with
iridescent beads belonging to the Aunt. Mr. Willy picked
it up and put it on a table, seeing the blue hair of the Aunt.
He would sit down and smoke for a while. But he found
that when, lately, he sat down in the evening beside the
window and fixed his eyes upon the golden shaft of the
Electric Building, in spite of his intention of reading or
smoking, his thoughts turned towards this subject of belief
which now teased him, eluded, yet compelled him. He
was brought up, every time, against the great stone wall,
how high, how wide he knew, but not how thick. If he
could, in some way, break through the wall which
bounded the area of his aridity and his comprehension, he
knew without question that there was a light (not darkness) beyond, and that this light could in some way come
through to him and alleviate the sterility and lead him,
lead him. If there were some way, even some conventional
way – although he did not care for convention – he would
take it in order to break the wall down and reach the light
so that it would enter his life; but he did not know the way.
So fixed did Mr. Willy become in contemplation that he
looked as though he were graven in stone.

Throughout the darkened latter part of the tea party, the man outside had lain or crouched near the window. From the sands, earlier, he had seen Mr. Willy open the glass door and go outside, followed by two or three men. They looked down talking, and soon went inside again together. The door was closed. From anything the watcher knew, it was not likely that the old guy would turn and lock the door when he took the other guys in. He'd just close it, see.

As night came on the man watched the increased animation of the guests preparing for departure. Like departing birds they moved here and there in the room before taking flight. The man was impatient but patient because when five were left, then three, then no one but the old guy who lived in the house, he knew his time was near. (How gay and how meaningless the scene had been, of these well-dressed persons talking and talking, like some kind of a show where nothing happened – or so it might seem, on the stage of the lighted room from the pit of the dark shore.)

The watcher saw the old guy pick up glasses and take them away. Then he came back into the room and looked around. He took something out of a chair and put it on a table. He stood still for a bit, and then he found some kind of a paper and sat down in the chair facing eastward. But the paper drooped in his hand and then it dropped to the floor as the old guy bent his head and then he put his elbows on his knees and rested his head in his hands as if he was thinking, or had some kind of a headache.

The watcher, with a sort of joy and a feeling of confidence that the moment had come, moved strongly and quietly to the glass door. He turned the handle expertly, slid inside, and slowly closed the door so that no draught should warn his victim. He moved cat-like to the back of Mr. Willy's chair and quickly raised his arm. At the selfsame moment that he raised his arm with a short blunt weapon in his hand, he was aware of the swift movement of another person in the room. The man stopped still, his arm remained high, every fear was aroused. He turned instantly and saw a scene clearly enacted beside him in the dark mirror of the window. At the moment and shock of turning, he drew a sharp intake of breath and it was this that Mr. Willy heard and that caused him to look up and around and see in the dark mirror the intruder, the danger, and the victim who was himself. At that still moment, the telephone rang shrilly, twice as loud in that still moment, on a small table near him.

It was not the movement of that figure in the dark mirror, it was not the bell ringing close at hand and insistently. It was an irrational and stupid fear lest his action, reproduced visibly beside him in the mirror, was being faithfully registered in some impossible way that filled the intruder with fright. The telephone ringing shrilly, Mr. Willy now facing him, the play enacted beside him, and this irrational momentary fear caused him to turn and bound towards the door, to escape into the dark, banging the glass door with a clash behind him. When he got well away from the place he was angry – everything was always against him, he never had no luck, and if he hadn'ta lost his head it was a cinch he coulda done it easy.

"Damn you!" shouted Mr. Willy in a rage, with his hand on the telephone, "you might have broken it! Yes?" he said into the telephone, moderating the anger that possessed him and continuing within himself a conversation that said It was eighteen inches away, I was within a minute of it and I didn't know, it's no use telephoning the police but I'd better do that, it was just above me and I'd have died not knowing. "Yes? Yes?" he said impatiently, trembling a little.

"Oh," said a surprised voice, "it *is* Mr. Willy, isn't it? Just for a minute it didn't sound like you Mr. Willy that was the *loveliest* party and what a lovely view and I'm sorry to be such a nuisance I kept on ringing and ringing because I thought you couldn't have gone out so soon" (tinkle tinkle) "and you couldn't have gone to bed so soon but I do believe I must have left my little bead bag it's not the *value* but ... " Mr. Willy found himself shaking more violently now, not only with death averted and the rage of the slammed glass door but with the powerful thoughts that had usurped him and were interrupted by the dangerous moment which was now receding, and the tinkling voice on the telephone.

"I have it here. I'll bring it tomorrow," he said shortly. He hung up the telephone and at the other end the Aunt turned and exclaimed "Well if he isn't the rudest man I never was treated like that in my whole life d'you know what he ... "

Mr. Willy was in a state of abstraction.

He went to the glass door and examined it. It was intact. He turned the key and drew the shutter down. Then he went back to the telephone in this state of abstraction. Death or near-death was still very close, though receding. It seemed to him at that moment that a crack had been coming in the great wall that shut him off from the light but perhaps he was wrong. He dialled the police, perfunctorily not urgently. He knew that before him lay the hardest work of his life – in his life but out of his country. He must in some way and very soon break the great wall that shut him off from whatever light there might be. Not for fear of death oh God not for fear of death but for fear of something else.

Afterword

BY DAVID STOUCK

Ethel Wilson's novels, with one exception, began as short stories. *The Innocent Traveller* was submitted to publishers in the 1930s and 1940s as a collection of stories about the Edgeworth and Hastings families, and although the manuscript was finally edited to create a continuous narrative, the discrete units of short-story writing remain evident. *Swamp Angel* had its genesis in three stories: one describing British Columbia's Chinese market gardeners living on the Fraser River delta, a second recording a woman's journey up the Fraser Canyon, and a third describing a powerful swimmer. *Love and Salt Water* started as the story of a violinist and was titled "Miss Cuppy." *Hetty Dorval* was the exception, but its length (shorter than "Tuesday and Wednesday" and much shorter than "Lilly's Story" which comprise *The Equations of Love*) suggests that novella is a more accurate formal category for this book.

"Your work is long on style and short on story," wrote John Gray, Wilson's editor at Macmillan, who pressed her repeatedly for what she called "The Big Bow Wow." Only when she stopped writing did Gray agree to publish a collection of her short stories. Accordingly, *Mrs. Golightly and Other Stories* holds a special place in the Wilson canon because here is the author in the abbreviated forms that she believed suited her talent best.

The stories in this collection span Wilson's writing

career, including "I just love dogs," first published in *New Statesman and Nation* in 1937, and "A drink with Adolphus," published in the *Tamarack Review* in 1960. The stories are not arranged chronologically and there is no evidence that they are organized by any principle other than theme and effect. The collection opens, for example, with two stories from the viewpoint of a travelling wife, followed by two stories about British Columbia landscape and weather. At the centre of the book is a pair of non-fiction pieces set in England, followed by four stories pervaded by fear and violence. Shrewd and witty insights into human behaviour characterize many of the pieces in the first half of the collection; sombre reflections on fear, estrangement, and despair colour most of the second half. A more clearly marked principle of arrangement is the alternation of stories with brief sketches of scenery ("On Nimpish Lake"), comic dialogue ("God help the young fishman"), diary-keeping ("Till death us do part"), and non-fiction.

Mrs. Golightly and Other Stories is peculiarly modernist in its formal elusiveness and fragmentation. It is also modernist in the details of its style. When a copy-editor at Macmillan altered the punctuation, Wilson offered to pay for fresh galleys to have the book "in the form that I wrote it." She was especially concerned that the quotation marks be removed from the text of certain stories (notably "God help the young fishman," "I just love dogs," and "Till death us do part") because, she said, they are "talked" and "race along in that fool-talking way without waiting for quotation marks." She explained to the editor that she had a strong feeling for punctuation as a form of modifying communication, and that is certainly evident in the extremes used here. There are places where the punctuation simulates the pace of the character's thoughts. In "Mr. Sleepwalker," for example, Mrs. Manly's attention is taken away from the movie she is watching by a frightening smell: "slight at first, then stronger, of, perhaps, an animal, or, perhaps, rotted wood, thick and dank (but how could it be rotted wood?)" Mrs. Manly lets her thoughts, marshalled by commas, inch forward only a word or two at a time, so terrified is she by the odour in the room. In the opposite vein Wilson omits commas altogether in long strings of adjectives (she describes a piece of salmon as "fine thick silver red-fleshed fish") in order to render in words what would be perceived all at once by the eye. And there are long monologues where the lack of all punctuation fittingly conveys the tedious loquacity of the speakers.

The stories are especially rich in Wilson's stylistic trademarks: oxymorons that bind together contraries (Mrs. Forrester's "good bad French"); non-sequiturs indicating gaps in communication ("in Spain we had too many eggs and she said Yes, but what about the el grecos"); repetitions which render characters and their actions cartoonlike ("I just love dogs. I'm crazy about dogs. I like dogs a lot better than I like people"). There is an identifiable narrator in these stories, a wordsmith endlessly fascinated with the power and pleasure of language. There is also a narrator who will use any number of strategies to tell a story, even the postrealist tactic in "Till death us do part" of confessing defeat as a storyteller, but continuing to make notes.

Most of Wilson's perennial themes and interests appear in these stories. Her life with her husband and their travels together provide an emotional setting for several of the pieces, whether in a convention hotel in California, a dark tomb in Egypt, or the streets of London. This life is sometimes the source of anxiety and fear when a loving husband and wife are separated, but in other places it provides a secure vantage point for Wilson's special kind of ironic comedy. "A drink with Adolphus" is a small masterpiece in this mode, a surreal blend of humour, social observation, and shrewd psychology that both entertains and disturbs.

The most valued setting in these stories is the landscape of British Columbia. Mrs. Gormley, on her way to

Adolphus's party, asks her taxidriver to stop and let her have ten cents' worth of view, of ocean and islands and mountains white with winter snow, "nearly all the glory of the world and no despair." Some of the pieces here, such as "On Nimpish Lake" and "Hurry, hurry," are almost entirely descriptions of the natural world. In others the crises in the lives of the characters are measured against a vividly rendered natural backdrop. Wilson believed in the "formidable power of geography," in the genius of place directing human actions and moulding the spirit. For example, convention-weary Mrs. Golightly is revived by a glimpse of seals disporting themselves on the rocks of the ocean; the blind man in "Beware the Jabberwock . . . " spends an idyllic few weeks fishing at an interior B.C. lake after deserting his wife; and in "The Window," Mr. Willy, who has also left a wife behind, comes close to answering the riddle of his existence by gazing for long hours at the magnificent scenery of ocean and mountains from the picture window of his Vancouver home.

Yet lurking in that beautiful scene from Mr. Willy's window is a man who will try to kill him. Similarly, the beautiful winter scenery on the delta marshes in "Hurry, hurry" discloses the body of a murdered woman. Just beneath the surface in Wilson's fictional world disasters await the unsuspecting – drownings, murders, maimings, sudden deaths. It was the experience and conviction of the author herself, who by the age of ten was twice orphaned and sent six thousand miles from England to live in Canada, that chaos lurks beneath the smooth surface of events, that humankind lives "on a brink." In such a world the fear of separation experienced by Mrs. Forrester and by Mrs. Manly is real and urgent.

The book's epigraph by Edwin Muir – "Life ' . . . is a difficult country and our home' " – points to a philosophical tension in the stories between existential uncertainty and the humanist's knowledge of certain truths. Repeatedly things happen without explanation: Why does Mr. Sleepwalker pursue Mrs. Manly? Did the writer and her husband actually see a singer and a dancer on the corner of X and Y streets? Wilson reminds us of epistemological uncertainties: "What is anybody like?" she asks. How can we know, how be certain? Mrs. Forrester confesses to her niece that her life is a masquerade. Mr. Willy fears that life has no meaning at all.

At the same time there are positive assertions in Wilson's fiction. In her depiction of the natural world, the beauty of blue summer ocean and violet islands and snow-capped mountains is a solid value, and the order and purpose she witnesses in a flight of wild geese or a display of Northern Lights softens the harshness of their teleological mystery. Similarly there are positive assertions in the world of human affairs where truth, transcending words, can exist in the love between husband and wife, where compassion heals injury, and where love and honour can bind men and women "to keep the memory of so worthy a friend."

BY ETHEL WILSON

FICTION
Hetty Dorval (1947)
The Innocent Traveller (1949)
The Equations of Love (1952)
Swamp Angel (1954)
Love and Salt Water (1956)
Mrs. Golightly and Other Stories (1961)

SELECTED WRITINGS
Ethel Wilson: Stories, Essays, and Letters
[ed. David Stouck] (1987)